P9-EFJ-192

NOT GUILTY OF LOVE

CHASE BRANCH LIBRARY
17731 W. SEVEN MILE
DETROIT. MICH. 48235

AUG 2009

CHASE BRANCH LIBRARY
17731 W. SEVEN MILE

NOT GUILTY OF LOVE

PAT SIMMONS

www.urbanchristianonline.net

Urban Books, LLC
1199 Straight Path
West Babylon, NY 11704

Not Guilty of Love copyright © 2009 Pat Simmons

All rights reserved. No part of this book may be reproduced in any
form or by any means without prior consent of the Publisher, ex-
cepting brief quotes used in reviews.

ISBN- 13: 978-1-60162-931-9
ISBN- 10: 1-60162-931-1

First Printing September 2009
Printed in the United States of America

10 9 8 7 6 5 4 3 2 1

*This is a work of fiction. Any references or similarities to actual
events, real people, living, or dead, or to real locales are intended
to give the novel a sense of reality. Any similarity in other
names, characters, places, and incidents is entirely coinciden-
tal.*

Distributed by Kensington Corp.
Submit Wholesale Orders to:
Kensington Publishing Corp.
C/O Penguin Group (USA) Inc.
Attention: Order Processing
405 Murray Hill Parkway
East Rutherford, NJ 07073-2316
Phone: 1-800-526-0275
Fax: 1-800-227-9604

Praises for Talk to Me . . .

I enjoyed *Talk to Me* because it was written from the point-of-view of a character that could not hear, and I was able to understand how difficult that could be, to a degree. I learned more about what a deaf person must deal with on a daily basis and how the written word and sign language does not always interpret what someone is feeling. Being able to talk to a deaf person is not always enough, and the ability to talk to them is not just in the interpretation. I recommend this book to anyone who enjoys a love story ordained by God.
Review by Sharel E. Gordon-Love for Apooo Book-Club, 4 Stars

A very good read with an atypical leading man. This is a pleasing Christian fiction novel with a fair balance of scripture, romance, and storytelling. I like the fact that parts are told from Noel's perspective and parts from Mackenzie's voice. I don't think you'll be disappointed at all with this story that has intriguingly different aspects from a run of the mill story—starting with an atypical, yet highly inviting male lead
Reviewed by reader B. Mar, 4 Stars

Within the pages of *Talk to Me*, Pat Simmons has done an admirable job of bringing attention to the trials of the deaf as they make their way through what we consider a normal day. With memorable prose and thought-provoking passages, Ms. Simmons sheds light on the necessity of vul-

nerability for all relationships we enter into; especially the one we must maintain with ourselves.
Reviewer by Dr. Linda Beed for On Assignment Reviews, 4 Stars

Praises for *Guilty of Love* . . .

Pat Simmons's sometimes whimsical approach to delivering the message of salvation is anchored by opportune scriptures. The author boldly tackles issues like abortion, child abuse, and anger toward God, adeptly guiding readers into romance, reconciliation, and restoration as this novel flows effortlessly from haunting pasts to delectable happiness.
Robin R. Pendleton for Romantic Times BOOKreviews, 4 Stars

Non-Christians could enjoy this story without feeling like that were being beat in the head about their sins and choices in life. The author really outdid herself with this novel . . . as her first novel, you can be sure that her gift is of God. I would have expected this work to have come from a more experienced author. And you know that a sequel is a MUST!
Idrissa Uqdah, AALBC.com Review Team, 5 Stars

Guilty of Love by Pat Simmons was my first experience with Christian fiction, and I must admit that I truly enjoyed reading this novel. I thought that Ms. Simmons did an excellent job of inserting the character's spirituality into the dialog in such a natural manner that didn't come across as being preachy, and she was also able to interlace a multitude of rich African American history in the process. I felt each and every emotion of the heroine, and it touched me deeply within. This story centered on a very difficult, heartbreaking issue and how Cheney dealt with it came across so incredibly real to me. It was astonishing to find such strong characters in a novel, even with the weaknesses evolved from their past experiences. I advise the reader to keep a big box of tissues handy because you will need them on numerous occasions. Thanks go to Ms. Simmons for a truly inspirational story. **Reviewed by Nikita for Joyfully Reviewed, 5 Stars**

Acknowledgments

To God's dependability: Hebrews 13:8
"Jesus Christ, the same yesterday, and today, and for ever."

To God's promise: Acts 2:38-39
"Then Peter said unto them, 'Repent, and be baptized every one of you in the name of Jesus Christ for the remission of sins, and ye shall receive the gift of the Holy Ghost. For the promise is unto you, and to your children, and to all who are afar off, even as many as the Lord our God shall call.'"

Thank you:
Jennifer Thomasson/Stems Florists, Florissant, MO
Ferguson PD Captain Dennis McBride and Joe Craig
Lenard E. Bell/Bell & Associates
Attorney Charles Kirksey

Bookstores
Barnes & Noble Booksellers/Florissant, MO
Not Just A Bookstore/St. Louis, MO
Books-A-Million/Hazelwood, MO
Boomerang Books/Texas
To every reader, church, and book club that supported me and shared your comments to make Book II: *Not Guilty of Love* possible.

Once again, special thanks to the expanding family and friends who make up my "Village People" staff, including

Chandra Sparks-Taylor, you guys have blessed me over and over again. UC Executive Editor, Joylynn Jossel.

Kerry, Jared, and Simi Simmons

My ancestors from my genealogy search: Coles, Scotts, Thompsons, Palmers, Wades, Browns, Jamisons; My in-laws: Simmons, Downers, Sinkfields, Stricklands, Sturdivants, and others.

My pastor and his wife: Bishop James A. Johnson and Lady Juana Johnson and the Bethesda Temple family.

Agent Judy Mikalonis with the Andrea Hurst Agency

A big shout out to Felecia and Renwick Ware at Goin Postal, Florissant, MO. We keep each other in business.

PROLOGUE

Sitting behind the desk in his office, Malcolm Jamieson snatched the receiver off his phone console and fumbled to get a grip. He punched in his ex-fiancée's work number and waited for the connection. Malcolm never expected Hallison to be an ex.

His heart ached for Hallison Dinkins's smile. His hands itched for his woman's soft perfumed skin and silky hair. He could never get enough of touching her. He grunted, remembering his older brother, Parke's wisecrack that Malcolm's hands were dry because they needed moisturizer. His world was upside down and Parke had jokes about hand lotion.

Hallison had the best assets God could give to a woman, and she didn't even know it. When she entered a room, other women bowed to her superiority. She was Malcolm's sole focus, his idol, his wife—well almost. Somehow doubt had insinuated itself into Hallison's head, and she questioned the magnitude of his love and walked away. To add to Malcolm's confusion, Hallison pointed a finger at God for her sudden decision. *What did God have to do with it?* He never received a satisfactory answer.

He replayed the scene in his mind: One Sunday morning, he escorted one woman into a church and a look-a-like emerged. By trade, Malcolm was a certified public accountant with Winfield & Young in St. Louis, Missouri. At the end of the day, everything balanced. Somehow he had miscalculated the bottom line with Hallison.

"Good morning, Bank of Missouri. May I help you?" greeted the customer service representative.

Malcolm gave the extension and waited impatiently. He had ceased calling her direct line and talking to her voicemail. After two rings, he was connected.

"Director of Human Resources."

He recognized Gloria's voice, the department's receptionist. "Hallison Dinkins, please."

She hesitated, causing Malcolm to wonder if he had been disconnected. "I'm sorry. She's doing payroll and can't be disturbed." Her patronizing tone annoyed him.

Malcolm was convinced Gloria was Hallison's watchdog. As efficient as Hallison was as personnel director, there was no way it would take her three days to approve a biweekly payroll report of three hundred employees. She supervised qualified department heads who thoroughly double-checked their staff's overtime hours, vacation times accrued, and comp days. As far as Malcolm was concerned, security was about to be breached.

"Thanks." He slammed down the receiver and stood, scattering pens and pencils. "Ten days is long enough." He pounded his desk. "You're going to see me, woman, with or without an audience. I'll no longer be refused." Malcolm stormed out his office without a word to his assistant, Miss Lilly, who lifted a bushy brow before she returned to pecking on her keyboard.

His assistant never verbally interfered in Malcolm's per-

sonal life, but her facial expressions read, "If you ask me,
I'm going to tell you what I think." This time she released
a heavy sigh before speaking her mind. "Come back in a
better mood, Mr. Jamieson. I get enough attitudes from
my boys, and they're looking for another place to live."

He ignored her remarks with his own musing. "Never
mess with a black man in love, and I'm a Jamieson too.
That's a hostile combination," he mumbled, suspecting
Miss Lilly "Radar" Brown probably heard every word.

Malcolm stalked across the marble floor to a pair of el-
evators. An empty one opened automatically as if sensing
his presence. The doors shut once he stepped inside, and
the car descended until it reached the lobby. Malcolm
hadn't pushed a button. He marched to revolving doors that
stood at attention, awaiting his command. As he crushed
the dirt on the sidewalk with each step, the crowd parted
for his entrance.

At the corner, Malcolm briefly marveled at the street-
light invented by Garrett Morgan, the son of a former slave.
Malcolm and his family considered themselves certified
genealogists, and they could recite historical facts and accomplishments of African Americans like Wikipedia. The
light turned green and flashed "walk," sparing Malcolm
the effort of looking both ways. He glanced anyway before crossing.

A health enthusiast, Malcolm didn't waste the effort to
get his car from a nearby parking garage. He needed the
exercise to temper his irritation. Eighteen minutes and
ten seconds later—a record speed—he yanked open the
door to the Metropolitan Circle Building. His heart pounded
heavier with each step down the corridor. When he entered
the personnel office, he used too much force opening the
glass door. Startled, Gloria, the dark-skinned department
receptionist, looked up and replaced the beginning of an
engaging smile with a surprised frown.

"I'm here to see Hali," he said. Malcolm didn't have time for a good morning, howdy doody, whatz up, or any other pleasantries.

Her face wrestled to form a response as she inched up from behind her desk. Barely reaching five feet, Malcolm wondered if she was standing or remained seated. "One moment. Let me see if she is available."

Shoving her chair to the side, it rolled in one direction and she began a backpedal jog in another. Somehow she weaved through several employment testing cubicles without looking. As soon as Gloria bypassed some offices, she turned and dashed down a long hall with plush tan carpet that signified an exclusive executive office. Malcolm trailed Gloria as she picked up speed. With little effort, he stretched his legs to easily overtake her strenuous pace. He entered Hallison's office without knocking seconds before the receptionist caught up and slammed into his solid body, causing her to ricochet off him.

"I'm sorry, Miss Dinkins. I tried to warn you," Gloria apologized, huffing before she retreated.

Hallison remained seated behind her mahogany desk. She was radiant in purple and seemingly unfazed by his appearance. Her straight, brown hair hung past her shoulders; her face glowed. It had nothing to do with cosmetics if she was wearing any.

How can she sit there, looking beautiful and acting so calm? Malcolm thought, further irritated. His peripheral vision closed in on Hallison's lips. Like a predator, he moved purposely toward her. Malcolm's eyes flashed, and his chest heaved as he tried to control his breathing.

He leaned against her desk. "Hallison Dinkins, how can we work out our differences if you refuse to see or talk to me?" Malcolm inhaled her perfume. It was the same one he had bought her the month before—sweet, subtle, and alluring. Malcolm's bold appraisal was meant to unravel Hallison. His tactic only drained his arrogance. *Do you know how much I love you? Of course, you don't*, he answered himself.

"Malcolm, I can't bear to see or talk to you. You embody every weakness known to women. For me, you're a double dose."

"Good." Focusing on her mouth, Malcolm proceeded closer until he could almost taste her minty breath. "And, you're my weakness."

"Malcolm, please—"

Kissing Hallison, he absorbed her words until she broke away, panting. "I'm not trying to make you cry, sweetheart. I'm trying to remove the blur in our relationship. You know I love you and will support whatever you need to do. I'll admit you caught me off guard weeks ago. We've dated for a year, and church was the farthest thing from our minds or conversations. Now, all of a sudden, it's as if you're on drugs, and you've got to have it after one visit. I can handle that addiction to a certain point. I'm just not convinced about this church makeover, and to be honest, I don't know if I'll ever be, or if I even want to."

Sniffing, Hallison jutted her chin after she cleared her throat. "Malcolm, I've run out of ways to explain. God spoke to me. I had no choice but to obey. My life depended on obeying. We have to be together in this Christian walk with Jesus. If not, I'll have to stroll with Christ by myself."

"Yeah, and just think, I had no choice in that decision." He balled his hand into a fist and frowned.

"But you did." Hallison massaged her temples, matching his frustration. "That was one of the reasons I balked at accepting an invitation to church. I was taking a gamble, not knowing if God would do—"

Malcolm pointed to his chest. "Oh, so this is my fault?"

She shook her head. "No, of course not. You didn't know we were walking right into God's trap. I had an uneasy feeling that once I was back on God's turf, He wasn't going to let me go that easily without reminding me of the consequences of sin."

"Hmm, interesting. Maybe I should've put up a bigger fight."

"It wasn't about you that day, Malcolm. When God's power hit me, I did an about-face. I tried to forget the cost of living a life without the Lord, but God suddenly revived every memory. This is bigger than you and me."

Why is she putting this distance between us? Malcolm was an honest, hard-working man, faithful to one woman. He had been taught since childhood and accepted that salvation was a given. At the time, he hadn't minded visiting churches. Now, he was dead set against stepping foot inside another for fear of God snatching him away too.

Malcolm's temper broke. "Hali," he managed through clenched teeth, "do you love me?" Malcolm hammered his fist on her desk. She jumped. "Hali, you know I love you, and I'd never hurt you."

Her eyes pleaded for understanding. "I know how special your love is, but I don't know how to balance you *and* God . . ." Her voice faded. "It's hard to put in words, but when I sat in church that Sunday, God showed me myself. It was a premonition of where I was headed." She shivered. "Malcolm, I had to make a choice either now, or never. I chose now."

"My sweet little woman got caught up in the moment." He paused and gathered his thoughts. "I'm not a man to be picked over, Hali." Malcolm released his fists and slid his hands into his pants pockets. "Again, do you love me?"

For a second time, Hallison didn't respond. Her eyes glossed over like lacquer. When she remained quiet, Malcolm nodded. He had his answer. Turning to leave, he heard a faint, "Yes."

Malcolm spun around, not realizing he had been holding his breath. "Remember that when you meet me at the altar." He believed Hallison was worth fighting for, even if the competition was God.

CHAPTER 1

Months later . . .

The party was in full swing. Hallison exhaled. She embraced the happiness as her eyes sparkled at the shower's turnout. She stopped counting the number of well-wishers who paraded through the door. The apprehension she had felt at the start of the gathering was fading. The excitement in the room was contagious. Judging from the elaborate gift-wrapped boxes, hidden treasures were sure to capture *oohs* and *ahhs*. She smiled.

"Don't you think you went a little overboard on the food and decorations? You must've paid the caterer a fortune," Hallison complained sarcastically to Malcolm's older brother.

Throwing his head back, Parke VI laughed and capped it with a satisfying grin. "You should know that when the Jamiesons throw a shindig, we go all the way, and this is a special occasion," he defended jubilantly as he encircled his wifes, Cheney's, somewhat protruding stomach before engaging her in a slow dance across the room until they disappeared.

Married almost two years, the couple considered themselves still on their honeymoon. Cheney was gorgeous, confident, and madly in love with her husband. Tall and shapely, her six feet height was a plus to camouflage the extra weight she had already gained. Her bright yellow skin glowed. Cheney's rich, dark features shined. She was the poster child for any mother-to-be magazine.

Parke VI and Malcolm had identical facial features: long noses, dimpled smiles, and fair skin. Each sported short, wavy, jet-black hair and thick, silky eyebrows. Whereas Parke preferred a long, thin mustache, Malcolm was dangerously handsome with a well-groomed beard. At thirty-three, Malcolm stood an inch taller than Parke's six feet five, plus Malcolm was buff. Women sometimes mistook them for the former NBA player-turned-actor, Rick Fox.

The Jamieson brothers, all three of them—Parke VI, Malcolm, and the youngest, Cameron, who lived in Boston— were intelligent connoisseurs of their ancestry, committed to their convictions, and faithful to their women to a fault, which had been the source of Hallison's problem.

Since Hallison and Cheney dated the Jamieson brothers, it was assumed they would become friends. That was an understatement. The women developed a bond closer than a set of twins, and their relationship continued after Cheney and Parke married. So, without argument, Hallison was designated to host the first of four baby showers. It wasn't the baby shower extravaganza that Parke's parents wanted to throw for their first biological grandchild, who, if male, would continue the Jamieson lineage that had been recorded in a tattered journal hundreds of years ago.

Cheney wanted something simple. To make everyone

NOT GUILTY OF LOVE 11

happy, she agreed to four baby showers over the next four months, given by her in-laws, her parents, her former neighbor's sassy seniors group, and finally the managers at her job. Parke and Cheney figured their baby would be partied out by the time he, or she, arrived.

Hallison was shaking her head at the absurdity of the multiple parties, when her heart skipped a beat. Laughter, lively conservations, and jazz spewing from the surround-sound speakers couldn't drown out Malcolm's trademark appearance. The doorbell buzzed twice, paused, and buzzed again. As if knowing Parke's door would be unlocked, Malcolm waltzed into the living room. His presence demanded attention. Without asking, he got it. Hallison's heartbeat accelerated.

It had been months since Hallison had seen him. She had purposely avoided him when she visited Parke and Cheney. A few times they had come face-to-face, but Hallison had a ready-made excuse to flee. "Oh. Hi, Malcolm. I'm on my way out. I don't want to be late for church," she would say, reciting a practiced line.

His speechless response was also preset with an amused expression, challenging her truthfulness. Twice, she had driven to the church and sat in the parking lot, repenting for the fib. She couldn't keep running away from her temptation, so she refused to bolt this time.

Months ago, she had invited Malcolm to what she considered their final, intimate dinner. Surrounded by the restaurant's romantic ambience, Hallison sobbed silently as she placed the four-carat diamond ring back into his palm with a shaky hand. Begrudgingly, Malcolm accepted more than the ring. It symbolized their engagement had officially terminated, and their couple status had been dissolved.

Malcolm wasn't the one who got away, but was instead the man God instructed Hallison to give away. The Lord had issued the ultimatum: Malcolm, the love of her life, or Him, the One who gave her life.

Women would be waiting on the sidelines, ready to steal Malcolm's affections, with a no-option-for-his-release clause in a relationship contract. On the outside, Hallison felt she was a fool to let a good man go, but spiritually, as a self-proclaimed backslider, her salvation clock was ticking. To her, the decision was a smart move, one she couldn't explain, except to a few church friends. God had let her know, loud and clear, she had to first deny herself of her fleshly desires, pick up her cross, and follow Him.

How long would I have to fast until I would be spiritually strong enough to quench my craving for Malcolm's voice, his touch, and his smothering eyes? she questioned God, as she controlled her breathing to keep Malcolm from seeing how much he affected her.

Glancing around the room, nothing seemed fascinating while her soul nagged God. *Was it so bad that I wanted to make love with the man I loved unconditionally and who faithfully loved me?* She tried to sway God's mind and plead her case, but the Lord responded, *I first loved you and gave my life for you. Trust me with your life. Fornicators will I judge.*

Hallison twisted her lips in defeat. God had her best interest, but Malcolm was her Biblical King David, her Solomon, and her Prince Paki. The latter, Prince Paki Kokumuo Jaja, was Malcolm's tenth great-grandfather, born December 1770, in Cote d'Ivoire, Africa. He was the firstborn son of King Seif of the Diomande tribe. Despite his warriors' protection, Paki was abducted and herded on a ship steered toward the Americas. Landing in Maryland, Paki was indoctrinated into servitude. He was automatically separated from his bodyguards and sold for a couple of hundred dollars in front of Sinner's Hotel, of all places. Ironically, the woman who would later become his wife was the slave master's daughter, Elaine.

Malcolm epitomized a contemporary version of an African warrior—strong, fearless, and determined. The only thing that kept Hallison from running back into Malcolm's arms had been part of Hebrews 12 . . . *let us lay aside every weight, and the sin which doth so easily beset us, and let us run with patience the race that is set before us.*

Hallison's shoulders slumped as guests, unknowingly, created a Red Sea path for Malcolm. He acknowledged them with a nod of generic hellos before hugging Parke and kissing Cheney on the cheek. Then she became his next destination.

"Hali," Malcolm greeted as he peeled off his black leather jacket and gloves, uncovering a black woolen turtleneck that squeezed his abs, biceps, and chest. He dropped them on the closest chair. If his cologne wasn't woozy enough, his pants stretched to fit his physique, and his highly polished boots would make any woman faint from appreciation of God's divine specimen.

"Hi," Hallison remembered to reply as her body debated if it would aid her to stand. She resolved that Malcolm's eyes would always be her weakness. They were a hypnotic brown.

She was defeated. How could she ever get over him, even if God paraded hundreds of princes before her? Malcolm, the dimple smiling, financially secure, and weightlifting competitor was a man whose DNA could not be cloned. *It's not funny, Lord, that you make me forsake the man I love, only to tempt me with him.*

Malcolm's nostrils flared as his breathing deepened. He didn't need words to communicate. Hallison knew exactly what he was thinking. This whole "Malcolm, you don't have a relationship with Christ, so we can't have a relationship" mantra was the craziest thing he had ever heard.

At first, he thought she was getting cold feet about their pending marriage. Evidently, they had frozen, but nothing a long, warm foot massage couldn't fix. He and Hallison didn't haphazardly fall in love. *Now, that was God's purpose*, he figured. Their emotions were woven so tightly that even a two-edged sword couldn't slice it.

He stepped closer, forcing them to share the same air. He allowed her time to adjust to his foray into her personal space. When she squirmed, he smirked. "Would you like for me to get you something to drink?" he asked, reversing his role as guest to Hallison's slave.

"Ah . . . no, no thank you," she stuttered. Her eyes were glazed with passion.

Malcolm frowned mockingly. "Are you sure? Because you look thirsty. As a matter of fact, I'm parched." Malcolm wasn't talking about water and Hallison knew it. Their explosive kisses were addictive, like mountain stream water.

He retreated, allowing Hallison enough room to escape. He loved her too much to continue making her uncomfortable, although he could strangle her for tormenting his body for want. For the rest of the night, Malcolm didn't confront her.

Instead, he appreciated her from afar. Hallison's two-piece outfit, with flared pants, flattered her shape. Malcolm didn't have to guess that her toes, hidden in fashionable ankle boots, were manicured. The liberty to rub his face in her hair was now denied, but he presumed it was freshly scented from a recent hair appointment. She believed in keeping herself groomed for him. *Man.* He bit his bottom lip.

Their relationship began to spiral out of control once

they set foot in the hotel for a weekend getaway. They were so close to making love for the first time. Malcolm thought he would suffer a heart attack when she suddenly backed out of occupying the same suite. That was a while ago, but his mind and body pegged it as yesterday. Everything had been planned—the suite, the roses, the sole activity.

"Do you want to get kidnapped?" he remembered asking her over the phone one night.

"Yes, I'd be your willing prisoner," Hallison whispered with a haughty chuckle.

For the next hour, they had exchanged all sorts of naughty ideas.

"Then I'll sweep you away for a romantic weekend getaway at the Ritz Carlton. We'll go after Parke's get-together tomorrow night. Pack very little. As a matter of fact, don't pack anything."

Malcolm's nostrils flared when he reflected on that night. He exhaled and squinted while Hallison continued to mingle with Parke and Cheney's friends and neighbors, without giving him a second glance. Malcolm didn't need to approach Hallison to release vibes. He read her body language. She was nervous.

Sometime later, Parke placed their adopted daughter, Kami, on his lap. She had been the first, and youngest, of three foster children Cheney, who was single at the time, had sponsored in her home. Although becoming a foster parent was initially Cheney's idea, Parke had gotten involved. He had adored Cheney and would've done anything to make her happy, which included assisting her with the care of the foster children, when Cheney had been at such a low point in her life, and she didn't know if God had the remedy.

Cheney had accepted Kami as a foster child when she

was two years old. A year later, one couldn't tell that Kami was once combative, out of control and possessive of her things, which somehow included Parke. When Kami was moved to another home, she terrorized her new foster parents. The toddler was promptly returned to the agency. After Parke and Cheney married, they formally adopted her. Now, fourteen months later, she was rambunctious, but obedient . . . sometimes.

Parke scooted closer to his wife. Hallison claimed Cheney's opposite side for the ceremonial unwrapping of baby gifts. Refusing to make eye contact with Malcolm, Hallison reached for a pad to record the gifts and the givers. Uninvited, Malcolm made himself comfortable next to Hallison to pass the presents. Trapping her between him and Cheney, he occasionally brushed his finger against Hallison's hand. *Accidently, of course,* he taunted.

His brother's eyes reacted to every expression on Cheney's face as she opened the boxes. Baby, wedding, and engagement showers weren't usually sentimental for men, but evidently Parke didn't get the memo.

More than a year ago, Cheney and Parke had been neighbors, separated by several blocks, in a historic St. Louis suburb called Old Town Ferguson. Parke had a reputation of having a long list of female acquaintances. Until he met his future wife, his claim was he couldn't decide on just one. Cheney was a naturally independent woman. When Parke barged into her life, Cheney began to shed her emotional armor until their romance became any woman's fairytale.

As their relationship progressed, Parke had confided to Malcolm that Cheney couldn't have kids, and for a time, that was enough of a reason for Parke to walk away. The Jamiesons took their family history seriously. Parke VI was responsible for continuing their heritage, which had been traced back to the firstborn African-American male. When an old friend of Parke shared her testimony about the Lord, Parke's family legacy was no longer the most important thing to him, compared to Cheney in his life. Eventually, they both accepted God's salvation and His blessings.

There had been a rumor about a boy possibly named Parke in foster care, but that couldn't be substantiated, so the child growing inside Cheney's womb was their hope for a Parke VII. Without the results of modern technology, Parke felt their unborn baby was a boy. Despite his protests of wanting it to be a surprise at birth, he was welcoming a son or another daughter into his family.

The only reason Parke repented, and was baptized the same day as Cheney, was to support her. Afterward, God revealed His plan for their lives. It was His will that Parke would unwittingly come to Christ by unknowingly bringing Cheney. Malcolm wasn't that soft. If God wanted Malcolm, then He should come to Malcolm man to man.

Tears welled in Cheney's eyes. "I'm going to have to change the baby's clothes every time I change his or her diapers to wear all of these adorable outfits."

"Correction," Parke interrupted, "I plan to have diaper duty with the little prince or princess too."

"You've got him trained already. I love it!" Mrs. Wright, a middle-aged woman said, clapping her hands, pleased.

The comment didn't register as Cheney and Parke shared a tender kiss while Kami struggled to separate them. "Ugh."

The couple ignored the snickers, but parted when clapping erupted. Hallison stole a glance at Malcolm; his eyes were trained, waiting to meet hers.

"Hey, you two, that's how Cheney got pregnant in the first place," another neighbor joked. "So do you know what you guys are going to have?"

Parke shook his head as he twisted strands of his wife's

hair around his finger. "Nope. We want to be surprised," they said in unison.

Malcolm bowed his head to keep from laughing. God was going to get Parke for lying. By the time Cheney opened the twentieth gift, Kami was on the floor, shredding discarded wrappings into mini napkins for her Bratz dolls. Parke unnecessarily assisted Cheney in standing as she swatted against his help. Chuckling, Parke struggled with Kami to disengage the makeshift napkins from her hands. He ignored her pleas.

"Thanks, everybody, for these gifts. What did everyone do? Raid the toy stores together?" Cheney teased. "That was work! You guys have worn me out. But seriously, I'm still dealing with bouts of fatigue. If you'll pardon me, I'm leaving my own party to take a power nap, but don't let my absence stop you from enjoying yourselves. Stay and stuff yourselves."

"Kami, let's help Mommy take the presents upstairs," Parke instructed.

Shaking her head in defiance, Kami squeezed two of the toys. "Can I keep these?"

"No, sweetheart; those aren't yours. It's for your baby brother or sister."

Kami pouted. "My baby won't mind if I played with them."

Parke sighed. "I am too tired to negotiate with you. C'mon," he said, tickling Kami's neck with his lips. Parke escorted his family up the stairs.

Despite the invitation to stay, most of the guests also stood and gathered their belongings.

"Hallison, baby, do you think Parke and Cheney would mind if I take a plate home to my husband?" an elderly neighbor asked.

"I'm sure they wouldn't." Hallison hurried into the kitchen. Minutes later, she returned with an aluminum foil-wrapped paper plate. She repeated the task for three other guests until the last one left. Malcolm waited a few minutes before he cornered Hallison as she began to cover the leftovers.

He moved closer until she was pinned against the wall. "So, you're over me, huh?" If she said no, Malcolm and God would call her a liar. "Are you over this?" Again, she didn't answer as he teased her with a kiss. When she moaned, he did, too. Malcolm clutched her shoulders as he trailed pecks down her face. Hallison didn't protest. He whispered naughty nothings in her ear.

"Yes," she whispered back, submitting to Malcolm and forsaking God. She didn't know if she meant yes, she was over Malcolm, or yes, she wanted more. All was forgotten until Parke raced down the steps like thunder. Hallison jumped and tried to detangle herself from Malcolm, but he refused to release her. Finally, Hallison broke away, panting.

Parke huffed. "I didn't see that." He grimaced. "But just in case I did, back off, Malcolm. Why are you all over her? The breakup wasn't an easy choice to make."

Malcolm mimicked Parke's stance and snarled. "You think my life is any easier without my woman? Do you really think Hali is happy without me? I doubt it. Your so-called Good News gospel has been the worst news I've heard in my life."

"And that attitude is why we're not together today, Malcolm," Hallison said.

He turned and was ready to explode when Parke stepped between them. "Save it. This isn't about you . . . I need your help." Parke glanced over his shoulder at the stairs. "I've got an emergency."

They gave Parke their attention. "What's up?"

"I just got a call from Cheney's mother on my cell phone. Cheney's father has been shot. I've got to get to the hospital."

Hallison gasped as tears sprang into her eyes. "What? Is he alive? What happened? Do the police know who did it?"

Parke growled. "Yes. Grandma BB."

CHAPTER 2

"What?" Hallison and Malcolm snapped in harmony as they shot questions at Parke.

"You've got to be kiddin' me. What—" Hallison reached out and gripped Parke's arm.

"I didn't know the woman owned a gun. Why . . ." Malcolm paused.

Parke held up his hands to ward off the firing squad. "Grandma BB sent me a text message stating she was about to be handcuffed for something nobody can prove. Then I received a call from Cheney's mother. She was crying and saying that Roland had been shot by some crazy woman. He was rushed to DePaul Hospital's emergency room. I put two and two together. Things are about to get ugly."

Malcolm glanced from Parke and Hallison. "I don't know what math you're using, but this is not adding up for me."

"It's not making sense to me either. How is Cheney holding up? I can't believe her day ended like this. Do you need me to stay with Kami while you two go the hospital?" Hallison asked, wiping tears from her face.

"She's not going to the hospital," Parke answered.

"Oh, okay. That's probably better. I guess I should stay with her," Hallison volunteered, already heading upstairs. "At least we can pray together while we wait for news."

Gritting his teeth, Parke shook his head and restrained her. "Hold on. I'm not about to upset my wife yet. I'll go to the hospital and find out what's going on before I break the news."

"Parke, I know she's pregnant, but that's her father, and he could die," Hallison argued.

"Then we'll have to pray he doesn't. I'll bet Grandma BB's not finished with him. Something tells me it was just a warning. That woman is having some serious issues conforming to holiness, man!" Parke rubbed his neck in frustration.

"You think?" Malcolm muttered sarcastically, folding his arms. "It sounds like you know what's going on, and it wasn't an accident."

Parke nodded. "It was only a matter of time before something like this happened. Listen," he said, lowering his voice as Hallison paced, "you know we consider Grandma BB part of this family, but I can't be with both of them at the same time. She is Kami's great-godgrandmother, god great-grandmother, or whatever she is. Anyway, she's family. I don't want her there alone. She's probably beside herself, realizing what she's done. I'm guessing the police probably took her to the Ferguson Police Department since the shooting happened near Wabash Park. She doesn't belong behind bars."

Mrs. Beatrice Tilley Beacon, aka Grandma BB, was Cheney's former next door neighbor. On the surface, people dismissed her as a harmless, childless, and senile old widow. It was a ploy to deceive everyone about her vulnerability. Mrs. Beacon had wrinkle-free mocha skin and snowy white strands mingled with silver hair. She was a small-framed woman whose height was five feet in heels, four-eleven in the trademark Stacy Adams shoes she wore like houseslippers.

She was known for taking catnaps during the day and terrorizing the neighborhood at night. From her living room window, she kept vigil over the normally tranquil street, shaded by mature trees and brick-covered walkways that winded to front doors. Her loaded shotgun was the incentive that caused intruders to think twice about committing burglaries, assaults, and car thefts on the block.

It wasn't Mrs. Beacon's age that earned her respect. It was her megawatt spotlight, which was bright enough to flag down a plane. More than a few robbers froze when the light was shone on them. Mrs. Beacon made her own decision whether to call the police. Depending on her mood, she often took matters into her own hands, using a so-called marked bullet to threaten anyone who gave her backtalk.

Cheney had slipped through her neighbor's intimidating façade. Mrs. Beacon's sweeter, gentler side flourished when Cheney accepted her first foster child, Kami. Mrs. Beacon stockpiled her house like a KB Toys store, and her backyard became a makeshift playground.

"I don't know, Parke. My girl still has a right to know." Hallison paused. "Wait a minute." Squinting, she cleared her throat. "If you don't need me to stay, you don't need me to go with him." She pointed nervously. "Malcolm can go alone."

"I need Malcolm to get her out of there. Pay her bond or bail or whatever. I don't want her spending the night in a cold cell. I think she's at Ferguson's jail. Bro, you know I'm good for it. Hali, you go for backup and quote Grandma BB whatever scriptures come to mind. I can't believe this happened." Parke didn't wait for their answer. He snatched his house keys off a wall hook. He continued fussing under his breath as he raced out the door then turned back. "Remember to lock up."

Hallison didn't feel confident about her scripture-quoting ability in Malcolm's presence. He reminded her of all that she gave up in the name of salvation. Parke and Cheney tried to stay out of Hallison and Malcolm's business, hoping they would resolve their religious differences. However, the longer the separation lasted, the more uncomfortable Hallison felt around them and Malcolm's family. She didn't want the couple to have to choose sides.

When Hallison would've backed off, Cheney always yanked her closer. "We're sisters, Hali. We were friends before, but God made us sisters forever."

Left standing in Parke's living room, Hallison tried to refocus as she quickly finished covering the leftovers. She raced to the kitchen and shoved dishes into the refrigerator. Malcolm trailed her without saying a word, or aiding in the clean up. *Just like a man.* His expression was unreadable. *What is he thinking?* she wondered.

"We'd better go, Hali," he said finally, reaching for her hand.

With nothing more to do in regard to the food, she reluctantly accepted his hand and walked to a foyer closet. She pulled her jacket from a hanger. Malcolm lifted it from her hands and wrapped it around her shoulders, waiting for her to slip her arms in the sleeves before he put on his own jacket. Hallison sighed and took one last look at the helium balloons teasing the ceiling and the misplaced furniture. Whatever time Parke returned, she knew he would restore the area before Cheney woke in the morning. As if confirming her silent thoughts, Malcolm nudged her out the door.

Once outside, Hallison ignored Malcolm's gleaming Monte Carlo and headed for her past-due-for-a-wash Toyota Camry. Heavy footsteps echoed behind her. Malcolm encircled her waist with his arm. "It's late. We're riding together."

She didn't put up a fight. She couldn't. Her mind was on Cheney's father, Dr. Reynolds, praying he would make it and Mrs. Beacon, wondering why she would shoot him. Even when she and Malcolm were a couple, they rarely argued, and if they did, their standoff ended before the sun descended. At the time, they were two soon-to-be lovers who could no longer wait to consummate their commitment. Hallison left Malcolm with many unanswered questions because she was waiting on God to explain things to her.

Retracing their steps to his car, Malcolm deactivated the alarm and opened her door. He swept a kiss against her cheek as she slid in her seat. Hallison didn't respond verbally, but her body did. She missed his comfort and attention.

When he got behind the wheel, he took his time removing his jacket. He made himself comfortable before putting the key in the ignition and reaching for a CD as if there was no emergency. Hallison refused to take the bait, ignoring the subtle reminders of their compatibility. It had been routine for one of them to load a CD and share a kiss while Malcolm fumbled to turn the ignition without looking. Hallison glanced out the window into the darkness as Malcolm pulled away from the curb en route to the Ferguson Police Department minutes away.

The R&B music was too hypnotic. It wasn't a coincidence that Malcolm played an old Earth, Wind, & Fire tune, knowing *Fantasy* was Hallison's favorite. She cleared her throat to drown out the song.

"I knew Cheney had a strained relationship with her family, but it wasn't that much of a threat for Grandma BB to shoot somebody," she commented.

Releasing the clutch, Malcolm squeezed her hand. "Baby, this proves my point, which is that church people are just as crazy as the rest of us."

CHAPTER 3

If Malcolm could've gotten away with it, he would've taken the scenic route to prolong the torture for both of them. The problem was most of the city of Ferguson was a small, basically picturesque municipality, filled with landmarks like those mansions built in the mid-1800s after the Emancipation Proclamation. Some homes were constructed with pieces from the 1904 World's Fair. One house was used to hold wakes, and several homes were built by Dr. George Case or his sons.

Later, famous barbecue sauce inventor Louis Maull, purchased one of the Case houses on Wesley. Not far away, another house was thought to be an original prefabricated Sears home bought from the catalog. The charm of Old Town Ferguson was one reason Parke had purchased his larger-than-life house on Darst.

When Malcolm parked in front of the police station, Hallison waited patiently for him to get out and come around to the passenger door for her. "Thank you," she mumbled.

Before Malcolm could respond with a seducing gesture

or phrase, his cell phone vibrated. Snatching it off his belt, Malcolm cursed under his breath after recognizing Parke's number. "Talk to me," he said, more annoyed than concerned. It was the first time he and Hallison had been alone in months, and he wanted to make her sweat. There used to be so much harmony between them. Now, the sweeter his former fiancée became, the angrier he became even months after their breakup. Malcolm wanted to lash out at Hallison for choosing Christ over him.

"Hey, man. Roland has superficial wounds to the shoulder and upper chest. He's going to be okay, but doctors are keeping him a few days for observation."

Malcolm digested the information, relayed the update to Hallison, and disconnected. Her hands flew in the air in silent praise. Afterward, she sniffed, but said nothing as she hurried inside the police station. The lobby was small with a metal counter and a few chairs against white walls. The counter's opening was protected by glass as if it were a drive-through bank teller's window.

"May I help you?" a woman behind the window asked as she sat at a desk. She didn't bother to look up.

As Malcolm opened his mouth, words spewed from Hallison's nonstop. "Yes. Our friend, Grandma BB—I mean Mrs. Beatrice Tilley Beacon—we think she shot somebody. I mean that's what we heard. We really don't know."

Malcolm contained his amusement. He loved it when Hallison was flustered. She was downright sexy. Malcolm gently scooted her over and took charge. Smiling, he winked at Hallison then cleared his throat. "We would like to pay Mrs. Beacon's bail."

The woman casually licked her fingers before flipping a page in a magazine. "She's at Christian Northeast Hospital."

Malcolm supported Hallison's body as she wavered. She searched Malcolm's eyes with hers before turning back to the window. "Oh my God. Was she shot too? What's her condition?"

The clerk shook her head, took a sip from a reusable Big Gulp cup, and sighed. "She looked okay to me. We've got a running tab up at the hospital because suspects feign heart, asthma, or bladder attacks. One woman even said she was having a baby. It turned out to be cocaine she swallowed. It's all stall tactics. The officer will finish the booking process when your grandma returns," she said dryly.

Facing Malcolm, Hallison's brows knitted with concern. She whispered, "She doesn't have a heart problem or asthma. I don't know about her bladder control. That woman is shooting at people and lying too."

"See, that's exactly what I'm talking about," the eavesdropping clerk interjected.

"Why be a saint when being a sinner will do?" Malcolm mocked, then brushed an unwelcome kiss against Hallison's ear.

Stepping aside, Hallison leaned unnecessarily closer to the security glass. "Thank you for the information. We'll head up to the hospital." They turned to leave.

"Ma'am, she's in police custody, so you won't be able to see her," the clerk said with finality, slurping from her empty cup.

Malcolm folded his arms, contemplating their next move. He didn't mind spending time with his ex. He just didn't want to do it at a police station. "Okay. We'll wait in the lobby."

"Unless you're her doctor, clergy, or attorney, you won't be able to see her here either. After she's charged and warrants are signed, she'll be transported over to the St. Louis County jail."

"Hali, we can go home and wait until tomorrow, but I

know you. You won't be able to sleep." Grimacing, he stroked the hairs on his beard. His behind was already protesting a wait longer than fifteen minutes in an antique chair, but with Hallison, he would have to tough it out. "Do you really want to wait?" He knew the answer when she gave him her bring-a-man-to-his-knees angelic expression.

"Please, Malcolm."

He counted to three as he appeared to consider her request. "Okay. C'mon, girl. I'll try to hang." With Hallison's hand still latched on to his, Malcolm allowed her to lead him to a set of chairs pushed into a corner, and they took a seat.

"Thank you."

"Hali, why are you thanking me?" He looked from their interlocking hands to the full lips he had kissed earlier. In the corner under a dimmed light and no audience was the perfect setting for a tryst, but he wasn't in the mood to fight with her over what she perceived as unwanted advances.

"Because I know I can't make you understand why I broke it off—"

"No, you can't," he said, shifting in his chair. He was starting not to recognize himself from the clipped tone he was using more and more with her. She was driving him insane.

Sighing, Hallison pleaded, "Please don't hold it against me, Malcolm."

One more request from his ex. He turned over their connected hands, admiring the slight contrast in skin tones, his—light toast, hers—medium toast. Hallison's back stiffened waiting for his response. Instead, he guided her head to his shoulder. Hallison complied without arguing. "I will always love you, Hali."

"I'll never stop loving you either."

Malcolm waited for her to say more, but she never did. Last New Year's Eve, he proposed, Hallison said yes. She loved him. He loved her back. They went to church. She came out converted. He didn't. She refused to marry him without a commitment to Christ. He refused to be forced. It was the beginning of the end. Hallison seemed happy. Malcolm was far from content with the women he had dated since their breakup.

Somehow, Hallison found enough peace in the so-called night's storm to fall asleep. Her light snoring lulled Malcolm to sleep. It was the same melody that caused him to doze during one of many of their late-night pillow talks.

Ninety minutes later, the clerk's booming voice echoed off the walls, jolting them awake. Malcolm jerked his head and braced himself to ward off any possible attack.

"Hey, hey, your grandma's back, and just as I thought, she's fine. Once the booking process is complete, you can bail her out at St. Louis County jail."

Standing, they stretched. Disoriented, Hallison searched for her purse while Malcolm texted Parke: *We haven't seen her yet, but we have to go to County to get her out. Oh, this is not my idea of a date.* Escorting Hallison out the door, Malcolm led the stroll to his car. As he pulled off the lot, Hallison drifted back into her slumber.

They arrived at St. Louis County Jail and repeated their request. Hallison and Malcolm were instructed to have a seat, this time, in cushion-covered chairs. By two o'clock in the morning, Malcolm's behind felt disfigured from sitting in one spot for hours. Yet, he was content as Hallison dozed, snuggled in his arms. He inhaled the clean scent of her hair. Malcolm was somewhat content despite Cheney's father being shot and Mrs. Beacon somewhere between jails. Maybe the night's event was a blessing in disguise. He didn't know how many women he had dated since Hallison, but at the moment, only her presence satiated him.

An hour and a half later, after learning of Mrs. Beacon's bail amount, he posted her bond. She signed the necessary paperwork and walked out into the lobby with no visible signs of anguish. "Thanks for coming to get me."

The trio was barely outside the building when Hallison unleashed her fury. "What is wrong with you? Grandma BB, did you purposely shoot Cheney's father? I can't believe you—"

"Hold up. Unless there are witnesses, I ain't guilty of nothing." Mrs. Beacon lifted her chin and dared either to disagree. When they said nothing, she straightened her seventy-seven-year-old body, then she switched all the way to Malcolm's Monte Carlo, strutting in pink stilettos instead of her Stacy Adams shoes, until they heard a bone crack. Mrs. Beacon continued with a slight limp that didn't slow her down.

Hallison never opened the pocket Bible that Malcolm knew she carried in her purse. She appeared to be too troubled. "Six days ago, we were sitting in church and singing praises unto the Lord. Tonight, we're leaving jail after bailing you out. What is going on?"

"I didn't ask you to bail me out. Personally, I liked the pink walls inside my cell at the Ferguson jail. It matched my pantsuit. Plus I had another female roommate—I mean cellmate to keep me company. She was sixty-nine years old and slashed the tires of her fifty-year-old lover's car for cheating on her. She's probably home by now."

"Great. A kindred spirit. Jail is not a social networking event," Hallison stated, agitated.

"Let me tell you something, young lady." She did her roll-your-neck thing. "First of all, you didn't bail me out. Judge Matthews released me on my own recognizance." Mrs. Beacon wagged her finger.

"Wrong. It's a good thing that place had an ATM machine. Parke and I put up ten percent of your bail, and I will get my money back," Malcolm stated, walking past her.

Mrs. Beacon ignored him and fussed at Hallison. "I don't need you keeping a daily diary of my whereabouts. On my good days, both of my feet are planted in the church. Yep, I got baptized and laid across the carpet, speaking in a language I had never heard before, and it sounded good too. Now this is personal. All bets are off. I've got one foot in church with one dangling out. If I need to, I'll consult with God later."

Malcolm would have laughed if the situation weren't so serious. *If her sins are washed away, then she needs a second rinse*, he thought. The bickering didn't stop as Malcolm assisted Mrs. Beacon into the backseat.

"Grandma BB, you can't have it both ways. I should know . . ." Hallison stole a glance at Malcolm who was listening with interest. "I don't know why you would want to aim a gun at Mr. Reynolds anyway. People are looking at us, watching churchgoers to see if we really are what we profess to be. There's more at stake than just you or me going to glory. We have to convince others glory is worth sacrificing everything in the world."

Hallison heard God's warning that Sunday at church. *Are you ready? I call many, but I choose few. Search Matthew 22. Is it evil for you to serve me? Declare, Hallison, this day who you will serve. If you deny me, I will deny you before the Father. Choose . . . choose this day who you will serve. Search Joshua 24 . . . choose . . .*

She remembered God's fading voice, but the warning intensified within her spirit. Hallison thought she was glued to the pew, but she sprang up with a force that chains couldn't confine. As God beckoned her to the altar, Hallison kept moving without looking back. She felt the moment when God had restored her spiritually after ministers surrounded her with prayer. Later, when she walked out the church doors, it seemed as if she'd never left God.

The only child of middle-aged parents, Harold and Addison Dinkins, Hallison was reared in the church. During her youth, she loved the atmosphere: church functions, other children, and the many mothers whom she called play-mommas or play-grandmas. Her only blood relatives in the church were her aunt Norma and Norma's daughters, Faye and Tammy.

Once Hallison returned from Xavier University in New Orleans with a business degree in hand, she felt it was time to put away childish things. She heard the rumor about how the pastor counseled couples to stay in God's will and minimize temptation in order to stay pure. *Impossible*, she had thought. When the pastor advised a close girlfriend, Octavia, to wait before marrying her boyfriend, Hallison balked. When her friend rebelled and married anyway, Hallison cheered.

She had been nitpicking for a while, trying to find any little fault in God. Hallison considered her former pastor's meddling in a couple's relationship the final straw. She left God's house a nomad, always searching for a new home, but never settling. At that point, the more God reached out to bring her back into the fold, the more Hallison resisted, snubbing the saints, their testimonies, and praises.

Hallison later learned that Octavia survived through a nightmarish marriage. Octavia's husband had been on drugs and physically abusive. The only rainbow after the storm was David dying in a shootout during a drug bust, freeing Octavia. Hallison sighed. It was the wrong time to think about that when she had another drama unfolding from the backseat.

Once their seatbelts were in place, Mrs. Beacon leaned forward. "Does Cheney know what happened to her old man?"

Hallison shook her head. "Not yet."

"Good. I'll be more than happy to give her the scoop." Mrs. Beacon nodded, crossing her arms.

Mrs. Beacon refused to say another word as they drove to her house. Hallison doubted scriptures could fix the situation anyway. Once they arrived on Benton Street, Mrs. Beacon got out the car unassisted. Turning back, she smiled and waved goodnight, as if she had been on a date. They waited for Mrs. Beacon to flash her porch light, signaling she was safely inside.

"So, back to us, Hali," Malcolm said a moment later, releasing an annoying sigh. He tapped the steering wheel until she made eye contact. "After all these months of soul searching, you're positive there's no way we can coexist with your beliefs and mine?"

Hallison shook her head. This wasn't the first time they'd had this conversation. To a warm-blooded woman, Hallison's reasons didn't make sense. To a warm-blooded church woman, it sounded good to confess, but in reality, God was asking too much of her to give up this man. She shivered as she recalled her first argument with Malcolm after the Lord restored His relationship with her.

"Okay, Hali, tell me who is the real woman I fell in love with—the one I escorted to church, or the one who ignored me afterward," Malcolm demanded, his voice threatening.

Hallison's shoulders slumped. "Both, I guess. I never mentioned church in our relationship because at the time that wasn't my concern. Neither of us had heavenly thoughts on our mind, just earthly desires. Maybe my mistake was I made you my world. I couldn't get enough of you."

He sighed. "You're talking as if you were an undercover church agent. Tell me this. You said you loved me, but—" He held up his hand to keep Hallison from inter-

rupting. "—*you forgot I don't drink, smoke, gamble, or whatever else is in the sinners' handbook. I'm a CPA with a healthy, steady income. I'm in high demand, baby. I'm not boasting, but I pack the good looks that my ancestors sent me. I'm a man who doesn't play games unless they're on a board. My personal résumé is full of accomplishments, so don't you see, baby? God made me self-sufficient. I have need of nothing but you.*"

"Our relationship was headed down a path I knew God wouldn't approve, but I wanted it anyway. I'm still soul searching."

Malcolm didn't respond as he drove the few blocks to Parke's house. When he pulled across the street from her car, he nodded. "Okay, I love you, but I'm my own man. Today was a test. We've both passed and failed. We're still compatible and desirable to each other even after all these months. We've failed, because we're both at a stalemate. It's time for us to move on.

"Evidently, your church obsession hasn't fizzled. I told you, I don't have a problem with church. You do. If we're meant to be with each other, we'll find our way back. If not, that means that there's a love stronger out there than what we have. My prayer is that you'll never find one."

CHAPTER 4

"She did what?" Cheney yelled, springing up in bed. The news interrupted her Saturday afternoon nap. Despite being somewhat drained from her pregnancy, she was fully alert. "What did you say?"

Parke sat on the bed and massaged her arms in a subtle way to keep her calm. This was not the way he wanted to wake his wife. Usually, he would massage her stomach until Cheney slowly woke refreshed. He swallowed before repeating, "Baby, I said Grandma BB shot your dad."

"When?"

Parke cringed. "Last night."

Cheney's lips moved before any words came out. "And I'm just now finding out?"

Please help my wife, Lord. She's going to need it, and there's good reason, Parke thought. Months before he married Cheney, Roland Reynolds approached Parke with a startling confession. The strained relationship with his daughter had less to do with her long-ago decision to have an abortion, but more to do with the sins of his own past.

"Twenty years earlier, I was the hit-and-run driver

*who killed Cheney's next-door neighbor's husband,
Henry Beacon. It's ironic that I could point the finger at
Cheney's sin, but couldn't acknowledge my own. After
all, I was in residency, preparing to become a doctor, an
obstetrician, when the accident happened.*

*"I was supportive about her returning home until she
moved next door to the woman I had wronged. I knew
where the woman lived for years and avoided the area. I
couldn't face Mrs. Beacon, knowing my cowardly act, so
I let my baby girl believe I shunned her because of her
secret abortion that wasn't so secret after I became suspicious and snooped around, enlisting the help of a col-
league to disclose confidential information from Cheney's
file.*

Roland had been drunk the night of the accident. The
next morning he had read about the hit-and-run in the
newspaper. Without any witnesses, Roland suppressed
any remorse, believing luck was on his side. He had told
Parke he was prepared to take his secret to the grave until
Cheney embraced a closer walk with God. Roland craved
it too, since the guilt had returned. Still, he remained
silent.

It wasn't easy for Parke to withhold the truth from
Cheney, especially since Mrs. Beacon had become a surrogate grandmother to her, but Roland pleaded for more
time. The two agreed to wait until after the wedding to tell
Cheney and Mrs. Beacon, who was sure to lynch Roland
before he would be able to turn himself into authorities.
Months later, Roland wasn't ready to admit the truth and
risk losing the closeness he was regaining with his daughter. Evidently, time caught up with him.

"Cheney, I don't want you to upset yourself. He's alive.
He's alert and talking. It was a small wound to his shoulder."

"Well, that should make me feel better," she bit out. "I

don't care if it was his shoulder! It could've been his head or heart. Grandma BB is out of control." Cheney sighed to compose herself, rubbing her stomach to ease the baby's kicking. "Missouri should've never passed that conceal-and-carry ordinance and granted Grandma BB a gun permit . . . I can't believe this." Tears streamed down her face. "Wait a minute. Daddy was over this way? He lives in the city. He didn't tell me he was stopping by for the baby shower—"

He had no choice but to go in for the kill. "It wasn't an accident, honey. I believe she was purposely trying to take him out."

Tilting her head, she squinted. "What do you mean?"

Parke sighed, knowing he was about to ignite a firecracker. "Grandma BB thinks Roland is guilty of something—"

"What?" Cheney grimaced as she wrestled with the covers, finally throwing them back. She didn't wait for Parke to finish explaining, nor did she welcome his daily pampering that had begun the day they learned she was pregnant. She was becoming hysterical. Despite her protruding stomach, she rushed into the bathroom.

With a little more than three months to go, Cheney had cut back her hours at work as a building manager for Missouri Telephone and worked afternoons from their home, which was less than ten minutes away. The purpose was to get rest, not to be stressed.

"Going somewhere?" He attempted to remain composed as he stood. He suspected her dash to the bathroom wasn't a nature call.

"Yep, to get dressed. First, I'm going to see my dad." She paused. "Nope, scratch that. Let's do a drive-by Grandma BB's." She balled her fist. "Then I'm going to the hospital to see my dad. Now who's driving, you or me?"

"I guess I am," Parke resigned, grimacing. He patted his

pants pockets for his keys, and then he went to wake Kami. Within twenty minutes, Cheney had freshened up. She performed her best speed-walk imitation out the door.

Parke was in no rush to strap Kami into her booster seat. Once the task was completed, he tussled with his own seatbelt to stall the inevitable. Taking a deep breath, he hesitantly drove the five blocks to Cheney's former next door neighbor's. Too soon, they turned off Darst to Benton Street and parked. "Let me make sure she's at home before you get out," he said, hoping for the contrary. When Mrs. Beacon didn't answer after three tries, Parke grinned to himself in relief. He returned to the SUV with his face draped in disappointment. "I'm sorry, she wasn't home, baby." He feigned frustration. "You want to head to the hospital and come back later?"

Cheney twisted and manipulated her body out of her seatbelt. "No. We're on a stake-out. I'll wait until my bladder starts talking." Scanning the block, Cheney admired the changes to her former house, courtesy of her friend. Imani was a flight attendant who purchased it after Cheney married Parke. Too bad Imani was never home to enjoy it. Cheney had lovingly restored the abandoned three-bedroom house with a sunroom over the garage. The landscape and outdoor lighting were projects she had done before she met Parke.

Her reminiscing ceased. Cheney wasn't on a sightseeing expedition. She squinted at her husband who seemed way too quiet in the middle of her drama. He was about to slide in a CD when she touched his hand to stop him. "Parke, tell me what's going on now before I deliver this baby right here in my seat," she ordered.

"I . . . look!" Parke pointed. "There's the little criminal now." He scrambled out the vehicle and jogged around the bumper to the passenger side. Cheney was already opening her door and getting out the vehicle.

"Parke, stay with Kami."

Sure enough, while the Boyz II Men ballad grew louder, Mrs. Beacon's Cadillac cruised by and turned into the driveway. Parke unfastened Kami's buckle, and they trailed Cheney to Mrs. Beacon's car. Both women stared at each other, waiting for the other to cower.

Tapping her foot, Cheney folded her arms. "Please, please tell me it's not true."

"Okay." Mrs. Beacon shrugged fearlessly as she resembled Goliath's height. The sassy senior wasn't intimidated. She jutted her chin. "It's not true."

"What were you thinking? You owe me some answers, Grandma, and I ain't leaving until you tell me the truth, and I mean the whole truth, or so help you God. You don't want to share a jail cell with me." Cheney's fair skin reddened as she balled her hand. Although she was angry, her baby was sitting on a vital organ and the pain was adding to her current stress.

Parke squeezed his wife's shoulder. "Sweetheart, remember your condition," he whispered in her ear before he kissed her.

Cheney elbowed her husband. "She better remember my condition." She pointed at her former neighbor.

"Humph! You always were a snooty thang," Mrs. Beacon sassed, then did an about face to her front porch. "C'mon." Kami was the first to follow.

Parke snickered until Cheney shot him an evil eye. He cleared his throat and mumbled an apology. Mrs. Beacon was known for her seesaw personalities. She could appear frail or be as energetic as a teenager. Either way, she was convincing.

Inside her meticulous home, Mrs. Beacon's living room

was decorated with contemporary furniture and accents—
unlike the plastic-covered sofa and chairs associated with
many senior citizens' homes. Bold colors mixed with white
suede sectional pieces: throw pillows, vases, and artwork.
Mrs. Beacon had the newest trend in window treatments,
and her dining room set looked like it came from a Thomas-
ville showroom.

"Might as well get comfortable while I go change clothes,"
Mrs. Beacon casually said.

Cheney barely cleared the doorway when she shouted,
"I don't need you to change clothes to explain why you
shot my daddy. Believe me. I won't be offended if you
were naked, although Parke might pass out."

"Daddy, can I go with BB? I like her big box of jewelry."
Kami gave Parke an angelic face, which contradicted her
feisty personality.

He nodded, and his daughter skipped behind Mrs. Beacon.

"Listen, girl, my body is sacred. Only the privileged get
to see it," Mrs. Beacon argued with Cheney while taking
Kami's hand.

Cheney rolled her eyes. "Umm-hmm. Don't use Kami to
stall. I do know where your bedroom is located."

"Yeah, but who's bad enough to barge into it? Umm-hmm,
that's what I thought. Nobody. I'll be back." Mrs. Beacon
turned around and switched her hips out the room.

Parke sat unusually quiet, avoiding eye contact. Mrs. Beacon reappeared clothed in a floral housedress and wearing her legendary oversized Stacy Adams shoes, which once
belonged to her deceased husband, Henry. After more than
twenty years, Mrs. Beacon kept the shoes cleaned and
polished. Her explanation for wearing them was vague except they once belonged to him. Kami followed Mrs. Beacon with bright red lipstick smeared around her mouth,
and clusters of white pearl earrings clipped on her ears.

"Did you, or didn't you shoot my father?" Cheney asked, manipulating herself to stand. Big for six months, the doctor warned her about picking up too much weight. She couldn't imagine what she would look like at nine months.

"Unless there were witnesses, no," Mrs. Beacon said, lifting a brow and daring Cheney to state otherwise.

"And if there were witnesses?" Cheney challenged. Going ballistic on her surrogate grandmother, former neighbor, and confidante wouldn't yield any direct answers because Mrs. Beacon thrived on drama. Yet, there was no excuse for the woman's behavior.

Mrs. Beacon tilted her head and squinted. "Then I would boast, 'Yeah, I shot the sucker.'"

"You're crazy!" As Cheney punched the sectional sofa in frustration, she swiped the side of Parke's jaw when he leaned in to calm her down. When he yelped, she asked, "What is wrong with you?"

"Me? You smacked me," Parke said, stunned.

Cheney blinked and looked at her husband. "Not you, her." She pointed to Mrs. Beacon. "Grandma BB, you've gone too far with your antics. Are you sure you repented before you were baptized? Your actions and words don't sound like you know Jesus."

"Look, Heney," Mrs. Beacon said, reverting to her pet name for Cheney. "I'm going to say this once, because this whole conversation is tiring. Your father saw me at a market. We chatted for a few minutes. He said he needed to speak with me privately. I didn't suspect anything amiss, so I suggested we go over to the pond at Wabash Park. You know I like to stroll in my heels until my feet start hurting, then I wish for my old Stacy Adams shoes. It was a good thing I packed my Smith & Wesson. When he confessed he was the hit-and-run driver who killed my Henry, I nodded okay, then I opened my purse, reached for my gun, and shot him."

In horror, Cheney patted her chest to control the palpitations and glanced back at her husband. Disbelief marred her face. "You've lost your mind. My father would never do such a thing! He's a doctor. He saves lives."

Mrs. Beacon shrugged. "Think what you want. I left him alive so he could confess a little louder. Go ask him for yourself. Your father's a murderer!"

"You're lying."

"Don't call me a liar, little girl. God is my witness and his too. Now if you'll excuse me, I'm going to pray and repent. You can let yourselves out."

"I woke with a headache. Now I'm going to bed with a headache and heartache," Cheney complained to Hallison over the phone late Saturday night.

"This isn't what you needed. It's just like the devil to show up uninvited to a party. I wondered where Grandma BB was the night of the shower. Have you spoken with your dad?" Hallison asked as she pushed the timer on the microwave for her nightly cup of herbal tea. She had slept most of the day after jail hopping most of the night, thanks to Mrs. Beacon.

"The doctors have him on some strong pain medicine. Here's the odd thing, Hali. When he was coherent, Daddy didn't deny killing Mr. Beacon. I kept waiting for him to say, 'I didn't do it.' Girl, this has been so much drama, I could go into labor."

"Please don't. I can't take a double scoop of anything else right now."

"Tell me about it. Mom was on the defensive, chiding me for thinking the worst of her husband, and blaming me for moving where I did. To top it off, my siblings provided secret-service protection by his bedside against me. I couldn't get any privacy if I bribed them. I needed answers, but . . . ooh." Cheney gasped.

"What's the matter?"

"The baby kicked."

Chuckling, Hallison could hear the smile in Cheney's voice. "What did I tell you? I've already exceeded my crisis level this weekend."

Parke's voice boomed in the background, arguing with Kami about which pajamas she wanted to wear to bed. Cheney muffled the phone to reply, then yawned. "I guess that's my cue to hang up. Please pray, Hali, that I can get through this."

Nodding, Hallison closed her eyes. "Lord, in the matchless name of Jesus, we need understanding, strength . . . we need you . . . " Hallison wanted to cry out so many things before God, unspoken requests she didn't want to share with Cheney, one of which concerned Malcolm.

It didn't take long for God to meet them at the crossroads. He touched her tongue, and a heavenly language poured out of Hallison's soul. Soon the power anointed Cheney to join in, speaking in unknown tongues controlled by the Spirit. For a few minutes, they indulged in one praise party, and God listened to both petitioners.

"Finally, Father, we thank you for meeting us here. I ask that you bless my dear friend and my family. Give us peace, love, and wisdom. Save all who don't know you, in Jesus' name we ask," Cheney ended, "Amen."

"Amen."

"Hali, I know all of the prayer wasn't about me. You'll be all right with or without Malcolm."

"How did you know?"

"Because I've prayed like that before over a man," Cheney explained.

When Hallison hung up the phone, she cried again.

CHAPTER 5

"Who told you to let peace go? Speak up! God can't hear you," the pastor of Faith Miracle Church preached the following morning. Hallison sat in her usual pew next to Parke and Cheney, but one familiar reserved spot remained empty. Hallison scanned the sanctuary and spotted Mrs. Beacon on the opposite side near the back.

"What part of Exodus 14:14 don't you understand? The Lord shall fight your battle, or ye shall hold your peace? This is not an *if* scripture. It's a *just do it by faith* scripture. If you drop peace, the only thing you'll pick up is discord . . ." Elder Baylor Scott ministered to the congregation. At the end of service, Mrs. Beacon, with her head high, headed for the west exit as Cheney chatted with Hallison.

"We needed that message, sister," Hallison said, hugging Cheney. "Hey, where's your husband?"

Squinting, Cheney looked around until she saw him. "You know Parke. It seems he can't leave church without speaking to at least one hundred people. C'mon. He'll meet us at the SUV."

They walked out the building to the parking lot. Hallison found a piece of candy for Kami as Parke's heavy footsteps caught up with them. He was snarling.

Cheney lifted her brow at Hallison's frown. "What's wrong with you? We're still on church property and you look like you left peace inside."

Parke waved off his wife. "Never mind. Come on, let's go."

Cheney didn't move. "I don't know what attitude you slipped into just now, but go take it back to the devil." She pointed to nowhere. "What is wrong with you, Parke Kokumuo Jamieson VI?"

"Oh, no, not that K word," Hallison joked, snickering. When she couldn't contain herself, a hearty laugh escaped.

"I'm glad you think it's funny because I find it downright irritating," Parke said.

"What?" Cheney squinted.

"That's the second guy this week. First in Bible class. Now today." Parke disarmed his vehicle. "Brother Carr and now Brother Thomas asked if Hallison was my sister and if she were available." He frowned.

"What did you tell them?" Hallison hadn't thought about other men expressing interest in dating her or them asking her former boyfriend's brother to intercede on their behalf.

"You don't want to know." When Parke opened the SUV's back door, Kami insisted on climbing in unassisted.

"Yes, we do," they snapped in unison.

He cleared his voice. "Well, the short version is that you two are separated, and he just left jail this weekend."

Giggling, Hallison slapped his arm. "Why would you say that?"

"Honestly, Brother Carr has changed jobs three times within the past six months. It had nothing to do with the economy. Brother Thomas, I just didn't like him, period. Either way, neither one passes my inspection."

* * *

Monday morning, Hallison walked into her office and groaned at the stack of work on her desk from Friday. For three hours, Hallison sequestered herself behind closed doors until her eyes blurred. She had scrutinized a two hundred-page plan on employee safety and training procedures.

Rubbing her stiff neck, she recalled Malcolm's departing words: *"If we're not meant to be, I pray that you'll never find a greater love."* Hallison cleared her head. Of all things to pray for, why that? "They were just words," she reminded herself, "and words can never hurt me."

"I wouldn't believe that, sister-girl. Proverbs eighteen says death and life are in the power of the tongue, so watch out," Paula Silas, coworker and friend, corrected as she popped her head inside Hallison's office.

Startled, Hallison looked up. Embarrassed, she shook her head, laughing. "You eavesdropper. What are you doing down here?"

"I'm inviting you to dine in the Boardroom. By the way, the next time you talk to yourself, whisper. It's more discreet." Paula displayed her trademark brilliant and contagious smile.

"Oh, if we get to use the executive conference room, that means the bigwigs are out of the building."

"You're a wise one, Hali." Paula gave a mocked bow.

Lunch with Paula was a luxury. Hallison always felt energized after a Christ-centered fellowship with her. With the demands of running their departments, coordinating their schedules wasn't easy, but it was worth it. When Hallison hired Paula a year ago as the bank's new chief credit manager, Hallison felt as if she were chatting with an old girlfriend. Within minutes, Hallison rejected the warm and cozy feeling as Paula praised God for the salary and job. It grated on Hallison's nerve at the time because she didn't want to hear the name Jesus more than twice in one month. That was before she returned to Christ.

"It all depends. What are we eating?" Hallison asked.

Paula came farther into the office. Her predictable attire always complemented the highlights in her hair in some way, whether it was a scarf or jacket, summer or fall, casual or dressy. She never missed the opportunity to make a fashion statement. Today she wore a shimmery soft green top under her blazer that complemented the shimmer in her makeup. "Ursula picked up Cecil Whittaker's sandwiches for us—the special."

Hallison's stomach growled at the mention of a St. Louis favorite—hot ham, roast beef, salami, and double cheese sandwiches, from a chain of family-owned restaurants.

"Can't have her waste her money."

"Works every time. C'mon. Let's head upstairs to the hide-out."

Standing, Hallison stretched and smoothed the creases from her winter pink wool suit, then shut down the computer. After locking her office, Hallison trailed Paula to the lobby. Stepping into the elevator, they acknowledged other riders with smiles.

"So how was Cheney's baby shower?" Paula asked, punching the button for the eleventh floor.

Hallison rolled her eyes and sighed. "Unbelievable. It started off good, but ended in a nightmare. As expected, Malcolm was at the baby shower. The sight of him made me want to renege on my promise to walk with the Lord in holiness, she said, getting off the elevator. The real surprise was Mrs. Beacon shooting Cheney's dad."

"Did I hear Malcolm's name mentioned?" Ursula Taylor asked. Her sonic ears beamed in on any gossip. As they entered their secluded meeting place, the legal department's executive boardroom, they quenched their conversation when they saw the food set up in the middle of a long cherry oak table. Ursula closed one of the styrofoam containers, dropped in a chair, and kicked up her heels in a nearby seat. "I'm waiting, and you know I don't like cold food." She shook her head with an added flair.

Hallison had recently hired Ursula as the new retirement and client solutions specialist. For some strange reason Hallison couldn't explain, they bonded. Ursula packaged herself as a conservative, but had a fondness for outrageous wigs. The three formed an odd on-the-job friendship triangle. Paula's faith increased daily. In contrast, Ursula's faith seemed to diminish by the hour. Paula grabbed a container and relaxed in a chair. Also sitting, Hallison reluctantly rehashed tidbits of the story.

"Didn't you say this Grandma BB attended your church?" Ursula queried between bites while Paula and Hallison bowed their heads in silent prayers. "Interesting. She must've taken a detour on her path to heaven." She shrugged as if she weren't surprised.

"Let me put it this way. Somewhere between the choir singing and the pastor preaching, she must've fallen asleep," Hallison shamefully answered after she said amen.

Ursula chuckled. "The woman is my idol."

On most days, Hallison overlooked her off-handed remarks, but Ursula had an uncanny talent of zeroing in on church hypocrisy. She thrived on it. She had a carbon copy attitude that Hallison possessed less than a year ago. Hallison compared herself to Saul—the pre-redemption Paul, who persecuted the Jews that followed Christ—to the forgiven Paul who proudly accepted persecution for following Christ.

"And," Ursula paused and waved her hand in air. "For months you've been professing you're over Malcolm. Instead of a testimony, a few hours with the man has your heart rate climbing and you giving a "lie-a-mony." Ask me, you would've done better keeping him and putting the witnessing stuff on hold. I put my money on Malcolm. You're going down, girl," Ursula said, slapping the table.

"But not without a fight this time," Hallison countered.

"A good man is hard to find," Ursula said.

You're telling me, Hallison thought.

"I'm married, and I'm still trying to find a good man," Ursula continued.

"See, that's your flesh talking, Ursula. Anthony was good enough for you to marry. Plus, we can't cut a deal with God," Paula explained.

For a half hour, Hallison listened as Paula and Ursula played volleyball with their opinions. She shook her head as she swallowed the last bite of her sandwich.

"Every now and then, I feel that God has asked too much of me. I would've gladly given up anything else but Malcolm."

It wasn't the first time God told Hallison to give up something after she defiantly left the church. Her addiction to cigarettes was short-lived after recovering from several wheezing episodes and visiting the St. Louis Science Center's cadaver exhibition. The urge vanished when she viewed a swollen, black tar-covered lung. God whispered, *Give me your body as a living sacrifice.* Cigarettes forgotten, Hallison decided to get a cutesy tattoo. Again, the Lord spoke, *Your body is my temple. Glorify me in your body, my temple is holy. . . .* As she walked farther away from God, the more spiritually deprogrammed she became. More than once, she partied all night and got drunk twice. There was no limit as Hallison seriously considered the advances of married men. God never stopped reminding her of the scriptures.

Then Malcolm Jamieson stepped into her world. At the time, both she and Malcolm were minority recruiters for their respective companies at a job fair. With little effort, they sold the other on the benefits of a relationship.

Throughout the daylong event, sparks flew and engulfed them. It wasn't long before he exhilarated Hallison's weary spirit and calmed her stormy moods. Her heart rejoiced. Malcolm was the package, and she was ready to unwrap her gift. Within two weeks, they had fit six dates into their busy schedules. By the end of the third date, they shared several passionate kisses, and Hallison had enjoyed every one of them.

Soon they began to undress each other, but God shouted at her, *The body is not for fornication, but for the Lord.* The following months had been torture for them as she delayed their physical fulfillment. Malcolm didn't balk. Although he always respected her decision, the temptation was becoming unbearable. Hallison's flesh constantly warred against her spirit, which she couldn't quench.

On New Year's Day, at one minute past midnight, they celebrated their official one-year-and-three-week dating anniversary. Malcolm had proposed. She could've shouted for the victory. It had been close, but she was going to make it to the altar without fornicating. Yet, God still wasn't satisfied. The Lord warned, *Be not unequally yoked with the unbeliever.* She was so mad; it seemed as if she couldn't win with God. Finally, when the Lord spoke to her about spending eternity in hell, she listened.

"Well, it doesn't make sense to me," Ursula countered. "I was under the impression God only stepped in when a person actually did something bad, like stealing or killing. Girl, if you're in a committed relationship it isn't lusting. Humph! I can't believe you're still sticking to that story that God told you to walk away from Malcolm. How do you know it was God? That's when you should've gotten a second opinion." Ursula's repetitious taunt surfaced every time Malcolm's name was mentioned.

Sometimes, you know that you know, Hallison thought. During that sermon a year ago, Hallison knew.

An hour later after lunch, the encounter with Malcolm was the furthest thing from Hallison's mind. She had two department managers quit. One gave two weeks notice. The other packed up his desk, dropped off his resignation letter to Hallison's administrative assistant, and walked out. Hallison had to replace the software support specialist and marketing assistant immediately. By five o'clock on Tuesday, the vacancies were posted on the bank's website and circulated through various networks.

By the time Hallison arrived at church for Wednesday night Bible class, she was exhausted. Before the week was over, she had more than thirty qualified applications on her desk. She loved her job, but she disliked the hiring process, mostly because she had to choose one out of many talented professionals. Since the economy was slow, the majority of the candidates were over-qualified and their salary requirements backed it up.

Saturday morning, Hallison prayed and danced around her bedroom, happy for some down time. After she showered and dressed, she pulled her hair into a ponytail and left for her hair appointment.

"I need the works: a facial, nails, hair. Make me beautiful, Alexis," Hallison stated minutes after walking through the doors of The Workout, the Workup, and Workin' Hair and Body Boutique.

The petite woman, with more earrings in an ear than ear space, grabbed her clipboard and checked off Hallison's requests. "You look like you need a massage."

"How could you tell? Yes, put me down for that too."

"Good. After you're dolled up, you'll need to go shopping," Alexis suggested, leading Hallison across the marble floor to a spacious shampoo room. Once Hallison was seated, the stylist prepped her for a deep scrub and conditioner. "Since you were in last, I found this new shoe store hidden in the Central West End. It's exclusive—a membership is required," Alexis said in a hushed tone.

"Get out of here. And how did you gain admittance?" Hallison cringed as Alexis twisted and jerked her head around during a deep scrub and rinse.

"Through a friend of a friend's cousin married to an executive who owned a chain of auto dealerships."

"You and your connections." Hallison smirked, then shrugged. "Why not? Count me in."

"Hey, it's a perk from owning my business. Anyway, my last appointment is at three. I can be ready in an hour once I get home." She held Hallison's head still, thinking. "You know, I'll need two hours maximum for perfection." She started to sing, "A party ain't a party unless it's a shoe party."

* * *

"I want visitation rights, and I will go to court to get them," Mrs. Beacon demanded over the phone. "I became Kami's grandma the same day you became her mother. She's in my will and everything."

"You should've thought about our family ties before you shot my father. You're already going to jail for attempted murder," Cheney said, appalled at the woman's nerve. She massaged her temples. "You could've killed him." Her voice faded.

"He murdered my husband! Am I supposed to turn the other cheek? To do so would mean I didn't love my husband, and his life wasn't worth that much."

"But the Bible says, *Then came Peter to him, and said, Lord, how often shall my brother sin against me, and I forgive him? Till seven times? Jesus saith unto him, I say not unto thee, until seven times: but, until seventy times seven.*"

"Umm-hmm, I never read that."

"Crack open your Bible. It's in Mathew 18."

Mrs. Beacon cleared her throat. "Well, if it really says that, then I think you should listen to the Bible yourself and forgive me." They disconnected—or rather Mrs. Beacon abruptly hung up. Mrs. Beacon had turned the tables, and Cheney's judgment had backfired.

Parke walked into the kitchen from work and saw that tears were visible in Cheney's eyes. He brushed a kiss on her cheek. "Hey, wifey, are you in a hormonal mood? Kami hasn't gotten kicked out of pre-school, has she?" When she didn't respond, Parke became concerned. "You're scaring me. Is it your father? Is our little prince, or princess okay?"

Cheney held up her hand to stop her husband. She exhaled before explaining, "Nothing like that. Grandma BB called and threatened to take us to court for visitation rights to see Kami."

Parke had learned a while back to expect surprise attacks from Mrs. Beacon, so most times, he didn't overreact. Leaning against the counter, he rubbed the residual sweat from his forehead as a result of his recent jog. "Every day seems to get crazier and crazier. Whatever happened to peace on earth and goodwill to all men? Baby, what are we supposed to do, choose sides? Your dad is family, and Grandma BB . . . well, uh, Grandma BB is nuts, period, but she loves you and had your back when your family shut you out."

Wrapping her arms around Parke's waist, Cheney laid her head against his damp T-shirt. "You know, I threw a scripture at Grandma BB about forgiving Daddy. She had the gall to hurl it back at me and demand that I apply it to myself." She paused. "Being a Christian seems to be an endless circle of forgiveness."

As Cheney vented, Parke looked down at his wife. He loved the shape of her face since her pregnancy. She was more gorgeous. He tightened his embrace, making sure he didn't hurt her. "What do you mean, baby?" he mumbled, tuning in again.

She sighed, and Parke smiled, when their baby stretched in her stomach.

"Parke, I know the Bible says we're to love people, even the ones we can't stand, but it's the forgiveness I'm having the real issue with. Once I forgive, I find myself repenting for something else, then I'm back on track again. I just wish this never happened."

"Me, too, baby. I'm sure God has His reasons. I wonder if He'll ever share them with us."

She looked up and wrinkled her nose. "Parkay, let me share this. You need a shower. You stink."

CHAPTER 6

Malcolm didn't know if he would ever get over Halli-son, but he was going to give it his best shot. He didn't necessarily believe in premonitions, but there was always a first time. Malcolm didn't care how much he loved Hallison. There would be another woman to replace her. He had already begun the search.

His secretary, Lilly, opened his office door without knocking. "Malcolm, you have an appointment in five minutes."

He scanned his desk calendar. "No, I don't."

"Yep, you do. Make that in four minutes. Mr. Winfield had to leave for a family emergency, and since you're the only other CPA in the office today, you're it in three and a half minutes."

"Do you want to hand me something, you know, a file to give me a heads-up to who it is I'm meeting?" Malcolm said, pointing to the folder in Lilly's hand.

"Oh, yeah." She walked farther into his office and tossed the file on his desk. She grinned when it landed intact, then left.

He gritted his teeth in disbelief. If Lilly wasn't years

older than his mother, he would've hired the next temp who walked through the door. Opening the folder, Malcolm quickly scanned the one-page form, naming the business that requested the audit: Gertie's Garden. He shook his head at the thought of some little old lady with a secondhand store overrun with junk, two employees, herself, and a cat. When he finished reading the company's summary, he learned that it was actually a flower shop with twelve employees.

Lilly buzzed him. "Mr. Jamieson, your appointment is here."

"Thank you." Standing from behind his desk, he smoothed his tie against his starched shirt.

The client wasn't an old Gertie-looking woman. She was young, petite, and dressed in black, which signified "I'm dangerous." She strutted into the room with a purpose. Malcolm could only describe her as hot. He blinked to keep from staring and lifted his brow in appreciation. *Whoa. Hallison who?* He held in a chuckle and stretched out his hand. "Good morning."

She accepted. "Good morning, Mr. Jamieson. Thanks for seeing me. I'm sorry about Mr. Winfield's emergency, but I had already set this time aside."

Malcolm smiled. Despite the woman's flustered voice, she appeared composed. "Not a problem, Miss . . ." He looked down at the opened folder. "Miss Nixon. Please have a seat."

Adjusting her skirt, she laid a purse, the size of a shopping bag, on her lap. "Please call me Lisa. There's a time and place for titles. This is not one of them," she said, seemingly amused by her own statement.

A woman with a sense of humor, he thought, settling into his chair. "You've got a point. Please call me Malcolm. I'm not sure what you discussed with my boss, but we usually suggest a review instead of an audit for small companies. He noted a staff accountant could be available next week to visit her shop. So," Malcolm paused, sat straighter, and folded his hands, "how can I help you?"

"I'm not in the habit of letting just anybody walk into my office and look over my books. I prefer to get a feel for people before I cut a check." Lisa leaned forward. "Three things, Malcolm. My bank wants a certified audit before they will approve a new loan for an expansion. I don't want to wait until next week, and I don't want a staff accountant. If you are a senior certified accountant, I prefer to have you."

Of course, you do. Every client wants a CPA. Most people don't know that in many cases, entry-level college grad accountants do the grunt work. Malcolm stroked his beard to hide his grin. She was a firecracker waiting to be lit. He had asked, and she told him exactly what she wanted without batting an eye. He was intrigued.

"Sounds like you need a financial statement," Malcolm stated. "I sign off on the accountants' reports. I'm also tied up with some previous client commitments for the next week. I'm sorry."

Tilting her head, she flashed a peek of a smile. "This is one of those times where the use of a title is necessary. Mr. Jamieson, your firm comes highly recommended by several clients. I was told you're thorough, professional, and can do the job in record, billable hours."

He nodded. "That is correct. Our reputation is our business." The woman had done some homework. "Miss Nixon, I apologize for any misunderstanding. I've been supervising staff accountants for almost a year now." Picking up a pen, he tapped it on his desk, in thought. Although the firm's business was flourishing, it didn't balk at accepting new accounts, but the partners were selective about taking on new clients. One of their five accountants was on his honeymoon for two weeks; the others were tied up with government audits. "Lisa, when is the last time Gertie's Garden had an audit?"

"About six years ago, when I applied for a business loan that I paid off six months ago."

He glanced at the woman again. Her game face didn't hide the hopefulness in her eyes. Malcolm didn't doubt he could perform the audit in a timely manner, but somehow he had an odd feeling he was getting in over his head. "If you'll indulge me to play devil's advocate for a few minutes, I don't know much about a flower shop."

"Floral business," she corrected.

He cleared his throat. "I apologize. Are you sure you want to expand with the current instability of the economy?" As the financial planner in the family, Parke had advised his family to monitor their portfolio and limit risky investments until the U.S. dollar bounced back.

"Babies are born every minute, couples exchange vows every week, and as long as boyfriends and husbands are sentenced to the dog house, there are always good reasons to buy flowers every day."

Malcolm couldn't keep from chuckling. Lisa made a valid argument. "Okay," he said, almost convinced.

"Listen, the floriculture generated gross sales of more than twenty billion dollars last year. Gertie's Garden contributed about a million to that number."

"Then running a test through your invoices will back up your profits. It's the future cost of yearly expenses that could be unpredictable."

"Don't insult me. I wouldn't be successful if I weren't aware of that," Lisa snapped indignantly.

For the next half hour, Lisa Nixon proved to be an astute business owner. Malcolm deduced her age to be about thirty. She said she had taken over Gertie's Garden eight years previously, right out of college. Her short hair and short stature didn't take away from her larger-than-life confidence. Her smile—men were suckers for lips that didn't dare hide glossy white teeth.

She checked her wrist and frowned. An interesting piece of silver circles looped together served as a watch. The accessory matched the hoops dangling from her ears.

"Malcolm, I've been up since five this morning. I've got to eat something. Is your answer yes, or do I need to visit another firm?"

Malcolm considered his light workload for the remainder of the day. "Why don't *we* break for lunch? Once we return, I'll give you a list of documents we need to review and work on an outline for an engagement letter of billable hours." Pushing aside the file, he grinned. "It won't hurt to learn the difference between carnations and daffodils."

She twisted her lips in amusement. "Sounds fair, but in all sincerity, thank you, Malcolm. This was my grandmother's business she started with nothing more than plants in the ground. It's important to me to keep what she started going. My cousins want no part of it."

A kindred spirit. He nodded his understanding. His tenth generation grandmother, Elaine, who was the only daughter of a white slaveholder, set in motion the Jamieson legacy. It began the day she witnessed Paki, a slave, being tied to a tree and beaten. She ordered him down, and after dark, applied salve to his wounds. Their life story was well documented and had been passed down to future family members.

It wasn't out of the ordinary for male slaves to refuse to marry female slaves owned by the same master because they couldn't bear to see their wives whipped unmercifully when they didn't move fast enough for the overseer, or for the women to be sexually violated. If slaveholders did recognize unions, sometimes they would sell wives and children to other plantations to punish the husbands.

When Paki escaped, he became a fugitive, taking Elaine with him. If authorities found him, Paki was a dead man. Together, they journeyed toward Kansas, a free state. Changing their mind, they settled in Illinois, deciding not to risk capture in Missouri, another slave territory.

"Legacies are what strengthen families." Turning off his computer, Malcolm stood and grabbed his jacket. Lisa remained seated until Malcolm pulled her chair back, allowing her to stand. "I'll tell you about mine, if you'll share something about your family."

Lisa adjusted her purse strap on her shoulder as Malcolm towered over her. Looking up, she offered another gleaming smile. "There's not much to tell. My great-grandmother grew flowers in her backyard. She began selling them on her tattered front porch, and her best customers were men on their way home from work. She encouraged me to believe in myself and my natural gifts to affect positive changes by studying my craft."

"So, there's a school for florists?" he asked, concentrating more on her body's curves than her answer.

"The American Institute of Floral Design isn't really a school, but it's a place where florists can get accreditation—for a fee—which gives them clout. Each year the organization holds a national symposium. Talk about the themes, techniques, and networking. It's not an event to miss. I also attend lectures, and I'm part of garden club associations."

Multi-tasking, Malcolm listened and considered where they would eat. "There's a place about five short blocks away from here. I haven't eaten anything from there that I didn't like."

"Malcolm, I hope you can keep up. I walk three miles every morning, so don't let my heels fool you," Lisa tossed back.

"Really?" He smirked. "Is that a challenge?"

"Only if you take the bait, Mr. Jamieson."

Interesting, Malcolm thought. On the way, they chatted. Each word, each sentence bonded them as friends. Once they arrived at their destination, Lisa lifted a brow in curiosity. Although she didn't voice it, Malcolm knew what she was apparently thinking—a church?

As they walked through a side gate between the Abbey and the Old Rectory, a courtyard patio came into view. "I never thought a church could be the backdrop for something so whimsical."

"Correction, former church. Besides lunch, the Abbey is a popular place for special gatherings," Malcolm boasted the historical facts. The Ninth Street Abbey in Soulard was built in the 1850s as the St. Paul's German Evangelical Church, and then another denomination worshiped there.

In the early nineties, Patty Long Catering purchased and converted it. The Southside eatery, known for its good food and ambience, was just minutes from downtown. Malcolm had never taken Hallison there because he preferred meeting her on her job for lunch whenever she could break away. He never had any issues with church until Hallison came out of one brainwashed about Christ wanting all of her, and anything less wasn't an option.

Water gushing from a fountain distracted Lisa, causing her to almost trip as they climbed stone steps that introduced a patio deck. Malcolm's hand reached out and grabbed her elbow, steadying her. She nodded her thanks, then froze as a pergola waited to romance its guests. Lisa inhaled her surroundings and smiled.

"Wow, Malcolm. I'll have to remember to come back here."

"With a friend?" he asked, pulling her chair back.

"I don't need a friend to go where I want to go," Lisa said, snickering as she opened a menu.

Whoa. An independent woman didn't threaten Malcolm. His soon-to-be client was turning out to be quite captivating indeed. After taking his seat, Malcolm considered his choices before the waiter came to the table. He nodded for Lisa to go first. She ordered a chicken salad and so did he, but deluxe.

Malcolm glanced around, admiring the scenery that excited Lisa. "Tell me more about your great-grandmother."

"Well, Gertrude Thomas was a remarkable woman. She enjoyed the scent of fresh flowers throughout the house. She appreciated the beauty of Mother Nature. She found a use for everything, dead or alive. Her favorite thing was potpourri—a mixture of pine cones, colorful fall leaves and feathers. With determination, she mastered a technique to preserve her creations longer."

"Determination, now that's a description I recognize from my dining partner."

She laughed and slapped his arm, forcing him to join her. "Touché. You begged to hear my story," she teased.

He leaned closer. "I don't beg for anything." He thought about his breaking point with Hallison. Did he beg for her to choose him over God?

Lisa lifted a mocking brow and continued. "Anyway, she made beautiful bouquets in her mind before her hands duplicated the imaginary. When her front porch could no longer hold her collection of flowers, my great-grandma peddled her goods in a homemade kiosk—basically a large laundry cart. She stayed fit as she strolled through her neighborhood's streets like a paperboy. She never ran out of customers because she never stopped soliciting new business. I admire her entrepreneurial spirit, and I'm striving to duplicate it."

Malcolm was impressed. "Lisa, you're on the right track."

"I know. I'd like to corner the market in the floral business as Walter Knoll Florist has done locally. Of course, my stores would be smaller." Her eyes sparkled, clearly in a daydream. "Malcolm, I envision a Gertie's Garden on neighborhood corners like Walgreen's. Gertie's Gardens will be classy, storefront shops that steal business back from supermarkets with their pre-packaged bouquets."

New patrons joined them on the deck. Lisa and Malcolm remained chatting long after those customers were gone. Finally, they strolled back to Malcolm's office, unconcerned about the passage of time. Lisa completed the engagement letter, and as requested, returned it by mail within two days.

A week later, Malcolm hadn't stopped thinking about Lisa. He hadn't been at work ten minutes, when he walked out of his office. He scrutinized the brilliant flowers overtaking his assistant's desk. Malcolm snickered at the possibility of Lilly hiding behind them. *One of her sons must've been in the doghouse and sent a peace offering,* he reasoned.

"I guess your boys have made up with their momma," he said as he continued his stroll to the restroom.

"Nope. Actually they're for you—not Winfield & Young—from Miss Lisa Nixon. Hmm . . ."

"Hmm, what?" Stopping, Malcolm turned around and frowned.

She shrugged. "Just, hmm. I like to exercise my vocal cords."

"As long as you don't try and sing in the office again. You gave me a headache trying to hit some of Patti LaBelle's notes." Lilly rolled her eyes. "Since Lisa owns Gertie's Gardens, I'm sure it's her way to show her appreciation for our services."

Lilly fingered a delicate petal. "Humph. That's not what the note said. It sounded personal."

"And how do you know that?"

"Because I read it."

Twisting his mouth, Malcolm considered Lilly's answer.
He couldn't snap at his assistant. It was her job to open
his mail. Malcolm walked away toward the men's restroom, then he stopped. He didn't want to come across as
too eager, but now he was curious about Lisa's message.

Malcolm skipped the restroom. He could hold out a little longer as he backtracked to Lilly's desk and swiped up
the vase. He strolled into his office, carrying the arrangement as a makeshift dumbbell. With the back swing of his
foot, he kicked the door closed. After taking his seat, Malcolm indulged in a whiff before opening the miniature envelope and slipping out the card: *I don't believe in chances.
I believe in fate. Malcolm, I'm attracted to you. I'll let
you take it from here.*

Malcolm barked out a laugh, flattered. Evidently, Lilly
thought that was her cue to push open his door, forgoing
a knock. "Well?"

"Don't open anymore mail from Gertie's Garden."

She was about to say something when her phone rang.
Instead of going back to her desk, she walked to Malcolm's and lifted the receiver off the console before he
could protest.

"Winfield, Young & Associates, Mr. Jamieson's office,"
Lilly cooed into the phone. "One moment please." She
pressed the hold button and sauntered out of the office.
"It's for you. The flower lady," she said over her shoulder.

You'd better not call Lisa—our client—that to her face,
he thought. "Malcolm Jamieson." He smiled when he heard
Lisa's voice. It wasn't as husky as Hallison's, but he didn't
want a duplication of his former fiancée. "Good morning,
Lisa, and thank you for the flowers. They're nice, and
smell good too."

She dismissed any pleasantries and stated her intentions. "Would you like to accompany me to a Chuck Berry
concert at The Pageant tomorrow night? Although he's

local, I try to see him whenever he makes an appearance. I hope you can make yourself available."

Malcolm was amused. So the little woman liked taking the lead. He grinned. Come Monday, he planned to ask Mr. Winfield to remove him from the engagement contract. There came a time in a man's life where he had to decide whether to take the bait. Malcolm had his mouth wide open.

"Lisa, you do realize if we don't stop where this relationship is going, it won't be business." He waited for her response.

"I would welcome the development of a personal relationship over a business one. Next question."

The woman's confidence was exhilarating, but he refused to be put in another situation like the one with Hallison. He had to ask upfront, "Do you go to church? Lunching at the Abbey doesn't count."

She released a haughty snicker. "Only when I have to on C.M.E."

"What does that mean?"

"You know Christmas, Mother's Day, and Easter, plus weddings, funerals—only because it's good for my business. Why?"

"Oh, I'm curious. I wanted to know whether we were on the same page." *Yes. Lisa could be a woman after my heart.*

"We are, so let's turn it," Lisa stated.

CHAPTER 7

Hallison sucked in her breath when Samuel Smith walked into her office. Her Friday, four o'clock, appointment was multi-lingual, double-degreed, and fine. Hallison almost suffocated, forgetting to breathe. The tiredness, hunger, and crankiness she felt earlier evaporated when the door opened.

The deep-chocolate brother was larger than life. Hallison stood to greet him. She masked her appreciation in order to maintain her professionalism and to remind the applicant that the power of his future employment was in her hands.

"Hi, Samuel. Please, have a seat."

"Thank you. Please call me Sam." His baritone voice almost put Hallison into a trance as he did what she instructed. Samuel set his briefcase next to the chair, then reclined slightly. Crossing his ankle over a knee and folding his hands, he gave Hallison his full attention. He wore his confidence on his sleeve. She couldn't determine if he felt he already had the job, or if that was his normal demeanor.

Reclaiming her chair, Hallison sat straight as she fumbled with Samuel's folder. "Your credentials are impressive." He nodded in affirmation as she continued reading his accolades. "You were recently laid off after the InBev takeover of Anheuser-Busch.

"That is correct." His strong voice rumbled from his throat.

She asked him the tough questions about conflict resolutions, employee morale, and productivity. Samuel gave the right answers. She made notes on his résumé and listened intently for any flaws in his story. When he relaxed, they chatted about his preferred sport of rabbit hunting and sailing on the Lake of the Ozarks, located a few hours from St. Louis. Hallison enjoyed the repartee.

Thirty minutes later, she noted the time and closed his file. "Samuel, thank you for applying for the software support specialist position. Do you have any questions?"

Samuel's presence reminded Hallison that she was indeed an available single woman; a Christian woman. She wondered about Samuel's commitment to Christ, but of course, she wouldn't dare introduce that subject in an interview without compromising the fairness-in-hiring laws. That still didn't keep Samuel's mustache-trimmed lip from flirting with her every time he talked about the recognition awards he had received on the job.

"Yes. You mentioned medical, vision, and dental benefits. Does that include partners of employees? That's the deciding factor if I will entertain an offer. The insurance premiums at Jerome's job are too costly."

Hallison had to keep her jaw from becoming unhinged to maintain a professional demeanor. "The bank does offer benefits to qualified partners of eligible employees. The premiums are reasonable." She wanted to hand him a gospel tract. Instead, she stood and reached across her desk. "Samuel, as of this moment, you're the most qualified for the position, but I have three more interviews on Monday. I'll be in touch."

"Thank you." Samuel stood and accepted Hallison's firm handshake before retrieving his briefcase. He gave her one final grin before leaving, adding a slight switch to his hips.

When her door shut, Hallison yelled to her empty office, "Jesus!" *Not only does Samuel need a job with great benefits, he needs salvation with the best benefits.*

Cheney inhaled and slowly exhaled as she stared up at her parents' stately Westmoreland Place mansion. After stopping at a wrought-iron security gate, she was allowed to proceed, once an elderly guard, Mr. Yates, cleared her. The two-story, narrow, watch tower built before the fifty-plus custom-built homes were completed was meant to deter unwanted gawkers.

Leaving work early, Cheney had arranged for late pick up for Kami after pre-school in hopes of having an uninterrupted conversation with her father. She parked in one of five spaces in the semi-circle driveway. The pampered lawn and flower beds failed to grab her usual admiration. She had moved back to St. Louis a couple of years ago from Raleigh, North Carolina. Cheney's visits to the three-story, fifteen-room house she had once called home were fewer than she had hoped. The term "strained relationship" wasn't the half of it. The Reynoldses could develop grudges, maintain them, and then take them to the grave. Her so-called secret abortion started the process.

Her mother, whose walk with God was short lived, didn't offer Cheney a new key to the house, and Cheney didn't ask for one. Mattie, the longtime housekeeper, snuck Cheney a key anyway. Hoping to forego an unwarranted argument with her mother, Cheney slipped the key into the lock.

It was a drastic measure, but Cheney had called every morning since Roland was released from the hospital, wanting answers to her unspoken questions. Gayle Reynolds had immediately dismissed any mention that her upstanding and beloved husband was a criminal. Her mother had warned Cheney if she so much as implied that Roland was responsible for any of the mess caused by her deranged neighbor, she would be removed from the premises.

She dodged a confrontation by ducking into the living room like a prowler. The quick motion made her dizzy until she composed herself. Finally, she crossed the foyer to a large, paneled room used to entertain a gathering of up to seventy guests. She pushed open the door, and Roland looked up from reading a hardcover book. Through an unbuttoned shirt, his bandages were visible.

Initially, Roland's response was surprise, then caution. "Hello, daughter." He mustered a carefree smile as Cheney walked into the room, her shoes sunk into the carpet. When she bent to kiss his steel gray, permanently curled hair, he patted her stomach as if he were performing a medical examination. No words were exchanged as he nodded his satisfaction before she sat near his recliner.

They held stares until Cheney looked away. Clearing her throat, she squinted. "Who are you?" She opted to forgo inquiring about his health.

"I'm your father who loves you, and a man who made a terrible mistake."

"Mistakes aren't allowed in the Reynolds family, or at least that's what you've drilled into our heads." Cheney didn't want to be hateful, bitter, or disgusted, but she was engaged in a flesh and spirit battle. She prayed she wouldn't say anything she would have to repent for later. "You've killed a man, and I killed my baby. I guess we're even," she said, snarling through clenched teeth.

Finding a temporary distraction outside the double patio doors, Roland was slow to respond. The fifty-two-year-old gynecologist was known for his intimidating, opinionated remarks. Roland and Gayle had recently celebrated thirty years of marriage. They earned the respect of the children: twins, Cheney and Rainey, and Janae, the eldest, but when their instructions were ignored, punishments were swift and their memories long, in contrast to their tender love that always lingered beyond the discipline. "Were you ever going to say anything? Does Momma know?"

"I never told your mother." The strong man she knew seemed to shrink under her chastisement. "I never planned to, but that didn't mean the memories didn't slap me across my face from time to time. When I saw the peace God had given you after so many years, I craved it too, but to embrace that tranquility, I knew I had to unload some dark things in my past. I was on my way to Mrs. Beacon's house when I stopped at Wabash Park to rehearse my confession one last time." Roland sighed. "I didn't expect her to be there with a loaded gun in her purse." He rubbed his head. "I can understand you being angry."

"Angry?" Cheney gripped the chair in restraint. "How about shocked, betrayed, and disappointed? Did I mention how guilty I felt when I heard that you were the person who stole something so precious from a woman who gave me laughter when I felt like crying? How could you, Daddy?"

"How could I? You were the pregnant, unwed mother-to-be," he defended. "You could've mortified our family's good name. My grandfather, father, and I strived to maintain a blemish-free reputation within the medical community."

Cheney wanted to throw up, and it had nothing to do with her condition. Her dad's hypocrisy made her stomach knot and heave.

"Then you used your upstanding reputation to violate my rights to privacy. As a patient, my medical records were supposed to be confidential. I was an independent adult, and student, who had earned a scholarship to Duke University. I was handling the situation the best way I knew how at the time."

Clearly shaken by his daughter's outburst, Roland lifted a finger to point, but Cheney cut him off.

"You're an imposter! Were you pretending to come to Christ? Daddy, I love you and desperately wanted to restore your faith in me. Ha! What a wasted effort on my part."

"Cheney, is that you in there? Don't you dare upset your father. I'll be in there in a minute, Roland dear," Gayle yelled from somewhere in the house. Cheney could set her watch. Her mother would be by her husband's side soon.

She lowered her voice, but not her anger. God took advantage of the interruption and whispered, *Forgive as I have forgiven you.* She silently defended her actions. *You've got to be kiddin', God. This is different. He's been living on Wall Street while I rented space on Torment Alley.*

"Mrs. Beacon had every right to retaliate for the wrong I caused her, but I'm asking for your forgiveness, baby," he pleaded. "I had made up my mind to come clean. It just so happened to be the same night of your first shower. I was trying to catch Mrs. Beacon and ask for her forgiveness . . . well, you know what happened after that."

"Why aren't you in jail?" *Lord, I'm trying not to be mean. I'm trying to hold my tongue, but my hormones won't let me.*

"My attorney assured me I could continue practicing medicine while the police re-open the investigation."

The baby moved and stretched Cheney's stomach muscle at the same time she stood. Roland smiled tenderly. She frowned. Holding the weight of her stomach, she stilled her movement to ward off a sudden bout of dizziness. "It looks like it's you who has to restore my faith in you, and next time, please leave my husband out of this. We don't keep secrets from each other, and you should've never asked him to hold his tongue. " Grabbing her purse, she gave an emotionless wave. She walked out of the front door without bothering to find her mother and speak.

Once inside her Altima, Cheney started the car, clicked her seat belt, and checked the rearview mirrors. As she shifted the gears, the Lord spoke. *Have you forgotten about your own prayers for me to forgive you of your sins, yet you deny forgiveness to another?* Sighing, she stared out the car window. She didn't track the amount of time. Ashamed and teary-eyed, Cheney bowed her head. How many times after the abortion had she sought forgiveness? How many? How long did she walk with the guilt?

If she ignored the reprimand and left, she could repent later, but her hand turned off the engine. Removing her seat belt, she retraced her steps to the house. She would at least speak to her condescending mother this time. Unlocking the door, she returned to the entertainment room where her daddy was slumped in the chair, worry lines etching his forehead.

"Daddy, I'm sorry."

He turned around and offered a weak smile. "Me, too, Cheney. Me too."

CHAPTER 8

"Hali, I'm not seeing how my trials are making me stronger," Cheney complained over the phone as she put away the leftovers from dinner. "I don't know if I can do this. I thought everything would be so much easier with Christ, but I wasn't prepared for the unsolved mystery of the century. Daddy killed Grandma BB's husband, then Grandma BB tried to kill him." She paused. "I really don't feel up to forgiving."

"But you do have a reason. Eternity," Hallison encouraged as she scanned her closet, searching for an outfit for church. "Cheney, this is my second, and last, go-round walking with God. As bad as it is, it's not worth straying away from the Lord for one minute."

Cheney sighed heavily into the receiver. "I don't know if I'm going to make it through this."

Pushing aside purses and hats on her shelf, she grabbed one of three shoeboxes she purchased at the private showing with her hairdresser, Alexis. Satisfied with her choice of champagne-colored leather sling backs, Hallison laid them on her bed and sat down. "C'mon, Cheney.

We've got to have each other's back on this, remember?" Hallison tried to quote a scripture, but she couldn't get the words right. "Hold on, let me grab my Bible."

She stood and walked into the living room and picked it up. Unzipping the cover, she flipped through the pages until she found Ecclesiastes 4:9-10. "Okay, here's the scripture I'm thinking of: *Two are better than one; because they have a good reward for their labour. For if they fall, the one will lift up his fellow: but woe to him that is alone when he falleth; for he hath not another to help him up.* We're a team—"

"Cheney, Kami's ready to say her prayers," Parke shouted in the background. "Tell Hali goodnight and goodbye."

Hallison chuckled and shook her head. "Now, how does that man know you're talking to me?"

"He says he knows your ring," Cheney whispered, sniffling. "One thing I thank God for is a friend who allows me to vent, yet loves me anyway."

"That's not one-sided, sister. I was literally willing to burn in hell just to hold on to Malcolm . . . well, not willing to burn, but willing to ignore hell even existed to be with Malcolm. It seems like I worried you about him forever. I may not talk about him that much now, but he'll always occupy a part of my heart that I hope God will never ask me to give up." Hallison sighed. "Anyway, like I said, you always listened and never told me to shut up."

Hallison's reason didn't make sense except to Parke, Cheney, and Hallison's mother who knew that God doesn't always reveal His plan up front. She still shivered recalling the glimpse God set before her in church, burning in hell, over and over. Heaven and hell were real, and she was scared. The Lord had let Hallison know she had sugar-coated disobedience long enough.

"Hey, I was close." They laughed until Cheney cleared

her throat. "Love ya." She covered the mouthpiece and yelled, "I'm coming" to Parke.

"Love you, too." Hallison hung up, smiling. Cheney was one of the best things that had come out of her relationship with Malcolm.

The smell and sights of spring drifted in the air before the calendar made the official announcement. Hallison dressed lighter in a short-sleeved, pastel-print dress that flared at the knees. Malcolm's eyes had always appreciated her molded legs, and he freely gave compliments, so short skirts had dominated her closet. Since she returned to Christ, she had become shy about showing off her God-given assets, but not today, although it wasn't thigh-length short.

Winking at her reflection in the mirror, Hallison slipped into a pair of new shoes. She grabbed her purse, a coordinating linen jacket, and her Bible. Within minutes, she was driving to service.

Hallison walked into Faith Miracle Church as the praise and worship team led the congregation in a rendition of gospel artist, Marvin Sapp's "Never Would Have Made It." Her presence interrupted a conversation between two men, including Brother Thomas who Parke had complained about a week earlier. Hallison had to agree with Parke. Brother Thomas looked to be nearing fifty, more than fifteen years her senior. She waved a salutation and kept walking.

After kneeling in prayer, she stood and raised her hands to join in the praise. Long after the song ended, the chorus continued to circulate in her mind. When small fingers poked at her legs, Hallison looked down and identified the culprit. Kami gave her a toothy grin. "Hi, Auntee," she whispered loudly and lifted her foot to show off her lilac, patent leather Mary Janes. "I got new shoes."

Evidently, Hallison wasn't the only one who went on a shopping spree. Hallison smiled and nodded, tugging on Kami's ponytail. Cheney entered the pew followed by Parke. The women exchanged air kisses. Parke winked at Hallison. While he knelt to pray, Cheney bowed her head. Kami got on her knees and covered her face, but kept one eye on Hallison, saying, "God bless me. Amen," loud enough for those nearby to chuckle.

Pastor Scott walked to the podium and addressed the members. "Whew, we got off to a good start this morning. We've talked to God. Now let's hear what the Lord has to say." After echoes of amen, he opened his Bible. "Let's turn to Matthew 18:12: *How think ye? if a man have an hundred sheep, and one of them be gone astray, doth he not leave the ninety and nine, and goeth into the mountains, and seeketh that which is gone astray? And if so be that he find it, verily I say unto you, he rejoiceth more of that sheep, than of the ninety and nine which went not astray. Even so it is not the will of your Father which is in heaven, that one of these little ones should perish.* God has a watchful eye," the pastor preached. "While we're looking one way, He's looking both ways. What's lost to you is not to God. There is no hiding place, no peek-a-boo. God's arms are so long, they can go around curves . . ."

Tears sprang to Hallison's eyes whenever she read or heard that passage. "Lord, thank you for not allowing me to get away."

Cheney reached over and clutched one of Hallison's hands, holding it until Pastor Scott finished his sermon and closed his Bible.

"Now, this is the part of the service where God allows you to make a choice: stay in the pasture or go off on your own. If you're tired of running away, tell God about your sins and repent. Take it a step farther and walk down this aisle to be baptized in the name that signifies power, deliverance, and forgiveness—Jesus. We have a change of clothing waiting for you, and since you'll be a clean vessel, God wants to pour His Holy Ghost into you." Pastor Scott stretched out his hands. "Won't you come?"

Many did, and Hallison felt renewed after the service. She chatted with a few churchgoers she had come to know over the months, steering away from Brother Thomas. Finally, hugging Cheney, Parke, and Kami goodbye, she headed for her car.

Before she pulled out of the parking lot, Hallison took her cell phone, tapped in a number and made reservations. "Hi, Mom. I'm inviting myself to dinner," she joked. But as the only child of Addison Dinkins, her visits were always welcomed.

Ten minutes later, Hallison exited I-170 at Olive. Her mother's white brick colonial house sat on a cozy cul-de-sac in Olivette, a St. Louis suburb that was minutes away from the city. The neighborhood was easily hidden by a cluster of leafy trees.

Addison opened the decorated carved wooden door after one knock. She reached up to receive her customary hug from her daughter. "Hungry?"

At sixty-one years old, Addison was a petite widow who stood five-two and favored actress, Della Reese. Hallison's five-eight height was a gift from her deceased father, who had died of a massive heart attack during her junior year in college.

"Why do you think I stopped by? I could smell the collard greens before you even opened the door." She strolled in and laid her purse on the hall table before washing her hands in the powder room. As was her routine, Hallison slipped off her heels and padded in stocking feet into the updated kitchen. As a gift to her mother, after Hallison received a hefty bonus, she had paid for much of the renovations, which included a stainless steel refrigerator, stove, microwave, ceramic-tiled floor, and granite countertops.

Rubbing her hands, Hallison grinned at the large chunk of cornbread, next to a healthy serving of greens and fried chicken, already on a plate. "Yes," she said, seeing the jar of beets and a bottle of vinegar. Hallison kissed her mother's cheek as a reward. They sat at the same time. "Remind me again why I left home and missed out on this good cooking?"

"You wanted to be grown," Addison said, laughing.

Hallison unfolded a napkin and laid it on her lap. "I'm glad you hadn't eaten."

"I was about to before you called. I decided to wait for my distinguished guest."

After linking hands, Hallison closed her eyes. She always enjoyed listening to her mother pray, except when she was dating Malcolm. During that time in her life, Hallison literally begged her mother not to pray for her and Malcolm. Thank God her mother had ignored her foolish request.

"Lord Jesus, we thank you for this day, this time, and this place. God, I'm grateful for everything you've given us and for those things you've withheld from us. I ask that you sanctify our food, bless my daughter, and bless the cook, in the name of Jesus. Amen."

"Yes, bless the cook. Amen," Hallison added as she reached for her fork.

Addison winked. "If you want a good meal, you better believe it."

Hallison moaned as she bit into the fried chicken, then dove into her greens. "So, Momma, what did Pastor King preach on this morning?"

"The Holy City."

Chuckling, Hallison held up her hand. "Revelation 21.

The new Jerusalem. I don't know how many times I heard him preach that when I was younger, but he's about eighty, eighty-five now, isn't he?"

"Eighty-three. It seems that lately, his sermons have been from that text whenever he preaches. Soon his son will take the reins. The young minister preaches most of the time anyway. I can tell he's very studious."

Their conversation ceased as they continued to eat. Minutes later, Addison pushed away her empty plate and folded her arms. "How's work?"

"Busy, but good," Hallison answered with a nonchalant shrug as she stood and returned to the stove for a second, bigger helping of greens with a smaller slice of cornbread.

"How's Hali?"

A simple question, but her mother was scooping for detailed answers. Hallison reclaimed her chair and scrunched up her nose to begin their cat-and-mouse game. "You're looking at me. I'm fine, wouldn't you say?"

Her mother squinted. "I'll ask the questions. You could stand to pick up some more weight. Now, how's your love life?"

"Terrible, but I've got time. How old were you when you married Daddy?"

Addison swatted Hallison's arm. "Smart aleck. I told you, I'm asking the questions." Their lighthearted banter included how many dates Hallison had been on, which were none. The topic then moved to how Cheney and her family were handling the crisis of the shooting. Finally, they discussed Hallison's plans for the upcoming week.

"Thanks for dinner, Momma, but I'd better head home. I've got another week of interviewing candidates before I narrow the selection down." Together, they cleared the table and cleaned the kitchen.

"Too bad that Samuel guy you were telling me about

turned out to be a homosexual—or gay, as people say. If he would've been saved, and from the way you described him . . . whew, he could've made that office dating thing interesting."

"No comment," Hallison said, laughing as she slipped back into her shoes to leave.

CHAPTER 9

"Who are you trying to impress?" Alexis asked, fingering through Hallison's hair the following Saturday.

"I just want something different," Hallison said, shrugging.

"Hmm-mm. Different? You've been wearing that same look for years. Live a little and add some curls and body." Alexis popped a piece of gum in her mouth. "However, I notice you're wearing those wedge shoes you got from our shoe rendezvous. Ooh, and where did you get that outfit? That reminds me, there's this exclusive club where guests can sample food from around the world—from fish dishes cooked in small African villages to cuisines served on Mediterranean cruise liners. A big treat is the wine tasting."

"Alexis, you know I don't drink."

"That's too bad, because girl, the hunks who attend are—"

"Not tonight," Hallison interrupted. "Where do you find out about these places anyway?"

The stylist whirled a comb in her hands. "You know, a friend of a friend of an exclusive—"

"Okay, okay, I'm sorry I asked." Hallison laughed until she squeezed a single tear from her eye. "I want a new attitude, a new look without going drastic." Hallison scrutinized her features in the mirror at Alexis's station.

Alexis angled her hand on her hips. "Is that all? Girl, that's easy. I've always told you to try highlights. I can lighten your hair and give you a few layers without taking away too much length off the back." Alexis prepped Hallison while talking nonstop. "Last week you mentioned something about a prayer luncheon this afternoon. That doesn't give us much time for a new attitude."

"That was before I found out about the doll convention that's in town. I would like to see what the exhibitors have and buy something. I used to tag along with a girlfriend years ago."

"Hmm," Alexis mumbled, stretching a streaking cap on Hallison's thick hair. Satisfied with the tight fit, she began the process of pulling strands through pin-sized holes with a crochet-type instrument.

"Hey," Hallison yelled. "Leave me some hair."

"Right. You're in the hands of an artisan. Once I brush on golden blond . . ."

Hallison whipped her head and was about to voice her concern when Alexis held up her hand.

"It's not the same intensity as us white girls' bleach-blond, but against your skin tone, you'll be a goddess. So, if you don't have one already, go buy a little pink book to write down men's numbers. If I had your skin tone, I wouldn't have to sit in a tanning bed."

They shared a few laughs before Hallison wrenched again.

"Hey, stop it before you scare my other customers,"

Alexis warned. "What's this about you skipping out on church? Isn't that a no-no for Christians?"

"I don't have to be in church every time the door opens. It's living for Jesus when the church doors are locked that counts."

"Preach," Alexis teased as she worked on Hallison's transformation.

Three hours later, Hallison was in awe of Alexis's finished product. Her brows were arched by a threading method instead of waxing. Hallison agreed to fake lashes, but not the thick ones or the eyelash extensions Alexis recommended. Strands of Hallison's curls were shiny, burnt gold. The reflection staring back at Hallison didn't look real. It was too perfect, yet natural. "Wow. You've been holding out on me, Lexi."

"Don't *Lexi* me. I've just uncovered what was hidden. Now, get out of my chair," she told Hallison, grinning. "My next appointment is here. In case you're writing out a check, which includes my generous tip, my full legal name is Alexandra Van Doverhoff."

"You're kiddin'." A laugh escaped. "No wonder you go by Alexis." She scribbled two hundred and fifty dollars across the check. Minutes later, Hallison practically pranced out of The Workout, The Workup, and Workin' Hair and Body Boutique to her Camry. "Alexandra Van Doverhoff outdid herself."

Once behind the wheel, and strapped in her seat belt, Hallison called Cheney. "Hey, I know you're on an outing picnic, but I have to tell you; Alexis pulled out my alter ego today at the salon. Cheney, I'm not vain, but I'll be the first to say I'm gorgeously unrecognizable."

"I want to see this makeover for myself. I'd stop by later, but I'm sure I'll be wiped out by the time this outing is over." Cheney said.

Turning the ignition, Hallison checked the rearview mirror and did a double-take at her reflection. "Lord willing, you'll see me tomorrow at church. Right now, I'm leaving the boutique going to check out that doll exhibition."

"Oh, that's right. You did mention that the other day. Have fun. If you see anything reasonable, grab it for Kami, and I'll reimburse you. Love you."

Hallison disconnected and exited onto Interstate 70 toward downtown. A half hour later, she drove into the parking garage across from the convention center. As she pushed the button to retrieve a ticket, a male attendant stared in appreciation. He winked and puckered his lips for a kiss. Hallison giggled and thought, *Oh yeah . . . a little attention does a girl good.*

Once inside the massive showroom, she started in row one, then began her mission. Crisscrossing across the aisle from table to table, Hallison's eyes grew wider in fascination. She wasn't interested in the seminars, lectures, or auctions. Her pure interest was to browse and maybe purchase a collector's doll or two.

"Hallison? Hali, is that you?"

Recognizing the voice, Hallison whirled around. "Tavia." The women screamed their greeting, then squeezed the other in a bear hug. "Octavia Ford, how are ya, girl?"

Standing back, her friend scanned Hallison from head to toe. "I would ask the same about you, but I can see for myself. Girl, you are wearing married life royally," the five feet two, former college sorority queen commented, with her hands on her hips, naturally enhanced.

Octavia and Hallison had been friends since high school, and at one time worshipped at the same church. Hallison spent a lot of time at Octavia's house, admiring her unbelievable collection of beautiful, black, porcelain dolls. Octavia started the hobby when she couldn't find any black dolls with features representing people of color.

They parted ways when Octavia unknowingly married, against the pastor's counsel, an abusive man who practically cut Octavia off from the outside world. Those had been her dark days, and Octavia couldn't bring herself to confide in Hallison that their pastor had been right. She should've never married David, who was later killed while trying to buy crack cocaine.

Once Hallison found out, she blamed herself for not doing more to stay in contact. Hallison assumed their longtime friendship was forgotten after Octavia married the supposed man of her dreams.

Hallison wasn't an avid collector like Octavia and only collected when she stumbled across a black porcelain doll in a specialty store that didn't bear the trademarks of a white cookie-cutter mold. When Hallison heard about the doll convention, she thought it would be fun. "I didn't get married," she stated with a brave face, but a sinking heart.

Octavia halted her steps and stared. "What? Okay." She placed her purse on a nearby vendor's table as if she had rented the space. "What did Malcolm do? All I need to know is where he lives."

Looping her arm through Octavia's, Hallison tugged her along to the next table, barely allowing her time to snatch up her purse. "C'mon. Get your stuff. We'll walk and talk."

"The last time we spoke, you were singing Malcolm's praises so I made those Hal and Mal couple dolls as an engagement present and sent them. What happened, and why didn't I know?"

Hallison bowed her head in shame. "You were diagnosed with breast cancer. Every time I picked up the phone, I hung up because I didn't know what to say. I couldn't say

I was praying for you because I wasn't even praying for myself, but you were always in my thoughts. Then when I returned to the Lord, I was praying for you. Despite my return to church, I was scared to call because of what you might say about, you know, your cancer."

Octavia nodded and hugged Hallison without reprimand. Hallison sighed in relief. They resumed their stroll until Hallison froze at a vendor with African American dolls. Several caught their eyes, but Hallison reached out and fingered the limited edition. Jacie was an African American, all-porcelain doll with wild curls and a white ballerina dress. Her skin was creamy and eyes sparkling.

"She's beautiful. I should buy it."

Octavia pulled her from the table. "Did you see the price tag? It's one hundred and fifty dollars."

"That's not bad."

Through gritted teeth and her back to the vendor, Octavia corrected her. "Hali, you can make that for one-third of the price."

"I'm not that creative." Hallison tried to walk around her to get back to the vendor, but her short friend kept a firm grip on Hallison's arm. "Look at you. Your makeup is flawless."

"I just came from the salon. My stylist did it."

"Hali, will you listen? If you can apply makeup, you can make a doll. I've shown you how easy it is," she said, nudging Hallison to the next table. "Now don't even think about buying anything until you tell me what happened between you and Malcolm. It's a good thing I came to St. Louis for the show, or I might've never known."

"Tavia, I gave Malcolm up freely to serve God. I still hurt because more than anything else, I wanted to be his wife and have his babies, but God spoke. My ears heard it. My heart felt it, and God left it up to my mouth to say it." She briefly bowed her head. "You had just told me about your breast cancer. I...I..." she stuttered. "I didn't know what to say, and I couldn't burden you with my problems. Plus, you hadn't come back to the Lord, so I didn't feel like you would've believed God had spoken to me."

"God talked to me too; during my chemo." After being jostled by an eager crowd, they stepped aside. "Anyway, it looks like you've recovered. You've been hiding your beauty all these years."

"Don't let my appearance fool you. I paid good money for this look. There isn't a day that goes by without me missing Malcolm, but...." She shrugged. "My soul is more important. I try to stay busy to fill the void."

"Well, God keeps talking to me, and I haven't budged yet. You'd think that with a near death scare, a bad marriage, and a murdered ex, I would've been the first one in the Holy Ghost checkout line. I honestly don't know what's keeping me away. "Well." She shivered. "Are you going to buy anything?"

"Sure. I want to get something for my goddaughter, Kami. There are at least ten more aisles we haven't seen."

Octavia yanked Hallison's hand. "I'm getting hungry, and you're going to eat with me. I guess I'd better go with you so you don't get ripped off. Plus, I want to stop by the mall before I catch my flight home in the morning. Victoria's Secret is having a sale."

"Do you have anything to put in a bra?" Hallison whispered, scrutinizing Octavia's chest.

"The bra won't know the difference." Octavia gave Hallison a Marilyn Monroe imitation of shaking her boobs.

Laughing, Hallison admired Octavia's sense of humor. Even without allegiance to Jesus, Octavia was good-hearted, successful, and self-assured. Hallison couldn't imagine her friend dying so young.

"C'mon. Let me help you spend your money," Octavia said as they returned to the table showcasing the African

American collection. When Octavia finished bargaining with the maker, Hallison purchased the Jacie doll for ninety dollars. They left the convention center. Octavia followed Hallison to her car in the parking garage, since she was staying at the adjacent hotel.

At the Galleria, their first priority in the mall was the atrium to the food court. They ordered sub sandwich combo meals. Octavia said grace, then attacked her fries. They conversed for more than an hour.

"So your cancer's in remission?" Hallison asked.

Octavia nodded. "Yes. After two years, I can officially say I'm a cancer survivor, but it wasn't easy. When I reach the five-year mark, doctors will consider me cancer-free."

Reaching across the table, Hallison touched Octavia's hand. "I'm sorry I wasn't there for you."

She waved her hand in the air. "I'd rather talk about more pleasant things. Hali, I'm sitting across from a stunning woman. Your face would make a perfect model for a porcelain mold. Why aren't you dating? There may not be many, but there are men in the church and some good ones."

"Why aren't you? You're two years older than I am. The doctors did say you can still have children, right?"

Wiping her mouth, Octavia started counting on her fingers. "One, I would get married again in a heartbeat if I could find a man who didn't have a problem with my cancer recovery. Two, I'm only fourteen months older than you are. Three, the doctors say it's a possibility, not one hundred percent, but a chance I could have children, and four, every man who has passed by this table has stopped and taken a second look—at you, so flaunt it."

Malcolm saw her. *If she isn't Hali, then she is definitely an improved version.* Malcolm recalled the vision Monday morning as he waited in the conference room.

The partners were scheduled to discuss the findings of a recent audit before a report would be released.

His mind drifted again. Malcolm could've been mistaken about the woman, but she had the same harmonious laugh. He shrugged as the staff entered. *If people could copy voices, mimicking a laugh had to be a piece of cake.*

"We have two audits to discuss today," Mr. Winfield stated after everyone had taken their seats. "Mr. Benson's recordkeeping at his three cleaners concerns me. He issues credit memos as if he's handing out candy. Plus he has a habit of advancing money to himself and his wife with no record of putting the money back."

"It's clear then that we shouldn't sign off on this report," Mr. Young, his partner, advised. "We'll make client recommendations, but that's all we can offer him." He signaled to move on. "Gertie's Garden. Malcolm, you have the floor."

Nodding, Malcolm leaned back in his seat and made eye contact with each staffer and partner. "Thank you. In Mr. Winfield's absence, I met with potential client, Lisa Nixon, owner of Gertie's Garden. We verbally agreed on the types of services she needs. I mailed her a letter of engagement, which she signed and returned. Since that time, I have handed over the project to another staffer to oversee the auditing. I made this request after I found Lisa to be an intriguing and attractive lady. This is a formal announcement to my colleagues to refrain from divulging any information about Gertie's Garden to me."

"Wise choice," Mr. Winfield agreed. Mr. Young granted the request.

Later that evening, Malcolm shared the news with Parke.

"You did what?" Parke shouted in his cell phone while driving. Malcolm heard brakes screeching in the background. "Was that wise? Since when did you begin to allow pleasure to interfere with business?" He huffed. "Hold on, so I can pull over."

Flopping on his couch, Malcolm reached for the remote. "My pleasure isn't interfering. You haven't met Lisa yet, but it's been on since she first came into my office. She's drugging me with her beauty."

"Hmm-mm. All this after two weeks," Parke stated sarcastically.

"Yes." *After all, I gave Hallison months and acres of space to work through her church obsessions.* He had called his brother, former playboy Parke, to cheer him on, not to question his sanity.

"So I guess you're really over Hali?"

"Doesn't it sound like it to you? Peace." Malcolm disconnected and turned up the volume on his TV.

CHAPTER 10

Hallison could thank Alexis, a.k.a Alexandra Van Dover-hoff's, makeover for the male interest she received over the weekend. Alexis brought out Hallison's new attitude. As she and Octavia walked through the Galleria, people stared. Through Hallison's peripheral vision, she caught a few gawkers. Hallison and Octavia visited shoe stores and shopped for bargains at clothing shops. They were exhausted. Claiming an unoccupied bench, they rested their purchases and people-watched for a while.

Finally, Octavia had dragged Hallison inside Victoria's Secret. Hallison chuckled at the scenario. Octavia had to practically push Hallison away from the sleepwear clearance rack. Coming out of the store, laughing, Hallison almost tripped when she glanced at a guy who was Malcolm's height, had his swagger, and was dressed in comfortable clothes that proved his fitness. Dark shades concealed any verification, plus he was accompanied by a petite woman.

Her imagination was running wild. Malcolm was never attracted to short women. Hallison dismissed the possible

Malcolm Jamieson sighting when Octavia begged to stop at one more place. Afterward, Hallison demanded that Octavia check out of her hotel and spend the night at her apartment.

Sunday morning, they had woken up to a non-alcoholic hangover after staying up most of the night, talking. It took a lot of effort, but they did make it to church before Hallison dropped Octavia at Lambert Airport for her flight. Both promised to do a better job of staying in contact.

"And don't forget to look into a doll-making class," Octavia shouted as she rolled her luggage to the check-in desk.

Monday morning, Hallison glanced at the clock as she reclined behind her desk. "Daydreaming over," she announced as she sat up. She smiled one last time at her fun-filled weekend while scanning three files in front of her. They were the top picks for one of the openings. Bowing her head, Hallison said a short prayer.

Her responsibility not only included hiring qualified candidates, but in the era of disgruntled and retaliatory workers, she had started asking God for guidance in selecting applicants who were mentally stable and spiritually starved for salvation. She finished praying, God spoke, and she listened. After an amen, Hallison picked up the phone and punched in the numbers.

"Smith and Jones residence," a man with an annoying drawl answered after the first ring.

"This is Hallison Dinkins, the director of human resources with Missouri Bank. Is Samuel Smith available?"

"Yes! Yes, he is . . . just a moment. Sammie," he yelled, muffling the phone. "I think you've got the job, hon. Pick up the phone. It's Allison Dingdong."

Hallison shook her head. That was the first time that

someone had butchered her last name. Usually it was the first name that gave people pause. *Lord, if you had not told me Samuel was the one, I'd have hired the other guy.*

"Good morning," Samuel said, coming on the line.

"Good morning, Mr. Smith. If you're still interested, I'd like to offer you the software support specialist position."

"Yes, I'm definitely interested. I just need to confirm that I'll have full benefits for my partner and me."

"After ninety days, you'll have coverage for any dependents who you've filed on recent tax returns," Hallison quoted the benefits, shaking her head in pity for Samuel. The only thing she could do was be a light for him.

"Thank you, Hallison. May I call you Hallison?" his voice dropped lower.

Why stop now? Hallison rubbed her temple. Already, Mr. Smith was taking liberties before filling out his W-4 forms at the bank. "Sure. The position starts at seventy-five thousand dollars. Is that acceptable?"

"That'll work. My partner and I were just discussing our finances. We're asking God to help us."

"And He answered your prayers. If you can come in and sign the paperwork and pass a drug test, you'll be able to start next week." They agreed on a time later that afternoon, then Hallison disconnected. "Jesus, you answered his prayer, now please answer mine. Save Samuel's soul. Before he starts would be my preference, while he's working here would be a blessing, or any time before he dies; in the name of Jesus. Amen."

As she reached for the other stack of résumés for the marketing assistant vacancy, her phone rang. "Hallison Dinkins, director of human resources," she answered.

"Your mother," Addison said cheerfully. "I didn't want you to forget about the family reunion picnic on Memorial Day. I just picked up our T-shirts."

"Oh." Hallison gritted her teeth. "I won't," she said, looking for a notepad.

"Okay, baby. You have a blessed day."

"I better write it down," she mumbled after hanging up. Hallison scuffled through papers, patted stacks of folders, and pushed aside reports. She tried to open a drawer, then remembered she hadn't unlocked it because Octavia had called first thing that morning, reminiscing about their good time. Hallison reached for her keys, in her purse, on the floor. As she juggled one strap, her purse tilted, spilling its contents: her makeup, pens, loose change, and wallet on the floor.

Getting on her knees, Hallison crawled under her desk and snagged her new Victoria's Secret pantyhose on a stray emery board. "My ten-dollar hose!" She groaned and continued gathering her things until she fingered something unfamiliar. She dragged it out of the shadow of the desk until she spied the magnifying glass. Picking it up, Hallison twirled the handle between her fingers as she sat back in her chair and recalled the day Malcolm had given it to her. It was a Friday, and they had met for lunch. He was toting a small bag.

"I brought you something."

"I know—you," she had teased.

"Great minds think alike. I love it when you focus on me, because God knows I enjoy every moment I focus on you."

Malcolm wasn't slack showering Hallison with traditional gifts—candy, flowers, perfume, and jewelry—but it was the personal things he shared about himself with her that were the most memorable.

He had lifted his bag. One by one, he pulled out items she needed in order to trace her family roots just as he had done, and continued to do, on both sides of his family: a magnifying glass to read old documents from hun-

dreds of years earlier; a hand-size notebook was filled
with definitions that was a lifesaver for every genealo-
gist; a note that professed his love for the first time.

"It'll take me until the end of our lifetime to stop needing and loving you. I don't want any secrets between
us," Malcolm had said. His voice shook with emotion.

Hallison sighed as tears filled her eyes. Sniffing, she
twirled the magnifying glass again. She closed her drawer
and tapped on her keyboard.

She typed in www.slcl.org for the St. Louis County Library, a trick Malcolm taught her to access records from
the comfort of any computer. From that moment on, she
was addicted to the hunt for her ancestors until she broke
it off with him. Hallison smiled, remembering how she and
Malcolm would celebrate her discoveries.

It had been from her office computer that she had
Googled her maternal great-grandmother's brother, Ellis
Brown. Unbelievably, Hallison had discovered an article
written a decade earlier. Ellis had perished in a house fire
in Kansas City, Kansas. He was a hundred years old. After
that, Hallison went on to locate Ellis's original draft regis-
tration card where his occupation was listed as a farmer
on Wyatt Palmer's property.

She couldn't believe he was listed among 150 Ellis Browns
on rootsweb.com. "Bingo," she had screamed, grabbing
her phone. After three attempts, she had punched in the
correct numbers for Malcolm's office.

"Winfield & Young Accounting, Mr. Jamieson's office,"
his sweet, older secretary answered.

"Hi, Lilly. Is Malcolm busy?" Hallison couldn't contain her excitement.

Lilly laughed without knowing the joke. "Hi, Hali. Does
it matter? He'll always want to talk to you." She trans-
ferred the call.

"Hi, baby," Malcolm *spoke into the phone after Lilly introduced the call.*

"Malcolm! I found a great-great . . . I mean a great-uncle. He actually lived in Kansas City . . ." She rambled in fragmented sentences.

He listened between humorous grunts. "When did he die?"

"March 1993, in a house fire. What a bummer." Her heart pounded in excitement and disappointment.

"I can't believe Ellis Brown lived to be one hundred and was only three hours away. Why couldn't he have held off that last cigarette until I found him, before he set the house on fire while he slept?" The online obit had led her to cousins she had never known existed.

Those were moments of bliss she didn't want to forget. It had been months since she searched through the Heritage Quest database. Although it held most records from 1790, Hallison's search for Ellis's grandmother, Minerva Palmer Lambert, prior to 1870 was stalled.

Minerva was born about 1848, and Hallison hadn't determined if her third great-grandmother was owned by Monroe County, Arkansas, attorney Jno Palmer. So, on the 1860 slave schedule, Hallison began searching for Minerva Palmer Lambert as a twelve-year-old slave girl. When she couldn't find any matches with his slave girls, Hallison gave up.

Pecking away on the keyboards, Hallison gnawed on her lip as she uncovered another possible prospect— Eliza Palmer. She had traveled from North Carolina in the 1850s to take possession of Palmer slaves that included three mulatto fugitives. Hallison grinned at the possibility of renegade ancestors.

Moving closer to the screen, she peered through the magnifying glass. "C'mon, Minerva Palmer, where are you? Who owned you last?"

"Who owned whom?" Ursula asked as she breezed into Hallison's office unannounced.

Hallison dropped her magnifying glass and lost her place. "Do you ever knock? I could've been in a meeting or interviewing a candidate."

Shrugging unapologetically, Ursula claimed a chair. She sported an auburn pageboy wig that happened to complement her tan suit. "Hey, I tapped on your door a few times. When your assistant walked by, she said it was okay for me to come in." She twisted her thin lips. "Now, who owned somebody, and since when do you need bifocals?"

Shaking her head, Hallison shoved the instrument back inside her desk drawer. "Oh, nothing."

Ursula pointed an unpolished finger, which meant she had an upcoming manicure appointment. "If it's 'oh nothing' from you, then I interpret that to mean it's 'oh something.'"

Hallison cleared her throat. "I had a genealogy urge, and I found something that might be connected to my ancestors, but I'm not sure. Malcolm could've found it in less than thirty seconds," Hallison mumbled.

"Malcolm. Umm-hmm, that name sounds familiar." Ursula worried one wayward hair strand that religiously sprouted on her chin the day before her hair appointment. Suddenly, she sat straighter and leaned forward. "Because it is familiar. Why don't you call the man?"

"And say what? Malcolm, you're perfect; and I've turned you into a monster since I chose God over you. I'm sorry, you're more important. Have you found a replacement for me, yet? Well, I haven't either, so do you want to get back together until God tells me to dump you again?"

"Humph, sounds good to me. You never know. A brief fling might do you two some good. Listen, Hallison, even I know what you want even if I never hear you say it."

Rocking back in her chair, Hallison closed her eyes. "Yeah, but it ain't what God wants."

Ursula stood and slammed her palms on Hallison's desk to get her attention. When she did, Ursula pointed from her eyes to Hallison, then back again. "Explain this to me again. How do you know it was God talking to you? What exactly did He say?" She shook her head, not waiting for an answer. "Personally, I still think it was just your imagination."

"Believe me, if it were my imagination, it would be filled with things I could do *with* Malcolm, not without him. Plus, there is a scripture in the Bible that says, God's sheep know His voice. Same as a pet, who after running away, hears its owner's voice and comes back."

Ursula tsked. "So, God has reduced you to a pet, huh? Hallison, this almost sounds like a cult." She sat back in her chair and crossed her legs.

As if for the first time, Hallison saw Malcolm's confusion through Ursula's eyes. Ursula wasn't convinced God would or could reach out and touch an individual. Hallison had failed to win over Malcolm; she hoped she did a better job with Ursula. "Believe me, I heard a personal message from God. I had to choose between my lifestyle or God's."

Ursula frowned, unconvinced. "Well, I think you made the wrong choice."

Balling her hands in irritation, Hallison leaned forward. "You're like a revolving door in my head. I wish it would stop and let you out. I'm entitled to my private—key word—private flashback moments." She squinted. "What are you doing here anyway? I thought Anthony was treating you to lunch."

"I canceled," Ursula said, fanning a hand in the air. "I'm considering filing for divorce."

Hallison gripped the desk, shaking her head as if to

clear it. "What? I like your husband." She paused before whispering, "You don't think Anthony's having an affair, do you?"

"Who cares?" She shrugged. "I just don't like him anymore."

"Ursula, that's not grounds for a divorce. If there's no cheatin', there shouldn't be any leavin'."

"I'll make it one. Changing the subject, did I hear you say something about the Palmers?"

"When Malcolm and I were together, he piqued my interest in researching my family tree. I had left this magnifying glass in my office. It must've fallen under the desk. Today, when I accidently found it, I thought about a project I hadn't finished. With some downtime, I was playing detective to see if I had overlooked something."

"And?"

"Malcolm reigns. He's the real-deal sleuth. It's in his blood. The Jamiesons have traced their ancestry to before the institution of slavery."

"Really? I say, let the dead rest in peace. My family did have some Palmers, but I believe most hail from South Carolina." Ursula swung a crossed leg.

"I'm researching North Carolina, not South. Did your family own slaves?"

"How would I know? If we did, I'm not apologizing, and I don't owe you a thing, especially a mule," she recited, as if she memorized the words on an index card for a class assignment.

Hallison felt her hair prickle. Malcolm had schooled her on how to respond to people who become emotionally offensive when discussing ancestry. "Ursula, when a friend loses a family member, do you ever say you're sorry, knowing you had nothing to do with the loved one's death?"

"Of course. I'm not insensitive," she snapped.

"Glad to hear it. What if a family loses their house in a fire? Would you say you're sorry for their loss even though you didn't strike the match?" Ursula looked as if she were about to answer. "Ah, ah, ah, don't interrupt. Let me finish. Weren't you out of sorts when three co-workers from another department were laid off, knowing you didn't have a decision in their terminations?"

Ursula stood to her feet. "Get to the point, Hallison."

Hallison took her time, making Ursula stew. "That is my point. Why is it so hard to say you're sorry to me, or anyone else, whose ancestors suffered such atrocities, whether the abuses came from your relatives or not? Saying you're sorry is an expression of compassion. I'm looking for my ancestors because I want to know who they were and how they lived, not to bring accusations against people today. Check yourself, Ursula, because although I genuinely like you as a friend, I wouldn't want to be related to you."

"Back at ya. I don't have any Christian relatives, and that's the way, uh-huh, uh-huh, I like it, uh-huh, uh-huh," Ursula sang, butchering K.C. and the Sunshine Band's hit.

CHAPTER 11

Malcolm couldn't stay away from Lisa. Evidently, she had read his mind as she swayed into his office without knocking, wearing another black outfit. Malcolm bit his tongue to keep from salivating. *Did the woman know how hot she was in black?* She carried a sack lunch and flowers. Standing from behind his desk, Malcolm crossed the room to free her hands.

"Food and flowers. You do know how to spoil a man." He kissed her hair and laid the items on a small table. Lisa waited as Malcolm pulled out her chair.

She jutted her chin and twisted her lips in thought. "Considering my dad is dead, I don't have any brothers and few male cousins, I would say you're a lucky man who I intend to keep," she complimented as Malcolm gently scooted her closer to the table.

Taking a seat, Malcolm mumbled a quick blessing then ripped open the bag. "You're not eating?"

"I did already." She smiled, stretched, and watched.

Malcolm licked his lips after he bit into his ham, turkey, and Swiss cheese on warm Ciabatta bread. He grinned.

"You're a woman after my own heart." He winked and gulped down a bottle of water without pausing. "Plus, you smell good."

"That's my flowers. I usually don't wear perfume, remember? I like the natural scent of my body."

He lifted a brow. "Is that so?"

Lisa nodded with a mischievous glint in her eye. Malcolm was falling hard. Getting up, she walked behind his chair. As if knowing his thoughts, she pinched his shoulders before administering a seducing massage. "Relax."

He did, closing his eyes and enjoying her massage. Malcolm wanted to kiss her, but it would've been considered an indecent act, especially if Lilly caught them.

"Better?" Lisa cooed as she tilted his head back and planted a kiss before guiding his head up and down in a silent yes. "I know you can't talk about the audit, but Malcolm, I have to share this. . . ."

Malcolm stiffened and turned around. "Lisa, I won't talk about the audit. We gave up our rights, or at least I did, to talk business when we became involved. Plus, we're in my office. There's no way I'm going to jeopardize my career with a casual conversation that could become misconstrued." His stern expression backed up the fact that he meant business. *I may be falling hard, but I haven't landed,* he thought.

The next few minutes were strained. Maybe his words were too harsh. Lisa was the first woman since Hallison who excited him. Before she left, he had to smooth things over.

"Well," she said with a sigh, "I hope you enjoyed lunch. I better go so we can both get some work done." When she made an attempt to walk around the table, Malcolm wrapped his hands around her wrist. "I'm sorry if I came across too strong. That was not my intention."

She rubbed his jaw. "Good. Be nice to me, and I'll be

nice to you," she taunted, then loosened his grip and
backed away.

"You little tease." Standing, Malcolm approached her as
if he were a predator about to pounce on his prey. Racing
to the door, she turned back and blew him kisses. Malcolm shook his head. "You're something else, you know
that? Call me later when you get home if you feel up to
going out for a few hours." *It's time to introduce Lisa to
the Jamiesons.*

Before leaving work, Malcolm called Parke on his cell
phone, not knowing if his brother was in the office with
the stock market playing jump rope, or working from his
home. "Busy?" he asked when Parke answered.

"Never too busy for my brother," he responded, then
paused. "Unless, of course, you want to whip me in a
game of b-ball, then I'm extremely busy."

They laughed. "Nothing like that, old man. I'm wondering if you're up to meeting Lisa tonight. We can run by—"

"Can't, Malcolm. It's Wednesday night, Bible class. You
two can join us, and we can grab a bite afterward."

"Here we go again. Parke, I love you and Cheney, but
church is the farthest thing from my mind with Lisa."

"Okay, my brother. Don't let your words come back to
bite *you.*"

"Yeah, right." Malcolm clicked off. He grabbed his briefcase and headed out his office to his car. An hour later,
Malcolm was settling in at home when Lisa phoned him.

"Hey, are you a risk taker?" she whispered.

Malcolm's nostrils flared. She was teasing him again.
"Absolutely."

"Pick me up in an hour," Lisa ordered, with a teasing
laugh, before she hung up.

He was early when he pulled up in front of Lisa's house.
When he rang the doorbell, she smiled and was ready to
go. They dined at Lumiere Place; a casino on Laclede's

Landing near the Mississippi River. Afterward, they strolled to the slot machines where Lisa acted like a kid in a candy store.

"You're going to let me play alone?" Lisa gave him her flirtiest pout. "I have special powers to win."

He stuffed one hand in his pocket and used the other to lean against the machine. "When I said risk taker, I wasn't talking about gambling. I don't like losing," he stated, referring to his car, money, and woman.

"Chicken. I'll put up your first twenty bucks." She reached for her purse.

"Lisa, I don't need your money." He waved away her offer, sliding in the seat next to her and inserting his own bill. Lisa knew when to call it quits. She was smart, beautiful, disciplined, and even more intriguing. An hour later, Lisa had spent twenty dollars, won two hundred, and only lost eighty dollars.

Unfortunately for Malcolm, he played ninety dollars and won thirteen. He was a risk taker in love, but not in slots. Some things were not worth gambling.

CHAPTER 12

Malcolm had been on Hallison's heart lately. She had learned months ago to stop praying for Malcolm's immediate salvation, but for God's will to be done in his life. Finishing her Monday morning prayer, she recalled the scripture for Sunday's sermon, Philippians 4:7: *And the peace of God, which passeth all understanding, shall keep your hearts and mind through Christ Jesus.*

Hallison was still reflecting on the scripture when she walked into her office one minute past eight. As if sensors noted her presence, her phone started ringing. Setting her briefcase and shoulder bag in a nearby chair, she reached across her desk to answer it. The caller didn't allow her to finish her standard greeting.

"Good morning. Got a sec?" Paula said as if she were out of breath.

Holding the phone between her left ear and shoulder, Hallison came around her desk and took a seat. She tapped on the keyboard to boot up her computer. "It's Monday. Applicants will be calling on job status and who knows what else."

"Do you remember me mentioning that The Blood of Christ Apostolic Church is fellowshipping all week with one of our sister churches?" Paula asked, then supplied the answer. "Some awesome evangelists will be preaching at Salvation is Free Pentecostal Temple all week. Let's go since I know your schedule is booked with blank pages. That means you're available every night."

Occasionally, she and Paula visited other churches to taste the Word preached with a different seasoning. "For your information, I'm helping my mother with some family reunion things tonight, and tomorrow, after work. I get free meals out the deal." They chuckled together. "Wednesday is my Bible class. Alexis is doing my hair on Thursday since I'll be at the family reunion picnic on Saturday. I have Friday open."

"Of all weeks . . . hold on." Paula's voice was muffled as she addressed one of her employees, then returned to the conversation. "Listen, my craziness has begun. Let's say I'm not planning to miss one day. I really could use clarity from God about some things."

Eyeing her company inbox, Hallison sighed at the twenty emails awaiting her attention. "I better hang up too. Make sure you take notes that I can read."

For the next three mornings, Paula relayed the nightly sermons to Hallison: Monday—Acts 15:28: *For it seemed good to the Holy Ghost, and to us, to lay upon you no greater burden than these necessary things;* Tuesday— Matthew 11:6: *And blessed is he who is not offended because of me;* Wednesday—James 1:3: *Knowing that the testing of your faith produces patience.*

Hallison was tempted to forgo her hair appointment on Thursday to hear the night's sermon. After Alexis's transformation the previous week, Hallison banished the thought. Besides, it was the only opening Alexis had during the week.

Friday morning, Hallison was ready to fast forward to the final night of the fellowship. She showered, then dressed in a powder blue, linen suit Octavia insisted she buy during their shopping spree. Hallison then selected a second pair of shoes she bought at the secret shoe club with Alexis, to complement the outfit. She opted to fluff her curls instead of using a comb before rambling through her jewelry box. Hallison located the soft blue pearl bracelet, a gift from Malcolm. She fingered it before deciding to slip it on.

Blinking away Memory Lane, Hallison glanced at the time and realized if she didn't hurry, she would be late. She rushed to the kitchen and grabbed an unhealthy breakfast of Pop-Tarts and Diet Coke, then prepared a deli sandwich, fruit, and chips.

Since Paula was fasting during the day all week, and Ursula was on vacation, Hallison was lunching solo. Her latest hire, Samuel Smith, had called a few times requesting her to join him for power lunches. Although she had previously declined, she had every intention on meeting with him, under auspices of the Holy Ghost power, to share God's redeeming power.

Most of Hallison's morning, and part of the afternoon, were spent on conference calls with other branch managers. It was almost one thirty before she took a break for lunch. Every time she faced the window, the warm weather beckoned for her to come outside. Hallison responded when she grabbed her bag, left her office, and headed out the building's revolving doors.

She strolled toward downtown's outdoor focal point— Keiner Plaza near Busch Stadium. On more than one occasion, photographers used the water fountain as a backdrop of wedding pictures. The luscious botanical garden offered rich, green grass and thriving, bold and colorful flowers. A meeting place for local sports teams' victory rallies was also a hangout for the homeless who needed a short respite.

She eyed a bench free of pigeons and beggars and claimed it. After she sat, a warm breeze embraced Hallison as the sun stood far off, playing hide-and-seek as it chased the dark clouds away. She blessed her food and nibbled on her sandwich. Sunrays winked at her again. Smiling, she recalled how the Lord had sent a cloud by day and fire by night to guide the Israelites to the Promise Land. "Lord, I need you to take the lead in my life because I sure don't know where I'm going."

Without any pressing appointments, meetings, or deadlines for the rest of the afternoon, Hallison took advantage of the free time. She followed the tourists' fascination with the tallest manmade monument in the country, the 630-feet-tall St. Louis Gateway Arch. Standing, Hallison balled up her trash and pitched it in an overflowing trash bin. Securing her purse on her shoulder, she wandered through downtown. When Hallison felt the first raindrop, she was in a crosswalk.

As more sprinkles followed, she raced across the street and ducked inside the Old Courthouse to wait it out. The weather had tricked her again. It never failed on the day of, or the day after, her hair was freshly coiffure.

The St. Louis Old Courthouse was a historical landmark because of a famous case. In the mid 1800s, a slave named Dred Scott filed a petition for his freedom, arguing he had lived in a free state longer than a slave state. He was bold enough to secure lawyers and hike the same steps that were used to auction slaves. To date, some of Scott's descendants still resided in St. Louis.

She was proud of herself at the wealth of information she could recall, another reminder of Malcolm Jamieson.

His hunger and thirst for African-American history was contagious. Before she dated Malcolm, she had passed the building without giving it a second glance. Now, it held good memories. She and Malcolm had shared lunch a few times inside. Although it was closer to her job, Malcolm said he enjoyed the exercise and would walk the distance for her.

The more she tried to forget about Malcolm, the more she remembered the wonderful moments between them. Sitting on a wooden bench in the rotunda, Hallison pulled out a small apple from her purse. Quietly, she reflected on someone's ancestors who had visited this building involuntarily. Malcolm had lit her fire of curiosity. Now it was up to Hallison to renew the search for the Palmers. She missed Malcolm's presence in her genealogy hunt.

The door squeaked open, but she ignored it. She didn't hear her name being called until his scent captured her.

"Hali."

She whirled around and met Malcolm's eyes, seconds before noticing a woman whose looks couldn't be ignored. Hallison mustered a tense smile for his companion. "Hi."

The woman returned Hallison's smile. "Hello."

"Hali, this is Lisa," Malcolm introduced as they were strangers.

He didn't offer an explanation of their relationship. Hallison nodded and tried to take a deep breath. While she demanded her body not to shake, she lost control of the rapid speed of her heartbeat.

"This is the last place I would've expected to find you," he said with genuine awe.

And me you. She nodded and swallowed any words that wanted to respond. Covering her apple core with a napkin, she stuffed it back in her purse and stood. She had made the decision to leave Malcolm. After all, God told her to walk away. She did it once, and she would do it again.

"Lisa, it was nice meeting you. Malcolm, have a blessed day." With one shoe in front of the other, her heels clicked in an off-beat pattern as she walked across the marble floor. Shoving open the thick wood double doors, she walked out into the pounding rain.

Hallison was not supposed to be there. Since Malcolm and Lisa had become almost inseparable, he'd pushed Hallison to the back of his heart. He craved Lisa now. When she sent him flowers, Malcolm had never realized how special they made him feel. Lisa enjoyed giving him attention. He wasn't complaining about being the recipient.

Since Lisa liked to walk, he suggested the Old Courthouse, never suspecting he would see a more stunning Hallison than his mind could remember. He had assumed her involvement in genealogy was to humor him. Under hooded lashes, it took Malcolm fifteen seconds to catalogue the new Hallison. Her hair was abundant—or maybe it was the curls—her face appeared so soft that if he touched it, she would melt. With less than three seconds left of his appraisal, he'd spotted the pearl bracelet wrapped around her slender wrist. Well, at least she hadn't thrown his gifts away. No . . . just him.

He blinked as the thunder clapped moments after Hallison disappeared. Frowning, he turned back to Lisa. Malcolm hoped his new lady hadn't noticed the air between him and Hallison, but she had.

"How special is she, Malcolm?"

"Past tense—was." Malcolm respected Lisa even more. She didn't ignore the obvious. "Believe me, the relationship was never meant to be. I am no longer guilty of loving her."

"But you *did* love her," she stated.

Malcolm didn't respond. When Lisa remained quiet, Malcolm wondered what she was thinking. When she smiled, Malcolm exhaled. There was no word to describe how different she was from Hallison. Lisa was drama-free. He might actually thank God one day for placing the right woman in his life. Hallison did have one thing over Lisa, besides height. Hallison was gorgeous, but Lisa was hot.

As she began to walk ahead, Malcolm reached out and linked his hand with hers. "I know you won't ask, but I want you to know. Hali broke it off with me. Yes, I have residual feelings for her, but I can assure you, my relationship with you is not on the rebound."

"That's good to know."

CHAPTER 13

Hallison was a mess, from her hair to her clothes, but her heart had taken the biggest hit. The truth was Hallison had a tiny seed of hope that it was God's will that she and Malcolm would find their way back to each other. After seeing Malcolm and Lisa, there was no hope to keep alive.

She had exactly three blocks to get her mind together before returning to work. That gave her less than a quarter of a mile for her tears to mingle with the downpour that had already drenched her. Hallison gave herself a pep talk. "This too shall pass." She forced a smile to curious onlookers who also had been targets from the rain. "That's it. I need someone too, Lord." Her only consolation was at least Alexis had dolled her up for the competition.

All she wanted to do was go home and climb in the bed, then pig out on ramen noodles and Oreos, followed by a half bottle of Pepto-Bismol. It dawned on her that she probably resembled Chaka Khan's sister. Hallison reached up to finger-comb the damage, but her hair wouldn't budge.

Agitated, she gritted her teeth. Hallison wished a hefty bonus could entice Alexis to skip an out-of-town wedding to redo her hair. Alexis would laugh at the offer.

"What about tonight? Oh, God, I can't miss the final night of the sermons," Hallison mumbled, groaning. She stood frozen at the entrance to the Metropolitan Circle building. No doubt her linen suit had absorbed water like a Bounty paper towel and shrunk. Straightening her shoulders, Hallison shrugged as she opened the door and entered the lobby.

Ignoring the stares, Hallison walked with her head held high like a runway model as her shoes squeaked across the floor. She had to steady herself as she slipped and glided across the marble floor, grabbing a doorknob to keep her from skating past her department. She nodded to her assistant as if she were dressed for an evening ball and headed to her office.

An explosion of laughter echoed from behind Hallison as she shook her hair like a shaggy dog. Putting on her game face, she slowly turned around to face her opponent, squinting. As her nostrils contracted, she snarled, "If you don't have a hair pik, Sammie, don't bother coming near me."

Hallison didn't try to restrain from making the unprofessional comment to Samuel Smith. Her mood had changed along with the weather. Hallison gritted her teeth. She had two callback interviewees for the marketing assistant position due within the next two hours. She couldn't afford to reschedule when the vacancy should've been filled a week ago.

Using the intercom, she informed her assistant to hold all calls or visitors until her scheduled appointments. She needed time to make herself presentable—at least as much as the director of the human resources department could. Next, she called upstairs to Paula. "I'm not going to be able to make it tonight."

"What?" Paula's squeal pierced Hallison's ear.

"I got caught up in that thunderstorm. I'm back to the afro."

"God doesn't care. Come as you are," Paula encouraged.

"If you saw my hair, you would take back your words before fainting. It's not going to happen for me tonight." Hallison sniffed her frustration. Her day was going downhill. She probably should go anyway, but she didn't want to put in the extra hours it would take to look halfway decent. "If you can buy a tape from tonight's service, I'll reimburse you."

Paula didn't reply at first. "It's not the same as being in the presence of God."

Hallison blinked as a drop of water ran from her hair into her eye. "I know. Listen, I've got to reinvent myself for my afternoon appointments. Get the CD, please." Once inside her office bathroom, Hallison peeled off her top and blazer. She had to shake her hips like Beyonce to loosen her slip and skirt.

With urgency, Hallison rummaged through her stash of extra clothing. She wasn't encouraged. Most items she either had taken home or to the cleaners. Besides her Victoria's Secret hosiery, there wasn't anything impressive.

At 3:25 p.m., Hallison sat behind her desk, swinging her leg and waiting for her appointment. She had stuffed most of her hair under a red baseball cap with a large portion of it hanging out the opening and was perspiring under an insulated Xavier University Alumni sweatshirt. Her hips were squeezed into a size ten pair of denim capris. Ankle socks and red tennis shoes finished her fashion statement. These were clothes she had used when she first moved into the office years ago.

After successfully repairing her makeup, Hallison tapped her manicured nails on her desk, waiting. She stood at the brief knock. "Come in." The applicant opened the door and blinked. "Good afternoon, Mrs. Green. Please have a seat." "Uh, hello," Mrs. Green stumbled over her words as her mouth twitched.

Hallison returned to her chair, crossed her legs, and examined the applicant's file. Hallison may not have looked like she was in control, but she was at the moment.

By Saturday morning, Hallison had done a bad imitation of Alexis's handiwork. This was her family, and most of them had seen her in diapers or worse. She managed to straighten her hair, and with bobby pins, comb it into two French braids.

The previous day's traitorous weather suggested a perfect forecast for Hallison to don the Reynolds-Brown family reunion T-shirt and pair of culottes for the picnic. Since Hallison couldn't show off her hair, her impeccable pedicure would have to speak for her grooming habits. Slipping her feet into flat, Roman sandals, she crisscrossed the straps and tied them slightly above her calves. She resembled a college student more than a bank's director of personnel. To be on the safe side, Hallison pulled a hooded rain jacket from her closet.

She refused to dwell on the scene of Malcolm and Lisa as she drove the short distance to Sioux Passage Park. She spotted the trail of parked cars, signaling the designated shelter. After maneuvering between two parked cars, Hallison stepped out at the same time the driver of a Range Rover honked the horn and distracted her. Turning around, Hallison grinned and waved, then adjusted her sunglasses on her face. Closing her door, she crossed her arms and leaned against her Camry, waiting for her two cousins.

The oldest at thirty-one, Faye, was a mechanical engineer and resided in Louisville, Kentucky. Tammy, twenty-six, the same age as Hallison, lived across the Mississippi River in Illinois and was the principal of a Metro East High School. Both had exotic dark features and spoke with an unlearned Caribbean accent, which most guessed they had inherited from a great-grandmother on their father's side. The sisters were considered fashion divas. Faye's family reunion T-shirt was tied in a side knot, exposing her navel's belly ring. Tammy took center stage with an eye-stopping straw hat and matching tote bag and culottes.

"Hey," Hallison shouted as the pair approached. They wrapped each other in a group hug, laughing. Standing back, Hallison nodded toward Faye's pricey SUV. "I see you're living large."

"And I see we've been shopping at the same place," Tammy interjected, pointing to Hallison's Roman sandals. They exchanged high-fives. "Fashion is our middle name," she told Hallison.

As they strolled to the sheltered area, the sisters gave Hallison an abbreviated update on their lives. By the time the trio reached the pavilion, a group of the male relatives had already attacked one plate and were feasting on a second one. The older women alternated between serving food and yelling at kids who were playing tag around the barbecue pits.

Faye, Tammy, and Hallison greeted their relatives, then formed a line, kissing and hugging every person within reach. Finally, they fixed their plates and sat next to their mothers, Addison and Norma. Their conversation was always the same—Jesus, His second coming, and the rapture. Hallison smiled, remembering a time when she wouldn't come near them. Now she appreciated their words of wisdom.

After completing two trips to the serving table, the three added their trash to a bin already filled with discarded paper plates. The group had thinned as the boys jammed cowboy hats on their heads and raced to the horse trails. A few girls ran to the empty tennis court. The swings and sliding board lured the younger children.

Hallison lifted her brow at how her skinny, long-legged, female cousins were suddenly transformed into beautiful young ladies. Her shy, male cousins boasted their muscular build. Some were engaged in the latest dance moves from their respective cities.

Hallison chuckled as she stretched her legs and rested her feet on a bench, then scooted down in a folding chair. Faye entertained a small audience with her rowdy victory after she had won her third round of spades. Her cousin's competitive streak was legendary. It was that quality in her older cousin that Hallison idolized when she was growing up.

The yelling startled Tammy out of her nap. She blinked, squinting at her watch. "Hey, it's almost four." She yawned. "Y'all going to play cards all night? There's a Memorial Day concert at We Love God Temple. We can get our praise on. Hali, Aunt Addie says you're back with the Lord. Praise God. I know you don't want to miss it. Maybe you can drag Faye with you."

"You've got to love my sister," Faye said. "She's always forgetting I'm older, and I call the shots." The three laughed, nodding their heads as they remembered. "I don't plan to set foot in church tonight or tomorrow. I'm on vacation, and I want to sightsee." Faye turned to Hallison. "Hey, cuz, want to play tourist? I heard The Loop has come back since I've moved away."

Tammy would not be trumped. "Momma said Aunt Addie said Hallison dumped her fiancé because he wasn't in church. Since you're not coming to church, Faye, you're on your own. We don't hang with sinners, right, cuz?"

Hallison cringed, and then leaned forward to keep them from arguing, "Actually, I didn't dump him, we—"

Tammy waved her off. "You don't have to sugarcoat it, Hali. Faye can go by herself."

Faye shrugged gracefully. "Makes no difference to me, my little sanctified sister. I have GPS, so I doubt that I'll get lost."

"C'mon, Tam, let's go to The Loop. It'll be fun. After-ward, we can go to the concert," Hallison said, trying to referee.

"Are you kidding? You wouldn't marry an unsaved man, why would you want to hang with a sinner? Faye needs to make a choice."

"Ladies, cousins, sisters, please," Hallison interrupted, standing. "First, I loved Malcolm. I chose to walk away. You two are my blood cousins. I didn't choose you, but God gave me you. Family is family." She unsuccessfully played the part of negotiator.

"Why you even got saved to mingle with the sinners is beyond me. Hali, we're supposed to set the example," Tammy instructed.

"Tammy, I don't think Faye and I strolling down five or six blocks of Delmar, visiting quaint shops and sampling food, will qualify as temptation. I read that an investor brought the struggling college hangout strip back to life, so I'm curious too."

"Somebody has to set the standard," Tammy snapped, also standing.

Hallison sighed. "Okay, group hug." Faye yanked her sister in the circle. Hallison prayed for peace. "Does this mean you're going with us?" Hallison smiled, hopeful.

"Not unless we're passing out gospel tracts," Tammy said defiantly.

CHAPTER 14

"Tammy's the very reason why I'm not in church today," Faye complained minutes after Hallison climbed into the Range Rover en route to University City. Then she mumbled some profanity.

Hallison didn't respond. She loved her cousins equally. Without any siblings, Hallison was inseparable with the sisters growing up. Once they reached adulthood, Hallison, Faye, and Tammy chose different careers, religious experiences, and social paths. If Hallison had one word to describe Faye, it would be irritating; Tammy could be overbearing. Of course, the sisters oftentimes labeled Hallison as "Miss Goody-two shoes." Both were shocked, hearing she had walked away from her church upbringing.

"Hmm-mm," Hallison mumbled, tuning her cousin out.

"I figured you weren't going to help me backstab my sister now since you've recovered your faith." Faye shook her head in defeat. She fumbled with the radio knob until she found jazz oozing from her satellite radio.

"Reclaimed my faith, Faye. Reclaimed," Hallison replied, laughing.

"Hey, if I can't talk about my sister, you're the next best target." Faye laughed too, as they skirted around the subject of Tammy.

Forty minutes later, Faye arrived in the heart of The Loop, originally known as the last stop on a bus line in University City, before it looped around and retraced its route to downtown. In recent years, the six-block strip had become a popular hot spot. Boasting forty-five restaurants, fifty-something boutiques and shops, and numerous entertainment venues, nearby Washington University students, city dwellers, and suburbanites didn't wait for the weekend or special occasions to partake in the buzz.

As they peeped through store windows and danced around patrons at sidewalk tables, Hallison noted the St. Louis Walk of Fame, highlighting local celebrities like Chuck Berry, Tina Turner, Nelly, and others.

"I see why this is a hot spot. I love it," Faye said in awe.

"I haven't been in this part of town in years." As they shuffled through the crowd, Hallison stopped cataloguing faces, letting her mind drift. "A person would think after dating Malcolm for more than a year, we would've toured these streets."

"So, do you miss him, or at least regret you gave up your man in the name of religion? Didn't that whole sacrifice thing go out with the Old Testament? What's the real story?" Faye asked without missing an opportunity to return smiles to men admiring her belly ring.

Hallison wondered if Faye owned any tops that weren't midriffs. If Hallison was keeping track, Faye was easily racking up twice as many stares as she. "In exchange for you telling me why you haven't given up to Christ."

Rolling her shoulders, Faye smirked. "Fair enough. I love my sister, family, and some saints. I'm emphasizing *some*. Even though I'm not in the habit of routinely going to church, I see the remnants of the devil, and not Christ, when folks aren't trying to play church."

They stepped to the side to keep from clashing with a waiter who was coming outside Cicero's, a restaurant known for its pizza. Hallison sniffed at the aroma.

"Faye, your feelings aren't isolated. The hypocrisy turned me off a while back, too. It fueled my argument for not going to church. As a matter of fact, I'd cross the street to keep from walking on the same sidewalk as a church." She laughed at her juvenile thinking as Faye nudged her. "Then God started turning up His pressure on me. He challenged me to clean up my spiritual health or go to hell where I would burn for eternity."

She frowned. "What a choice. Was Malcolm so bad, Hali?"

"Yes and no. I loved Malcolm, and there was no doubt that he loved me, but God had something else in mind. Malcolm didn't have anything against visiting churches. It was his refusal to even seek a commitment with God. Basically, he was okay being a visitor indefinitely. It's like settling for girlfriend status when God really wants a marriage certificate for His salvation. Faye, I've got to believe I made the right decision." Hallison paused. "Do you want to get an Espresso?"

"Sure . . . now, for argument's sake, is there any way you and Malcolm could get back together? I'm a romantic if not a churchgoer." She smiled.

Peering into Starbucks, Hallison tripped over her own feet. Malcolm was reclining in a chair at a table. A woman's back faced Hallison. She swallowed. "I've changed my mind. Let's keep going."

"Why?" Faye put her hands on her hips.

Hallison tugged on her cousin's arm. "The reason why Malcolm and I won't ever get back together is sitting in

Starbucks with him. That's twice in two days I've seen him with Lisa. God is trying to tell me something."

Faye grunted. "Or that she-devil is."

Hallison drew the line Saturday night when Faye wanted to go clubbing downtown. They said their good-byes, and Hallison told her to have a safe trip back to Louisville. "Love you, cousin. Stay safe."

"And you," Faye said, grinning, "stay saved."

The fun-filled day ended with a quiet, lonely night at home. Hallison closed her eyes and prayed. "God, I know you have a companion for me. Will you speed up the candidates? It's agony seeing Malcolm with someone and not me. I did what I know you told me to do." Needing something to do, Hallison grabbed a book, *Genealogy for Dummies*, as she answered her phone.

"Grandma BB, you've got to be kidding me?"

"I ain't." The old woman was insistent with her message. "Cheney threatened to have me arrested if I step my Stacy Adams shoes on her property. That kinda hurts an old woman's feelings. She won't even entertain the thought of coming to my house. She calls herself a Christian. That's where you come in, Hal," Mrs. Beacon said, abbreviating her nickname even further. "I need your help in picking a neutral battleground."

Hallison didn't feel qualified to act as a mediator between Cheney and Mrs. Beacon. The feisty woman seemed ready to do battle even in her sleep. *The battle is not yours, but mine*, God spoke II Chronicles 20 to Hallison. "How about the Whistle Stop?"

The eatery was known for its old fashioned custards. It was a former train depot and a popular meeting spot for Ferguson residents. Children were thrilled to wave at the conductor who blew the whistle for their entertainment.

More than twenty Norfolk Southern freight trains passed by the eatery daily.

Mrs. Beacon agreed, and the following weekend, she was sitting outside the Whistle Stop when Hallison and Cheney drove up. She looked harmless as she swung a leg over a knee, showcasing her choice of footwear. Residents had stopped raising a brow at her trademark Stacy Adams shoes.

Chin jutted, Mrs. Beacon eyed them suspiciously as they strolled up the slight ramp to the outdoor eating area. Mrs. Beacon straightened her shoulders to show superiority, but her imploring eyes betrayed her need for Cheney's mercy.

At the circular table shaded with a tilted umbrella, Hallison cleared her throat, wondering who would be the first to acknowledge the other. Even after Hallison and Cheney took their seats, it didn't happen.

"Well, why don't we begin in prayer?" Hallison reached for their hands. "Lord, in the name of Jesus. Your Word says where two or more are gathered in your name, you shall be in the midst. We all need you with us. We all have shortcomings, and this is bigger than us, oh, God. Only you can judge this situation." Hallison said amen and Cheney whispered amen. Grandma BB mumbled words which were indecipherable.

"Okay, okay, okay," Mrs. Beacon said, fanning her hand in the air. "Someone has to be the bigger person, and I'm not talking about size." She scrutinized Cheney's belly. "Cheney, I'm sorry it was your father who I shot. I love you as if you were my own daughter; you know that. And I would never, never do anything to hurt you, *but* I'm not sorry I shot the snake." Mrs. Beacon didn't blink.

Shocked, Cheney took a deep breath, readying for a comeback. "I knew an apology from you would be short-lived."

"Ladies, here are your orders," a worker interrupted as Hallison's heart pounded.

"Oh, but we didn't—"

Mrs. Beacon's hand stopped Cheney from protesting. "I ordered your favorite." She jabbed a finger at Hallison. "Hal, I guessed at your selection. I figured you'd eat anything to keep the peace."

You're right, Hallison agreed. With every bite Hallison took, she prayed for peace. Occasionally, freight trains and car horns interrupted their conversation, but there was plenty of eye contact as if Cheney and Mrs. Beacon were waiting for someone to light the match. Their composures were forced, betraying their stockpile of ammunition that was loaded and ready to take aim. When Cheney lifted her finger to shoot the first question, Mrs. Beacon wiped her mouth and threw down her napkin.

"Before you get started, let me tell you something. Chile, this had nothing to do with you. It was about me settling an old score. I would've shot him regardless," Mrs. Beacon nonchalantly explained.

Cheney repeated Mrs. Beacon's gesture as she threw her napkin on the table. Her brows knitted and her nostrils flared. "Do you hear what you're saying? On Sundays, you're Mother Beacon in church, a senile widow in the neighborhood and an endearing Grandma BB to all who love you. Let me add another attribute—you're crazy!"

Mrs. Beacon stood abruptly, and she slammed her fist on the wood table, causing Cheney's dessert spoon to twirl in the air before landing under the table. She attempted to retrieve it, but her unborn baby refused to shift. When Hallison pushed back to reach it, Mrs. Beacon sat and shooed her away.

"I'll get it," she said, but didn't move. Within minutes her legs moved as if she were tap dancing in her seat.

"Are you okay? What's the matter?" Hallison asked.

Mrs. Beacon waved one hand in the air. "I'm fine." She sat as if nothing had transpired and crossed her legs. Then she lifted her shoeless foot. "Got it," she repeated, displaying long, designer nail extensions on her toes. The plastic spoon dangled in the air between her big toe and another. Hallison choked as she sipped her water.

Cheney gawked in disbelief. "Ah, I'll pass. That's worse than when you attached pocket-size mirrors as flaps on your shoes." Gripping the edge of the table, Cheney leaned forward and held up a finger. "One scripture, *Vengeance is mine says the Lord, I will repay.* It's not for you or me to punish him." Cheney swallowed hard and massaged her temples. "I don't need this right now. After all these years, my dad and I were finally reconciling our differences, then you shoot him," she voiced as a tear fell down her cheek.

"The wino got behind the wheel of a car, ran over my dear husband, and left him dying in the street like a dog. He should be locked behind bars, waiting in the Catholic's purgatory, sitting on the hot seat in hell, and swimming in the lake of fire and grindstone," Mrs. Beacon said, gnarling.

Hallison corrected, "I think that's fire and brimstone."

"Whatever. Same neighborhood," Mrs. Beacon barked.

"Unfortunately, you both should be in jail," Cheney said.

Mrs. Beacon grunted. "If God can't understand my reason for an eye for an eye, a tooth for a tooth, and a bullet for a body. . . ." She turned to Hallison and dared her to argue. "Then I don't want to be saved."

As the mediator, Hallison had heard enough. Cheney was near tears while Mrs. Beacon's nostrils flared. Hallison cleared her throat. "This is a reconciliation meeting, remember?"

Sipping lemonade, Mrs. Beacon smacked her lips and

sighed. "It is. I've reconciled that God doesn't work for me. Otherwise, He would've held me back."

"That's where you're wrong. Sometimes, free will gets you in trouble. Ask Adam and Eve, ask David and Samson, and ask me," Hallison said.

CHAPTER 13

Malcolm escorted his guest up the sidewalk to his parents' home. This would be the first time his family would meet Lisa. Although he re-entered the dating pool a few months after he and Hallison broke up, he'd never bothered introducing them to any other acquaintances after Hallison. Things were different with Lisa. He had found a jewel, and he wanted to show her off.

"I thought you said it was a block party," she mumbled as guests spilled out the door to the front lawn.

"Nope. I said a black party where everything from the food, games, and attire have an African theme. Of all days, you didn't wear one of your little hot black outfits." He saw her confidence slip. Lisa was an impeccable dresser, whether casual or business. "I guarantee your skirt will flirt with every male here and those heels . . ." Malcolm smacked his lips. "Woman, your calves and toes are a man's weakness. You're gorgeous."

She smiled at the compliment. "Malcolm, I don't try to impress a man. If they're threatened by my intelligence and independence, then they need testosterone injections. It's your family I want to impress."

Winking, Malcolm squeezed her hand. "You'll easily accomplish your mission."

"Thank you. Now tell me about this party."

"It's part of our family's Juneteenth celebration. Next to our monthly family nights, which are filled with Afrocentric games and dialogue, I wouldn't miss this for anything."

"Ah, that's right, June 19, 1863."

"Not quite. President Lincoln signed the Emancipation Proclamation in January 1863. The Galveston slaves didn't get the news until June 1865. Major General Gordon Granger arrived in Galveston, Texas, and read the General Order Number 3."

"Is your mind always this sharp?" Lisa wrinkled her nose in a flirt.

"My family and I live and breathe history. So you're familiar with the celebration?"

"I'm a florist. It's my job to know every local, national, and ethnic holiday."

"Just a job?" he queried, giving her his full attention.

"Like you, I study my craft." Lisa frowned when something brushed up against her shoe as they entered the house. Looking down, she blinked in surprise. "I've seen everything . . . but a poodle wearing a green and gold plaid Kente tutu?" They chuckled.

White, Asian, and other nationalities, wrapped in their expressive African attires, mingled with no hint of awkwardness. For a black event, they outnumbered African American guests.

"We do have a tendency of going overboard. We discovered this black-owned business that specialized in Afrocentric themed characters for kids' parties, so we purchased their products for Kami's birthday party and some of our get-togethers. It's important for us to return more than five cents of every dollar back into the black community. We try to find one black-owned company a month to patronize for the life of their business. Of course the service has to be impeccable. Michelle Baptiste at Afro Party House loves us."

"Then you understand my plight to expand Gertie's Garden's business."

He nodded.

"Good. Would I be right to assume I have you for the life of my business?"

"Oh, you got me, baby; for sure." Gripping her tighter around the waist, Malcolm steered around friends. "Good evening, Mr. and Mrs. Rubin, I'm glad you two could make it," Malcolm greeted, then introduced Lisa.

Mr. Rubin laughed. "How long have we known you, Parke?" Oblivious of the wrong son, he pressed on. "We haven't missed a pre-Juneteenth celebration since you were a teenager. Besides," he confided, leaning closer, "your mom and dad always requests tickets for the Rosh Hoshana at my temple." He patted Malcolm's back. "See you around, Parke."

Lisa nudged Malcolm. "Why didn't you correct him?"

He shrugged. "It wouldn't do any good. People have always had trouble telling us apart, but clearly I'm better looking."

"Can you spell conceited?"

"Nope. Can't say I've seen that word on a vocabulary list."

"Your family celebrates the Jewish New Year, Rosh Hoshana?"

"Yep. Currently, June on the Jewish calendar is Sivan 5769. We also celebrate part of the month-long celebration of the Chinese New Year with our Asian friends who celebrate everyone's birthdays during that month. These parties are the norm for us."

"What about Hali? Was this normal for her too?"

Where did that question come from? "Lisa, whether we're together or not, I don't want to talk about old girlfriends."

"Although I don't lack confidence, I'm wondering about our similarities and differences because I want nothing less than all of you."

"There's no comparison."

"Good. I'm glad we're of one mind because . . . Malcolm, who is the woman in that dazzling green and gold outfit? She's gorgeous with that crown on her head."

He followed her eyes. "Oh, Nefertiti? That's my mom. C'mon. I want you to meet her." Sneaking up behind his mother, Malcolm wrapped his arms around her waist and kissed her cheek.

Startled, Charlotte Jamieson twirled around, laughing. "It's about time you arrive. Your niece has been asking about you," she scolded in her sing-song voice, then turned to Lisa and waited for an introduction.

"Momma," Malcolm said, pulling his date closer. "Lisa, this is my mother—"

"And his father," Parke V's rich baritone interrupted as he approached.

"Lisa, welcome to our black party. Don't be shy. Make sure you sample a little bit of this and that. You'll love the *braai*, which is a South African-style barbeque topped with *boerewors*, a spicy sausage," Charlotte explained.

Parke V squeezed his wife's shoulder. "That's Charlotte's favorite. All the African dishes are delicious with their blend of spices. Some have as many as thirty," he said and winked at Charlotte. He extended his hand to Lisa and she accepted the shake.

"Okay." Lisa displayed a polite grin. "I will. Thank you, Mrs. Jamieson."

Although Malcolm's parents were cordial to Lisa, it was dismal in comparison to their initial reaction to Hallison. They had loved Hallison almost instantly, and the feeling was mutual. His mother didn't extend an invitation for Lisa to call her by her first name, something she had automatically offered to Hallison. Malcolm decided not to make it an issue. He reached behind his mother and picked up two drinks from a table.

"My son tells us you have a unique family legacy," his father queried.

Accepting a cup from Malcolm, Lisa nodded before sampling the contents. Malcolm stuffed one hand in his pants pockets as he took a gulp. He waited for Lisa's reaction. Moments later, she blinked at the sweet concoction.

"That's Tej, made with honey from the beekeepers in Ethiopia," Charlotte offered.

He sensed Lisa was overwhelmed with information he had learned as easily as his ABC's. Clearing his throat, he came to her rescue. "Why don't you tell them about Gertie's Garden?"

"I would like to think it's unique. In the early 1900s, family businesses were commonplace. My great-grand-mother found a niche to provide for her children, and she uncovered a simple talent, using the fruits of Mother Nature, and it turned into a lucrative business. Since none of my cousins were interested in the floral industry, it was a no-brainer for me to step in, and I didn't have to start from scratch. I want to tweak my great-grandmother's perfection."

Fascinated and impressed, Malcolm's parents gave Lisa their full attention. When his mother's face became animated, Malcolm knew Lisa had won them over. "Lisa, pardon my ignorance, but how is the floral business doing in our non-official bad economy?"

"I'm still in business. I drive a Lexus, provide health insurance for my employees, and have long-time contracts from major businesses in the area. From my point of view, I won't go hungry."

Charlotte was visibly in awe. "I guess you don't have much overhead."

"Quite the contrary. The coolers I use to store the flowers cost about ten thousand dollars apiece. The life of some flowers is short. As a result of the high cost to maintain a perishable inventory, some florists won't survive. Our biggest competitors are grocery store chains that sell everything from produce to patio furniture. Anyone can grab a bouquet at the checkout, not knowing its sale-by date. When consumers value fresh flowers and original designs, they come to Gertie's Garden," she pitched before turning to Malcolm. "We get a feel for the recipient's personality to create the perfect arrangement."

Malcolm discarded his cup and stuffed his hands in his pants pocket. "Really?" His eyes twinkled. "What did you read into my personality for the flowers you sent me?"

She lifted her face to the sun, thinking. "Hmm. you need a lot of attention." She turned and held his stare. "You were worth every petal."

His parents exchanged cautious, but pleased expressions.

"Mrs. Jamieson, please feel free to come into my store any time, and I'll create something for your home—exotic, just like the lady of the house—my treat. If you don't have time, I encourage trying the FTD service online. What you see is what you should get if you jot down the item number. It keeps families, especially during bereavement, from receiving the same plant three or four times."

"I never thought about that. I usually pick up the phone, tell the clerk how much I want to spend, and leave the rest up to them." His mother waved at a few guests. For one moment, Charlotte's eyes trailed one couple adorned in colorful unisex attire. Realizing her rudeness, she returned to their conversation. "Sorry, Lisa. Please call me Charlotte, and I'll be happy to recommend Gertie's Garden to my circle of friends and use your business as my sole supplier of floral purchases."

Malcolm listened with pride as his new woman wrapped his parents around her finger. *Two down and two to go.* Malcolm wasn't worried about Parke. They always had each other's back. Cheney, on the other hand, might be a hard sell since she and Hallison had the girlfriends' allegiance thing going on. If he hadn't personally introduced them, he'd have believed they were born on the same day and grew up in the same house. Cheney professed to be a Christian, so she shouldn't have any problem accepting Lisa as the new lady in his life.

He tugged on Lisa's hand. "Time's up, Mom, Dad. There are other people I want Lisa to meet."

Malcolm lost track of the number of guests Lisa enthralled with her beauty, wit, and intelligence. He had made a wise choice. *Thank you, Hallison Dinkins.* They were heading toward Parke and Cheney when his niece spotted him.

"Uncle Malcolm! Uncle Malcolm," Kami shouted as she barreled into him. Picking her up, he kissed her cheek until she giggled. Secure in his arms, Kami talked nonstop, "I saw my Mommy's stomach move. She's says that our baby is stretching."

"I know." He grinned.

Lisa smiled at the same time Kami seemed to noticed her. "Aren't you cute? How old are you?"

"I'm three, how old are you?"

Malcolm frowned as Lisa gasped. She recovered. "I'm thirty-seven."

Kami tilted her head, thinking. "You look older than Uncle Malcolm." She squinted. "He's thirty-three."

Embarrassed, Malcolm squeezed his niece. "Kami! That's not nice."

She pointed to Lisa. "BB told me to always tell the truth and to call it like I see it." She glanced again at Malcolm's date. Cupping her small hands, she whispered loudly. "I don't like her, Uncle Malcolm. She's evil. Auntee is nice."

"Stop it, Kami. What is wrong with you?" Malcolm slightly shook her as his anger began to rise.

The toddler frowned and stared at Lisa. "But Uncle Malcolm, I don't like her."

Shocked at the outburst, Malcolm snarled. "Listen, little girl, you did not learn to act like that from your parents. Say you're sorry."

Kami shook her head. "BB said to call it like I see it."

"I should've left that woman in jail," Malcolm mumbled.

Lisa held up her hands. "It's okay. I don't have children, so naturally they don't warm up to me quickly."

"I don't know what's wrong with her. Usually, she's very affectionate." He turned to Kami. "I still might spank you later."

"No!" Wiggling out of his arms, she raced toward her parents. Malcolm yelled for her to come back, but she ignored him.

"That niece of mine, I feel like putting her on punishment for the rest of her life."

Lisa laughed uncomfortably. "I'm sure she's harmless. Don't worry about it."

Still fuming, Malcolm linked their fingers and resumed their trek toward his brother, who was standing near a stone figurine of a woman pouring water into a basin. Malcolm had helped his father install the water fountain the previous summer. "Once again, Lisa, I apologize."

Parke was sipping a drink with Kami stationed at her father's side. Cheney watched their approach as she gently rubbed her stomach. Malcolm debated being a tattletell, but concocted the perfect payback, eating a double scoop of bubblegum ice cream in front of her before her bedtime. He gave Kami a mischievous grin. "Parke, Cheney, I'd like for you to meet Lisa Nixon."

After Malcolm told them about Lisa's profession, Parke asked, "So, how is business? I guess it has slowed down since Mother's Day."

"Not really. There're always funerals and weddings to keep us busy, and Cheney, we do adorable arrangements for baby showers."

"Hmm. I wish I'd known. I've already had a baby shower," Cheney responded, looking away.

Malcolm had a soft spot for his sister-in-law. Everyone's plan to give Cheney more baby showers were on hold. Cheney's mother blamed it on the scandal Mrs. Beacon brought on the family. Cheney declined Mrs. Beacon's offer for a sassy senior shower, and asked Parke's parents to wait until after the baby was born to host their shower. Malcolm had thought it was too early to have a baby shower anyway. She was now seven months pregnant, and the craziness was still going on. That baby shower was the first time he had seen Hallison in months.

Since dating Lisa, Hallison seemed to pop up everywhere—the mall, the Old Courtroom—looking good, and he was pretty sure that was her in The Loop with another woman. He didn't want to think about Hallison. Lisa was on his arm now and in his life. Her unpretentious personality won everyone over except Kami who didn't count.

Charlotte reappeared and stole Lisa to introduce her to some of her friends. Parke used the opportunity to pull Malcolm aside. "She's definitely pretty. Hali—"

"I don't want to hear Hali's name," Malcolm cut him off.

Parke squinted, silently assessing his brother. "Ever again?"

"Never."

Parke's shock turned into disappointment, then shifted to compliance. "As you wish."

Then Malcolm confronted Cheney. "Before I leave, what's going on in your pretty little head?"

"I'm happy if you're happy. Not really, but I respect whomever you choose to have in your life," Cheney replied.

Crossing his arms, Malcolm snickered. "Okay, what do you really think?"

"She ain't Hali."

"That's exactly what I want," Malcolm mumbled as Lisa walked up to his side with her eyes sparkling. His nostrils flared in appreciation.

Parke had kept an eye on his brother as Lisa taste-tested several samples, then finger-fed Malcolm the remains. The chemistry did seem to exist between them.

"God, help me to be objective," Parke mumbled, then turned to his wife. "Hey, baby, what do you think about Malcolm's new brains and beauty?"

"God, help us," Cheney said, shifting her body as the baby made a rolling lunge for the second time in minutes. "There is so much going on in my life right now, Parke. I've got Daddy's admission to a homicide, Grandma BB's revenge, and Hallison's replacement. I don't even want to add my hormones into the mix."

"I know, baby," Parke whispered as he rubbed her arms. "I love my brother, but I love Hali just as much as a sister, and I'm not referring to just the body of Christ. You would think God would've rewarded Hali for being obedient without understanding why she had to sacrifice Malcolm for her salvation. I wished they'd made it because it appears Malcolm got the cookie out the cookie jar, and it isn't Hallison flavored."

"Well, I guess it's official." Cheney sighed. "Malcolm's moved on."

Parke folded his arms. He purposely exercised his bulging biceps to amuse his wife. "I'm not buying it. It's not as if he hasn't dated since his breakup. I give Malcolm's fling fifteen days, tops."

"I'm not seeing temporary in Malcolm or Lisa's eyes at all."

CHAPTER 15

"What?" Hallison was unprepared for the news pouring through the phone. *Why is it that other people's happiness causes another person's sadness?* she wondered.

"The same God who blessed me has the power to bless you too." Paula was bursting with news. "Unbeknownst to me, while I attended that church fellowship a few weeks ago for the Word, the Lord sent a man. Through hordes of worshippers, Emmanuel Washington noticed *me* as he was leaving that first night. For the next three nights, Emmanuel was persistent in finding me again.

"After services, he kept asking around to see if anyone knew me. When he saw a mutual friend from my church who did know me, Emmanuel pleaded with him to intercede on his behalf. When asked if Emmanuel could have my number, I said, 'Sure, why not?' We've talked every day this week. He knows what I look like. I know what he sounds like, but I need a favor," Paula said, bubbling with excitement.

"You need me to be a bridesmaid at your wedding?"
Hallison answered dryly as Alexis's manicurist lifted her
brow in question. Hallison mustered a smile as she tried
to keep her fingers steady. She was glad she had on her
earpiece.

"No, silly," Paula scolded jokingly. "I don't even know if
he's the one, but if he looks as handsome as he sounds,
then Hallelujah!"

Hallison smiled again to keep from crying. She ached
for a God-fearing clone of Malcolm. She missed the com-
panionship. Taking a deep breath, she shook her head of
curls to appreciate the fragrance of a recent hair appointment and regain emotional normalcy.

She may not have a man, but she had Jesus. Hallison
tried to convince herself that was enough for the moment.
That sounded good, but why did she still want to cry? Hallison forced herself to refocus. She was looking forward
to the communion and foot washing service later with her
mother. Her mind continued to drift as she thought about
Cheney being happily married. Ursula had a husband, although every few days she threatened to divorce him, and
now Paula. She may have to change her circle of friends.

"Hali, did you hear me?"

"Huh?' She blinked and smiled. "I'm sorry, Paula. What
did you say?"

"Emmanuel wants to meet face to face, and I'm a little
nervous. Do you mind chaperoning for our first meeting?"

Hallison frowned. Her earpiece slipped. "You're kidding, right?"

"I'm not. This may be my season for happiness. Remember what I told you right before I started working for
the bank? I gave up what I once called a good man for
Christ, but only on the outside. Now God's blessing me.
Emmanuel is six-three and two-fifty. He's enough man to

handle my full figure. I'm educated, independent, and the manager of the bank's credit department, yet I'm scared of meeting a man."

The manicurist seemed annoyed at Hallison's lack of co-operation. "Miss Dinkins, I want to keep my job. Miss Alexis demands perfection in this salon," she said through her protective nose mask.

"Listen, Paula, I've got to go. Whatever you need me to do, consider it done."

"Great! Monday at lunch," Paula rushed and discon-nected.

Afterward, Hallison was thankful the manicurist con-centrated on her handiwork and didn't try to engage her in idle talk. Her mind was occupied with what God had done in the midst of Paula's praise and worship. She would always wonder if she had missed her window of opportunity. Could she blame Malcolm and his lady friend for making her walk in the rain?

Later that evening, Hallison exchanged kisses with her mother as Addison got into Hallison's car. Soon they were en route for the monthly communion service.

"Baby, you're quiet. Your spirit seems heavy."

The emotion was thick in her throat. "Momma, despite the big talk of being an independent woman, I want to be loved. I want to be dependent on a man and for him to be there for me."

Addison reached over and rubbed her daughter's arm in loving strokes. "What brought on this melancholy?"

Hallison didn't take her misty eyes off the road. "My friend, Paula, from work, is meeting her secret admirer from a series of church fellowships that I missed. She wasn't looking, but it appears God placed Emmanuel there for her. I just hope I didn't make a mistake when I gave up Malcolm."

"Nonsense. Malcolm made his choice by rejecting God,

and you made the right choice by following Him. God has
a plan. We'll have to wait and see the details. As beautiful
as you are, no God-fearing man can resist you."

When they arrived at church, Hallison's spirit lifted
once she parked and walked inside. They selected a pew.
Both knelt and prayed. Addison finished first and sat as
Hallison continued to petition God, "Lord, I'm out of
words. I don't know what to pray so I ask you to take
over . . ." Before she got off her knees, God spoke from
Mark 11:24: *What so ever things ye desire, when ye pray,
believe that ye receive them, and ye shall have them.*

As the praise team stirred the spirit, few remained in
their seats. Even Addison was able to keep the beat with a
rendition of Israel & New Breed's "Breakthrough." Making good on Hallison's earlier prayer request, God spoke
to her in other tongues. As the tears streamed down Hallison's cheeks, the prayers reached God's ears.

Pastor Joshua Bellamy stepped to the pulpit, wiping his
forehead with a white handkerchief. "Let's continue in the
spirit of holiness tonight. Let God's praise be continuously
on our lips. God didn't tell us to celebrate Christmas,
Easter, Memorial Day, and on and on. He commanded us
to take His body and eat. Tonight is not a ceremony, it's a
celebration . . ." He preached from 1 Corinthians 11:25.
*This is my body, which is broken for you; this do in re-
membrance of me.* "God is ordering us to remember Him
in every part of our life. When you walk out these doors,
remember the communion, communication, championship
you have with Jesus. . . ."

Minutes after they had eaten His body and drank Jesus'
blood, praises exploded throughout the sanctuary and
continued as men removed their socks and shoes for foot
washing. The sisters gathered in an adjoining room to remove their pantyhose for foot washing among themselves. Afterward, they returned to the sanctuary. When

the services concluded, Hallison was still rejoicing, drunk in the Spirit, so Addison drove home.

Sunday morning, while others were dressing for church, Lisa and Malcolm were gliding their bikes along the Katy Bike Trail—an old route through the Missouri, Kansas, and Texas rail line. Although they didn't attempt the entire 225 miles through the state, the exercise was invigorating.

"My family and I are getting together to review some documents from the early 1900s about another side of our family. We're going to dig through a treasure box of draft cards, marriage certificates, and even an old phone book that my father bought on eBay. We're hoping the phone numbers, occupations, and addresses could be that of deceased relatives," Malcolm rambled as his heart pounded with excitement. He was almost salivating.

Lisa shook her head. "The only dead people I'm interested in are the ones whose funerals I'm paid to provide plants and flowers. Unfortunately, Gertie's Garden is supplying flowers for an event tomorrow afternoon. I need to make sure everything is in place."

Malcolm parked his bike, then steadied Lisa while she climbed off. "I hate to see you go." He grunted and twisted his lips.

Stepping closer to him, she encouraged and he accepted a kiss that wasn't meant for public display. "Let me make it up to you."

He focused on her lips. "I'm listening."

"A getaway—a day trip to Chicago. We can dine on the Navy Pier, ride the Ferris wheel, and fly back that night or stay there until the weekend," she cooed huskily.

Malcolm responded with a wicked grin.

"I'm ready, Malcolm, whenever you're ready to make love."

Lisa's admission echoed through Malcolm's head the following week. He didn't want to waste his energy talking to Parke when his brother called about the family gathering. Malcolm had other priorities—personal ones.

Arriving home one evening after work, Parke was camped outside Malcolm's house, manning his porch. Parke unfolded his arms and stood once Malcolm parked and was walking toward him. Before Malcolm's foot hit the step, Parke lit into him.

"Remember me? Let me introduce myself. I'm Parke Jamieson VI, the firstborn of Parke V and Charlotte Jamieson, the eldest brother of Malcolm and Cameron Jamieson, grandson of . . ."

"I know who you are, Parkay." Malcolm threw the nickname Cheney called him when Parke irritated her. Malcolm brushed past Parke to his front door.

"Great. With the formalities out of the way, you want to tell me why you haven't called me back? Are you even planning to come to our family night? Cheney could've had our baby, Mom or Dad may have been sick—"

"Did she?" When Parke shook his head, Malcolm unlocked the door and threw his keys on a counter that separated the kitchen from the family room. "Lisa and I—"

"Since when could we not bring a guest to a family night?"

Malcolm gritted his teeth, annoyed. "I'll think about it."

Parke slammed his fist on the counter. "Which part are you thinking about? Coming with or without Lisa?"

Undressing, Malcolm strolled into his bedroom. Parke followed. "Lisa has made plans. I'm skipping one little meeting." He held up a finger. "It's a simple family get-together that Cameron hasn't attended in months."

"Cameron's in school in Boston," Parke bit out in a snarl. "No wonder you're not thinking, because your brain is fried."

Malcolm shrugged. Lisa mentioned she really wasn't interested in genealogy and Malcolm wasn't going to force her. In any relationship there was give and take. Every woman didn't share her man's every passion. He could deal with it, and his family had to respect that.

Parke was rendered speechless. He grabbed a nearby pen and pad and started scribbling.

Malcolm stood still. "What are you doing?"

"Writing down our parents' address in case you decide to attend and need directions." Parke dropped the pen, walked out the bedroom, and slammed the front door behind him.

CHAPTER 16

On Thursday morning, Malcolm didn't feel contrite about Parke's foul mood when he and Lisa boarded their Southwest flight to Chicago. With their fingers linked, Malcolm observed Lisa as she looked out the window. She was beautiful. Not only that, Lisa was willing to make him her top priority next to her business.

He should offer her nothing less. Yes, he was irritated Parke didn't understand, but he was furious with Cameron. His younger brother thought he had the right to call and chasten Malcolm as if he were a child, reciting the virtues of a tightly-knit family. He never had undergone this much drama when he was with Hallison. Probably because Hallison enjoyed his family as much as he did.

Lisa had turned toward him, moving her lips although Malcolm didn't hear her. She snapped her finger. "What's got you frowning? I've called your name three times."

In a blink, he erased his musings. Instead of answering, he instructed her, "Close your eyes."

"What?"

"Close your eyes," he repeated.

When she complied, Malcolm inched closer and brushed a kiss against her lips. They both tried to end it, but their lips had a mind of their own until an attendant asked about a drink selection. Clearing their throats, they smiled.

"Malcolm, I'm so glad you could get away," she whispered minutes later as she sipped her ginger ale. "I meant what I said. I'm ready to take our relationship further, and I don't have a problem staying until the weekend."

"Stop tempting me, lady." Malcolm didn't sound convincing to his ears. As a matter of fact, he was feasting on her enticements. Granted, he didn't jump in and out of bed with women, nor did he profess loving them when he did, but Lisa had been seducing him since the first day she walked into his office.

He was careful to steer clear of possible entrapments. Sometimes she seemed rather eager, but Lisa was hot. He preferred the hunt, but Lisa had laid her trap open. It was all about the chase, but Lisa was the aggressor, the lioness. She hadn't seen him in his predator mode, but she would by the time their plane returned home.

"Hmm. I'll be good for right now. Let me tell you what's been going on at the store. I've been recalculating my—" she started.

He held up his hand to stop her. "Lisa, you know we have a don't ask, don't tell relationship. While my firm is auditing Gertie's Garden, I can't ask you any questions. It's better if you don't divulge anything about the store. I'm sorry, baby, but this is a pleasure trip, and I expect us to please each other."

Annoyed, she nodded and didn't say another word. Instead she stared at Malcolm as if deciding whether she should shoot darts his way. Finally, she lifted a brow and smirked. "I see, and I expect full pleasure."

"As you wish." He brushed a kiss against her hand. For

the remainder of their short flight to Chicago Midway Airport, Lisa leaned back and closed her eyes.

When they landed, Malcolm retrieved their carry-on bags from overhead and escorted Lisa off the plane. Once they were outside at ground transportation, Malcolm was surprised and impressed to see Lisa had reserved a limousine to take them to the hotel. Her pampering was consuming and almost scary.

"Since we only have this afternoon, let me show you how a Jamieson man wines and dines his woman. I can take you shopping on Michigan Avenue, have a late lunch on the Navy Pier, and cap off our outside activities at the top of the Ferris wheel. I hope you don't mind dessert in our bedroom." He winked.

"Malcolm, to be honest, I didn't come to Chicago for anything else but to make love to you all day, night, and until the weekend if you think you can hold up," she whispered in the backseat of the limo.

"You're making it hard for a man to say no."

"Then don't."

He didn't. They checked into a ritzy hotel on the lakefront. Lisa couldn't keep her hands off him during the ride up the elevator. When it stopped on their floor, Lisa led the way with a seductive switch. Malcolm couldn't do anything but lust. He had to calm himself down. She was about to slip the card into the door slot when Malcolm snatched it.

"Lisa, let me seduce you on this trip," he commanded.

"It's too late. I'm in control."

The next morning, Malcolm rolled out of bed and padded to the bathroom, thinking about his relationship with Lisa. He wasn't in love with her, and she didn't demand it. Malcolm had loved only one woman—Hallison—

and they should've been married by now. He stepped in the shower and tried to wash away any lingering feelings for Hallison.

He enjoyed a healthy sex life. The thrill of Lisa leading him like a sheep ready for slaughter was exhilarating. He was fearless, a strong Jamieson man . . . and terrified of bed bugs. He couldn't help it, and it was the second time in almost ten years he had seen any before making love to a woman.

When he was a boy, he had spent the night at a friend's house. The following morning he went home covered with a nasty red rash over his entire body. Ever since then, he double-checked mattresses wherever he planned to sleep. Lisa had been furious, but Malcolm was serious about checking into another hotel. She reluctantly agreed, but the sexual fire was drenched. To buy himself some time and recapture the mood, Malcolm had suggested dinner on the Navy Pier.

It took a little convincing, but she finally relented. Relieved, Malcolm chose the Riva Restaurant. Lisa had tossed him a saucy smile as their waiter showed them to their table. While perusing the selection, she winked at him over the menus. When their dishes arrived, she dug in, so he bypassed praying over his food, and he reached for a roll instead. Throughout the meal, she brushed up against his leg constantly.

Lisa swallowed her last bite and wiped her mouth. Malcolm chuckled. "You weren't kidding. You were hungry."

"I'm in a rush."

His nostrils flared as she leaned forward.

"Malcolm, sweetie . . ." She waited for his undivided attention. "I want to go over some things with you."

Grinning, he grumbled. "My woman has rules." He dropped his voice. "Anything you want."

"First, I left major accounts in the hands of my staff to plan a romantic trip with you. Second, unless you're gay, a virgin, or a sanctified fool, I don't see how a few bugs that were placed on this earth could cause you to lose your libido. Oh, let me go back to number one-and-a half. I wanted to engage in a casual discussion about my business with my man. I care about everything in your life, I expect the same courtesy."

Her brilliant eyes slanted. "On to the third thing. You will pay for this trip. I've never been so humiliated." Swiping the white linen napkin off her lap, she stood and dropped it on the table. Lisa checked her watch. "Now, if you'll pardon me." She stormed out without looking back.

Malcolm hadn't tried to stop her. She needed to cool off, and he needed to get professional help for his fear of bugs. After ordering and eating his dessert, he charged their meal to his credit card and left. Instead of walking, he hailed a cab for the couple of blocks to the hotel. When he went back to their room, she had checked out, leaving a message for him to cover the bill. Thursday night had turned into an expensive letdown.

Now back in St. Louis, it was Friday morning and a new day. He sighed as he brushed his teeth, glancing at his empty bed. Malcolm wished he could make the previous evening's fiasco disappear. He jumped in the shower, wondering what it would take to restore his reputation with Lisa. Twenty minutes later, he was out of the shower, dressed, and heading to the kitchen. He popped a frozen breakfast meal in the microwave, then ate quickly. Grabbing his briefcase, he left for work. Once there, Malcolm stepped off the elevator and made a beeline to his office without hearing Lilly speak to him as he passed her desk.

"Well, happy Friday to you too. That's why I wake up in the morning; to babysit a moody, grown man," she said to his back.

"Huh?" Malcolm waved. For fifteen minutes, he brainstormed an acceptable and dignified way to make up with Lisa. He wanted to send her flowers, but having them delivered from competitors would insult her. He signed on his computer and Googled flowers. He was directed to a Teleflora site. "Lilly," he yelled as if she were down the hall instead of another room, "I need help. Can you come here a minute?"

His assistant appeared in his doorway, but didn't make a move to enter.

"Okay, I'm sorry, Miss Lilly."

"Took you long enough," she scolded and approached his desk. "Apology accepted. If you're calling me Miss, you want something. What is it?"

Malcolm mustered his best puppy dog expression for a thirty-three-year-old man. "I need to order flowers . . . for Lisa." He pointed to his computer.

"Why am I not surprised? Be right back." She walked out and returned, flipping through a ledger. She scribbled a note, then glanced at his screen.

"Lilly, please pick an arrangement you think Lisa would like. There's no need for recordkeeping. I'm the accountant, remember?"

"Yeah, you are, but it's my tally sheet of your girlfriends: Sasha, Carmen, Hali, Regina, Rene, Kim, Ava, and now Lisa."

He frowned and sat straighter in his chair. "You're keeping tabs?" he asked incredulously. "Why would you do that?"

She shrugged without answering. Lilly gave him a pointed look that dared him to ask again because she was ready to unload a mouthful of something he would probably rather not hear.

Malcolm stretched to peek, but Lilly rested the ledger against her chest, then folded her arms. "What exactly are you noting?"

"Not much. Appearances, personalities, sincerity, mannerisms, positive influence, motherhood, loyalties . . ."

He loosened his tie. "Evidently, I'm not giving you enough work to do. Anyway, all these flowers look too small for the price. What do you think about this celebration bouquet?" Silently, Malcolm counted the names in his head. He hadn't realized he dated most of those women after Hallison. Well, Lilly might as well throw away her notepad because the buck was stopping at Lisa.

She squinted. "A hundred and fifty-something dollars?" Her eyes bulged.

"Yep." He put his arms behind his head, pleased.

"Okay, but you could get those cheaper at the grocery store." She shrugged, scribbling on her pad.

"Yeah, and that would be unacceptable to Lisa."

"Right, Lisa," Lilly said and turned to leave.

Malcolm disengaged his arms and leaned on his desk. "What did you just write down?"

She gnawed on the butt of her pen, thinking. "You told me to order flowers," she said in a scolding tone. "I jotted down the floral selection item number and price. You're spending a lot of money on this one, Malcolm." Puckering her lips, Lilly began to whistle as she headed to the door.

"Ah, out of curiosity, who's leading the list?" Malcolm twirled his pen as if he didn't care.

"You don't want to know."

"Humor me."

"Nah, it's a silly game I play."

"Lilly, tell me," he said, more forcefully.

"Hali." She paused. "Three to one."

Malcolm scowled. He shouldn't have asked.

Lilly buzzed his intercom. "I've placed order TF115-1. Do you want pick up or delivery?"

"Pick up."

She relayed the information and disconnected the call. "The deed is done," she told Malcolm using the intercom.

Malcolm nodded to himself and reached for a file to begin his day.

"It doesn't have to be Secretary's Day to bring your dutiful, efficient assistant flowers," Lilly yelled from her desk.

CHAPTER 17

"He's bringing a single red rose. Isn't that outdated?" Hallison asked Paula absentmindedly while reviewing the bank's monthly report on productivity against the payroll. "Today's not a good day. I've got three deadlines to meet. What happened to going to dinner, a movie, or a play? If your idea of meeting Emmanuel for the first time in the building is romantic, then please keep your dating tips to yourself."

Paula laughed. "At least it's a public place. Emmanuel understands my nervousness. Plus with all the talk of bank and company bailouts, I need to go over the credit department's assets and mortgage reports."

"I'm not the only one under pressure. If I can't make it, you know Ursula wouldn't have a problem with a ringside seat of being in your business."

They disconnected as a light knock at Hallison's door preceded Ursula's entrance. Today, she strutted in wearing spiked hair. The wig's color was a toss up between soft gray or dull blond. She could easily pass as a younger version of actress Sharon Stone. "Guess what?"

"Speak of the devil," Hallison mumbled, dropping a pen on her desk to rub her temples. "I don't have time to guess. If you don't have your report, you and your staff can prepare to work throughout the night."

Ursula twisted her lip and waved one hand. "Girl, pleez. What do you think this is? I brought it down myself. Here." She placed it on Hallison's desk and took a seat. Ursula crossed her legs, folded her hands, and smiled. The red two-piece pantsuit complemented her current hairpiece. Hallison wondered if she would recognize Ursula's natural hair one day.

"Thank you." Hallison tapped on her computer keys to hint she was busy, but Ursula didn't budge. Sighing, she stared at Ursula, waiting. "What?"

"I told you to guess." Her smile grew wider and her eyes brighter.

"You're divorced?"

"Humph, I wish." Ursula twisted her lips, then grinned. "No, you'll never guess."

"Then I won't try." Impatient, Hallison lifted a brow.

"I'm black."

"Umm-hmm. You look the same color as you did on Friday." She didn't need this distraction. She returned to her computer screen. "Ursula, how about we talk about your immigration status in about two hours? Barry Grossman, my boss, the vice president of the bank—you know the one whose signature is stamped on our checks?—wants my figures by five. Now *you* guess what. He'll get them on time."

Ursula stood with her shoulders slumped. "Okay, do you have time for lunch later?"

"If I do, I'm meeting Paula in the café."

"And you guys didn't tell me? I hope Samuel isn't joining us again. That man has a crush on you." Ursula shook her head.

Hallison had invited Samuel to lunch with her friends one time. He invited himself the other. "That man is a homosexual who is qualified to do his job. Don't harass him, because you'll be dismissed. I'd hate to sign your termination papers."

"All right, I'll keep my thoughts to myself, but I'm telling you if that man were straight, I'd leave Anthony."

"Close the door behind you." Hallison had to agree with Ursula. If Samuel was a delivered soul . . . she didn't finish the thought. Hallison had too much work to daydream.

Hallison really didn't have time to take a break, but she was a bit curious to see a man who could look through a crowd and pick out one woman. With one major task completed, she reached for another report that could determine if a department needed to be downsized due to a decline in check processing.

Glancing at her watch, Hallison realized she had lost track of time. It took her three attempts to save her document and log off her computer. She stood and fingered through her curls, adjusted her dress over her hips, then slipped back into her shoes. Hallison opened her drawer and took out her purse. She caught her reflection in the mirror as she walked to the door. Lime green would always be her favorite color.

Ursula had beaten Hallison to Paula. Both sat at a table near the window. Paula was holding her compact, scrutinizing her makeup. Her white two-piece outfit complemented Paula's glowing brown skin. Her freshly styled short hair and golden highlights added to her stunning looks.

"How can we be girlfriends when you and Paula leave me out of the loop like this?" was the first thing out Ursula's mouth as Hallison sat with them. "I'm curious to see how this is going to play out with Emmett." Ursula checked her watch, then stuffed lettuce into her mouth. "I hope he's on time. I've got to get back upstairs."

Paula lifted her hand. "Don't correct her, Hali. I don't think Ursula can remember Anthony's name half the time, either." She turned to Ursula. "Emmanuel will be on time, and then you can leave." Paula smiled sweetly.

Laughing, Hallison laid her purse down and stood. She strolled to the food counter and ordered a cup of soup and a deli sandwich. When Hallison returned to the table with her tray, Ursula had made a dent in her salad, and Paula was sipping on a can of 7-Up.

"Paula, aren't you going to eat?" Hallison asked after blessing her own food.

"I can't." She fanned her face. "I'm a nervous wreck. That's all I need is to get sauce on my clothes, eat something with garlic on it, or smear lipstick on my teeth."

"Good point. Although Malcolm and I had already met at the job fair, I was nervous on our first official date too."

Ursula slapped the table. "Oh, we're back to Malcolm again? What's the man's number? I'll call him for you. Anyway, don't you want to hear about why I may be no longer white?"

Whispering, Paula leaned toward Ursula. "What is wrong with you? Our company does have a policy for random drug testing."

"Nonsense. Hallison had me curious when I caught her in the act of digging up dead people. My grandmother left behind some old—and I mean old—pictures and papers." She looked around to make sure no one was listening before confessing, "My family owned fifty slaves." She faced Hallison. "See, I apologized."

"What?" Paula turned to Hallison.

Shaking her head, Hallison sighed. "Ursula's America's African History 101. Her people could've enslaved my people. Who knows?"

Ursula waved her hand. "You don't have to be so dramatic. I wouldn't phrase it like that. I'm sure it was purely for economical reasons. From what I read online, Blacks were traded and sold as currency. Many South Carolinian Freed Blacks owned slaves."

"I wouldn't say that too loudly. The term is just as bad as saying the 'n' word in my book," Paula warned.

"Don't let Ursula be a party pooper," Hallison advised "Remember, you're about to meet your black knight. Anyway, Malcolm taught me, regardless of our ancestry, we can change for the future. That's what President Obama said."

"Amen," Paula agreed.

"Enough of the church service, ladies. What does Emmett look like?"

"*Emmanuel* is tall, dark, and handsome. He'll be carrying a red rose." Paula smiled and her eyes sparkled.

"Well, I wouldn't miss this for the world, especially since Anthony and I are getting a divorce."

Paula lifted her brow. "Again? What is he guilty of this week?"

"He's developing a severe case of bad breath. I think he has gum disease."

Hallison and Paula laughed until their sides hurt. Paula was wiping away a lone tear when she looked up and stared. "Oh, my God. That's him. That's Emmanuel."

"Where?" Ursula whipped her neck around toward the door and swallowed. "Humph."

"Ditto," Hallison repeated, breathless.

"If he's a black man, I'm definitely getting a divorce," Ursula said with awe.

"Forget it," Paula and Hallison snapped in unison.

"Humph, I'm going to get me a DNA and see exactly how much black I've got," Ursula said.

"If the world is lucky, hopefully zero percent," Paula mumbled.

Sure enough, two eye-stopping men walked through the maze of tables. A white guy searched the faces. He discarded one after the other as he twirled a stem between his large, fair hands. No doubt he was on a mission. A black guy, without a flower, trailed him.

Paula said, without taking her eyes off the pair, "He can't be Emmanuel. I don't think he's white. I mean, he didn't sound white."

"Disappointed?" Hallison asked, rubbing Paula's hand. She tried to calm her own racing heart. This was one reason she didn't like blind dates, because there were too many surprises.

"Why would I be disappointed with anything or anyone God sends me?" Paula cleared her throat.

"Here we go again with God speaking and sending. He's not concerned about your love life. Look at what He hasn't done with mine, for example." Ursula didn't take her eyes off the two men while missing her mouth with a fork of lettuce. "What's up with the bodyguard? You should've asked for a background check."

The man dressed in the state patrol uniform was easily six-one, but not as tall as the white man he escorted. Both were buffed, but the white one could fit the profile Paula described to Hallison. The trooper showcased dreadlocks and had skin the color of mink. He walked with precision, as if he owned the world. The other strutted as if he were the co-owner. The women held their breaths as the men stopped in front of them.

"Ladies." The white man's rich voice spilled from his lips as he eyed Hallison, then Ursula. He finally zeroed in on Paula. "I'm Emmanuel." He paused, leaning closer. "Hi, baby." He reached for her hand, turned it up, and placed the flower in it. "God bless you abundantly."

Ursula almost slid out her chair. Hallison wanted to check her deodorant for a hot flash that was about to slap her. Paula forgot to exhale.

"I would like for you to meet my baby brother, Trooper Derrick Washington."

The trooper nodded with a smirk. "I haven't been his baby brother since I was five, and please call me Trey."

Claiming a nearby chair, Emmanuel dragged it next to Paula and left Trey standing. With the same finesse, Trey stole a chair and straddled it as he joined the group. Folding his arms, he shrugged nonchalantly.

Emmanuel chuckled, tilting his head. "I knew I wouldn't be able to shake him. Trey wanted to see the woman I've been raving about so he came—uninvited, I might add. He always did tag along when we were younger too."

Trey didn't respond. His eyes seemed to sparkle as he focused on Hallison. The scrutiny made her uncomfortable. Hallison was curious how Emmanuel, who looked every ounce of Caucasian, was related to the dread-wearing trooper who could possibly be a descendant of an African slave.

Ursula's cell phone rang. She snatched it off her waist and read the number, twisting her lips. "Man, Anthony always calls at the wrong time. Excuse me," she said, contrite, standing and marching away.

Amused, Hallison would've made eye contact with Paula, but her friend was completely smitten with Emmanuel. She frowned, suddenly self-conscious of her appearance as she sensed Trey's stare. "I'm sorry, do I remind you of someone, or should I be concerned with something unflattering stuck on my face?"

"I'm always looking. You never know what God wants you to see," he answered matter-of-factly.

CHAPTER 18

Malcolm was strolling through the doors of Gertie's Garden when Lisa was walking out of her office. She froze, but he continued his trek until he towered over her.

"What are you doing here?" Lisa hissed.

"I came to pick up an order. After all, my family and I believe in supporting black businesses."

"Well, I hope it is to your liking. If not, we'll be more than happy to give you a full refund."

"You be the judge." Malcolm walked to the sales counter. He gave the fake name he told Lilly to use. Minutes later, one of Lisa's clerks handed Malcolm his order.

"You ordered the Celebration?" she murmured, shaking her head in disbelief. "You're kiddin'. I thought a secret shopper ordered the TF 115-1 to see if our handiwork would pass Teleflora's quality control."

"You passed." He lowered his husky voice and presented her with the bouquet as if she had won the crown of a beauty pageant. "Have dinner with me, Lisa."

She hesitated before nodding. Malcolm grinned, then wrapped her in his arms and delivered a lustful kiss. They agreed on a time. Turning around, Malcolm swaggered out the door, whistling as he headed home.

An hour later, Malcolm was trimming his beard when his phone rang again. He chuckled because Lisa had already called twice before he stepped in the shower. "Talk to me," he answered.

"Are you coming tonight?"

Malcolm's jaw dropped in irritation. "No, Parke."

He sighed. "Okay, since you'll be a no-show, how about planning a double date so Cheney and I can really get to know this Lisa?"

Parke was always the peacemaker. Blessed are the peacemakers for they shall see God. *Where did that come from?* Malcolm wondered. "That's cool. I'll get back to you."

"Love you, man. We're brothers, remember that."

Malcolm frowned at Parke's cryptic statement. "Yeah." They disconnected. He refused to let any guilt eat at him. Not long after that, Malcolm was at Lisa's condo. She opened the door dressed in a hot little number. "You're trying to kill me."

Lisa stood on her toes and smacked a kiss on his lips. "Silly, I need you alive."

On the drive to Jazz at the Bistro, Malcolm tried to keep his eyes on the road and not Lisa's legs. They weren't as shapely as Hallison's, but second best was a good runner-up. After parking, they linked hands and strolled inside the club.

Once they ordered, Lisa reached across the table and grasped his hands.

"Malcolm, I want to make this work."

He lifted his finger to her lips. "Let me do the talking. I owe you an apology." She opened her mouth to interrupt, but Malcolm shook his head. "I was a fool to ruin the wonderful day you'd planned. By the way, I've put a check in the mail to cover all the expenses for the trip. I figured you wouldn't accept it if I put the money in your hand." He leaned in closer. "Don't return it, Lisa. How about I plan the next get-away? Let me woo you, beginning tonight. I do have a confession. I suffer from insectophobia. Bed bugs do bite."

"I can help you overcome it."

Malcolm wiggled his brows. "Hmm. Work your magic."

"I intend to."

They joked, laughed, and swayed in their seats to the music until their food arrived. Throughout their meal, Malcolm teased; Lisa taunted. He teased, she taunted. They were practically drunk with lust as they swallowed the last drop of wine from their glasses.

"You ready to go?" he asked and he motioned to the waiter for the check.

"Of course, and I almost forget to tell you, I received my financial audit letter today."

"Oh? And?" he said, relieved that hindrance between them was at least over. As the band began another tune, Malcolm relaxed.

"Your company says it can't certify that I have enough capital for an expansion. I was depending on that letter for a new loan."

"Hmm." Malcolm incorrectly judged Lisa. She wasn't as astute with her money as he thought. Now that the audit was complete, maybe he could take a look at her books and offer her some financial planning advice. "You probably need to monitor your cash flow and. . . ."

Lisa's smiling eyes turned furious. "Malcolm, do you hear what you're saying? You're talking about my livelihood. Can't you talk to them?"

"I removed myself from the case to be with you, remember? Winfield & Young reviews and signs off on every project before a report is written. We carefully consider every variable that could hinder a business down the line. I'm sure our letter outlined their findings."

She squinted as she leaned closer because of the drummer's beat. "Now, I don't want you to talk shop with me. You're supposed to hold me, and if I cry, wipe away my tears and tell me you can make it better."

"Unfortunately, in this instance, I can't make it better. I'm licensed and so is my company. We can't make figures appear and expenses disappear like magic." He snapped his fingers.

"Well, I can."

"Baby?" Malcolm reached out to draw her closer, but Lisa wouldn't budge.

"Not now, Malcolm," she whispered. "I've been known to curse like a sailor's twin brother when I'm upset. Once I say it, I won't take it back. Apologizing has never been my strong point. Please, take me home."

Their date ended forty-five minutes later at Lisa's front door. She hurled some profanities in the air before shutting the door in his face. Stuffing his hands in his pants pockets, Malcolm wondered if their relationship was cursed.

CHAPTER 19

Monday morning, Hallison walked into her office, humming lyrics to "We Shall Behold Him," the choir's A selection on Sunday. Pastor Scott took his sermon from Romans 8:28: *And we know that all things work together for the good to them that love the Lord and who are called according to your purpose.*

Shifting in her chair behind her desk, Hallison kicked off her shoes from her latest *Chadwick's* catalog. She praised God for reminding her of His promises. She was about to indulge in a mini-concert of worship behind closed doors when Paula almost skipped into her office without knocking. Although Paula was a full-figured sister, it was her four-inch heels that concerned Hallison. She didn't want to contend with completing a workman's comp claim.

"Why do you and Ursula barge into my office?" Hallison asked dryly, hoping Paula would find a seat soon.

"I checked with Gloria," Paula practically sang, "So . . ." She flopped in a chair much to Hallison's relief and glided beautiful, manicured nails across Hallison's desk. "What do you think of Emmanuel? I don't have much time."

"First, you interrupt me, and now you're rushing me?" Hallison stalled to irritate Paula. "Okay, besides being a sanctified version of sexy, he seems nice and infatuated with you. So, how was your weekend?" Hallison asked as she booted up her computer. "Did you know he was white?"

"With a voice like his? When he made his appearance in the café, I stopped thinking and started appreciating."

"Well, we know that was an understatement."

Paula smiled. "He's not all white. He's mixed."

"And so is all of America," Hallison joked. "Regardless of his race, I'm happy for you. If there was a mutual attraction between a good-looking man of another race and me, I'd be willing to explore it too. Even Moses had an Ethiopian wife despite some grumblings."

"It's something about blind dating on the phone. Your feelings are already rooted before looking into each other's eyes. Emmanuel does have beautiful eyes, by the way. We went out to breakfast Saturday morning, enjoyed Bible trivia at his friend's house that night, attended his church yesterday morning, and ate dinner together last night." Paula closed her eyes and sighed as if she'd forgotten she was in Hallison's office.

Hallison picked up a pen and played with it. She couldn't relate. She had to know what a man looked like before she opened her door for a date. How else could she visualize his expressions behind the words he professed?

"Hali, I'm glad you said you're willing to explore a relationship based on attraction. What do you think of Emmanuel's brother, Trey? He appeared very enthralled with you. Who knows? This could turn out to be a double blessing." Paula's eyes sparkled.

"Ah, don't you have a manager's meeting in . . ." Hallison checked her watch. "In fifteen minutes? I think you should prepare for that instead of starting a matchmaking service after one date with Emmanuel."

"I always have time for my dear sister, and technically, if you count Saturday's breakfast and dinner, Sunday's worship and dinner, that's four dates." A grin stretched across Paula's face.

"You've been unattached a year longer than me. It was your time for a blessing. Me, although I may not say it or look it, I have too many left over feelings for Malcolm."

"Get over it because Trey asked for your number, and I gave it to him." Paula shrugged. "Your work number, of course."

"You did what?" Hallison shot out her chair, snagging her pantyhose. She hoped she had a spare pair in her emergency box. "Paula, I don't even know this guy. If I could fire you on personal tampering or something, I would. You don't know this brother or Emmanuel really," Hallison fussed as she dropped the pen and stabbed the air with her finger.

Paula shrugged, showing little regard for her friend's fury. "But you will."

Nostrils flaring, Hallison rolled her eyes. She had too much work that needed her attention. Without another word, Paula stood and did a Hallelujah dance. In a Comedy Central moment, Hallison entertained the thought of Paula slipping and landing on her behind as the floor gave her one hard spank. Hallison shook her head. It was a naughty fantasy that she wouldn't want to turn into reality. She loved Paula, up until a minute ago.

Foregoing a break, Hallison's assistant picked up a salad for her at the St. Louis Bread Company. She worked nonstop to prepare insurance option packets for more than two hundred employees. At five minutes before five, she logged off her computer. Standing, Hallison stretched, then pulled open her desk drawer for her purse. That's when her office phone rang. Hallison's shoulders slumped in exhaustion. "Of all days for a late call," she fussed, snatching the phone off the receiver. "Hallison Dinkins, director of human resources."

"Good evening, Hallison. This is Trey Washington from the Missouri Highway Patrol."

She froze, then collapsed in her chair. Her heart pumped wildly before regulating its beat. She wanted to strangle Paula. Trey didn't wait for her to regain her composure.

"I hope you don't mind that I called."

"Well . . . well, I don't know what I mind right now. I don't know if I should be angry with Paula for giving you my work number or skeptical because you asked for it after meeting for what? At most, thirty minutes." Last Friday when she had stood to leave the café, so had Trey. His words had been so comforting.

"Hallison," he had pronounced affectionately, "May God give you a blessed day."

"Amen." It was her standard response when she didn't know what else to say. His voice was confident, kind, and non-threatening, a contrast to his intimidating uniform.

"Let me take the blame for both. You never know, I could be applying for a job. I majored in business with a minor in criminal psychology, and I understand you're the head of the department," he joked. "Unlike my brother, I'd never ask someone else for a woman's home number. I believe in making my intentions known to the intendee."

For the first time since Malcolm, Hallison blushed at another man's compliment. She took a deep breath and exhaled. "I do have one question. Are you and Emmanuel really brothers?"

Trey's chuckle was a deep rumble. "Yes. Everybody asks. Once you get to know us, you'll see the similarities.

We have the same dad, but different mothers. His mom was white and mine is black. He grew up in a black household after his mother passed away, so that's where he picked up his black mannerisms and dialect. Deep down, he's what he is, a white man on the outside with a dash of African American heritage on the inside. He's a good man who loves God and is willing to listen to His voice. I believe he's serious about your friend."

Surprisingly, for the next hour, Hallison enjoyed his conversation. She learned more about Trey than he knew about her. He didn't ask her probing questions, but he didn't wait for her questions, either.

"I'm thirty-five and perfectly settled in the Lord. Let's say, I've found my way. I wasn't always sanctified and walked as if I knew Jesus died and hung on a tree for me," he admitted with a bit of shame. The vulnerability was endearing. After a slight grunt, there was a lull in the conversation.

"Hello, you called me. Did you forget I was still on the other end, at my desk, and ready to go home?" she teased. "Why did you become so quiet?" Hallison really was curious.

"Just thinking about an article I stumbled across on lynching in America a while back. I'm not deep into that part of history, but I recall looking at pictures and becoming incensed over the 1930s lynching of Rubin Stacy and Lint Shaw. I was repulsed, angry, and ready for revenge. Then God spoke to me. 'Where's your reaction for me, my death, and my torture? Are you prepared to avenge my blood against spiritual warfare?' At that moment, I knew I had to repent, refocus, and return to my spiritual roots. The next day, I dragged my older brother to church, and together we walked down the aisle for prayer. Before we left Redemption Ministry Church, we were baptized, in Jesus' name. We came out the water rejoicing, not realizing we were speaking in other tongues until we listened to each other and couldn't recognize a phrase. It was a day and an experience I won't forget."

Thinking of Hallison's safety, Trey reluctantly ordered her off the phone so she could make it home before dark. He forced his home and cell numbers on her, but didn't ask for hers, nor did she offer.

By Friday, Trey had phoned her again at work. "You didn't call me."

"No, I didn't. I have relationship baggage. I was a backslider, but now I'm working overtime to catch up on my walk with God. I don't want any distractions. Knowing what God saved me from, I'm determined to ensure that my name is written in the Book of Life."

"Revelation 20, verse 12: *And I saw the dead, small and great stand before God and the books were opened, and another book was opened, which is the book of life. And the dead were judged out of those things which were written in the books, according to their works,*" he quoted.

Smiling, Hallison was impressed. *How can two walk unless they agree?* She thought about the scripture in Amos 3. Suddenly, in the background, static and hurried emergency calls interrupted their enjoyable conversation. "Where are you? I hope you're not talking and driving. That's not a good example for teenagers," she teased, and it felt good doing it.

"Guilty. I'm about to end my shift. Listen, Hallison, I want you to know that I'm strong mentally, physically, and spiritually. If you ever decide you want to let go of that baggage, I'm strong enough to carry it."

There was no doubt of the sincerity in his words. "Amen. Trey, let's be friends for right now." She needed to play it safe.

CHAPTER 20

"Is there something you want to tell me?" Cheney queried her friend over the phone.

"Nope, not really. Not yet anyway," Hallison said with a smile. She had briefly spoken to her mother, who Hallison suspected thought a man was behind Hallison's carefree disposition. If Addison and her church group hadn't been on their way to an afternoon stage production, the conversation would've been, at the minimum, an hour.

With her legs hanging over one arm of her living room sofa, Hallison scooted farther down until her head rested on a large throw pillow. Soft jazz floated from a kitchen radio. "How did you know you were truly over your ex? CliffsNotes only, please."

Cheney laughed, then exhaled. "You just know when that man fills up your heart. But hey, I'm on my way out to my doctor's appointment. When I get back, you better be near your cordless, land line, or cell phone." *Click.*

She beamed and stared at the ceiling. Was she actually close to getting over Malcolm? Hallison grabbed the remote and pointed at her TV. She didn't care what was on.

As she channel surfed, Malcolm's light-skinned, bearded face flashed in her mind instead of Trey's dark brown, clean-cut face and shoulder-length dreads. Hallison stopped smiling, wondering how Malcolm was doing. Did they really love each other as they had professed? Could she really get over her first love, and how long would it take? Somehow, she felt God was going to answer those questions soon.

Hallison stalled for time as she waited for Cheney to call her back. She called Octavia who was at another doll exhibition, this time in Dallas. "I'm in doll heaven. I'll call you back tomorrow," Octavia had said without saying goodbye.

Amused, Hallison grinned at Octavia's obsession. She considered calling Tammy or Faye, but each had a history of being long-winded and Hallison wouldn't be able to get rid of them. They would be like sharks on a trail of blood. Bored, she decided to drive to the library and try some more digging on the Palmers' genealogy. Standing, Hallison walked into her bedroom to change clothes. As she brushed her hair, the phone rang.

"Hi, Hallison. This is Trey. Were you busy?"

Two days earlier, the trooper had finally chiseled away at her resistance and she surrendered her cell number. Still, Hallison was surprised to hear from him. "I was going to run some errands."

"Would you like comp—"

Her phone beeped. "Hold on." She read the caller ID and clicked over to accept Cheney's returned call. Perfect timing. "Yes, Mrs. Jamieson?" Hallison cooed.

"Don't 'yes, Mrs. Jamieson' me. Start talking."

"Okay, hold on." She switched back to Trey. "I need to take this call." He accepted her excuse without question. After disconnecting Trey, she returned to Cheney. "All right, no questions. I want to listen."

"Okay. Larry was my first love. Because of my feelings for him, he had a stronghold on my heart. If Larry had said jump, not only would I have said how high, but how many times should I jump to prove my love. I was a fool. As I look back now, I realize I wasn't in love. Larry was my lust who I'd followed behind like a zombie. Girl, I was strung out on some serious Larry addiction." Cheney sighed. "Sadly, I had to go through that to find my prince in Parke. I'm not angry anymore, and I'm happy. What a blessing."

With Cheney's words ringing in her head, Hallison took that as a sign to allow a friendship with Trey to proceed. Days later, they shared, tasted, and compared various St. Louis frozen custards at Iggys, Fritz's, and Ted Drewes after church. They became inseparable outside work. Trey invited her to Bible classes at his church and Hallison accepted. When they couldn't get together, a phone call was the next best thing. One Saturday morning, Hallison had already spoken with Trey when Paula called.

"Do you think you can squeeze Emmanuel and me in for a double date?" she joked.

Laughing carefree, Hallison played along. "Let me check our schedule."

"Yeah, right. I told you God may have had a double blessing. Emmanuel not only fills my emptiness, but stimulates my spiritual awareness in Christ."

"Ooh," Hallison said, sucking in her breath. "I'm not prepared to say all that, yet. I do admit we're enjoying each other's company though. Trey is such a sweetheart."

"Good, because Emmanuel and I are challenging you and Trey to a skate-a-thon, and before you give me some lame excuse about checking schedules, Emmanuel already talked to Trey this morning. The first couple who lands on the floor buys the other dinner."

"Bet." Hallison couldn't get enough of the sport when

she was a teenager. Skating had been a weekend staple with Faye and Tammy.

Hours later, Trey treated her to a new pair of skates when she couldn't fit her old ones. "They were on sale," he said, shrugging. "My mama always told my dad, 'you can't beat a sale.' "

When she tried to pay him, Trey shook his head. His dreads bounced on his shoulders. "Don't insult me." His stare dared her to blink.

"I won't. Thank you." Hallison couldn't believe she had accepted a pricey gift from a guy she wasn't dating. Maybe they were dating, and she hadn't labeled it. It seemed as if Trey had crept into her life without her putting up much of a fight. He had proved to be more than a good listener. She actually enjoyed his company.

Once the couples met at Skate King, on the city's north side, the competition was on. To the women's surprise, the brothers put on a show, with Emmanuel steering Trey to the wall where he lost his balance. In the end, Trey and Hallison were the losers and paid for dinner at Qdoba, a Mexican restaurant.

The following week, Hallison's phone rang as she finished her last five seconds on the treadmill. "Hello." She pulled the hand towel from around her neck and wiped her face.

"Hi. Good morning," Trey struggled to say.

"What's wrong?" She panicked.

"Tired. I've worked a long shift, thanks to two brothers who decided to take up cooking lessons and start with a meth lab as their first experiment. It goes to show you why Jefferson County is considered tops for drug busts in the nation. The house exploded, and the men suffered second degree burns. Thank God the five children who lived there weren't hurt. When I left, the Hazmat crew was still on the scene. I'm beat, but I wanted to talk to you."

Flattered, Hallison smiled. "Ah, poor baby," she teased. "I'd better let you get some sleep."

"What are you planning to do today?" he slurred.

"Shop."

"Will you wait for me? I only need a few hours of sleep."

"You're kidding. Isn't that unmanly or something?" Hallison joked, but instantly she wanted to snatch back the statement. She and Malcolm didn't have limits on what they could enjoy together. "Ah, don't worry about it. I might not buy anything."

"Hali," Trey's husky voice whispered, "I don't care if you go shopping or not. I'm interested in everything about you. I'm asking you to wait for me for a few hours to get some sleep."

It was the first time he called her by her nickname. Trey Washington was endearing. "Yes. I'll wait."

"Thank you." He disconnected without saying goodbye.

Hallison closed her eyes. "Lord, if this is you, please let me know . . . please." She sat motionless, waiting to see if God would stir. When He didn't, she used the reprieve to study God's Word, which she hadn't done in a few days. After reading several passages from the Old Testament and making notes, she prayed and checked her watch. Trey hadn't phoned, which meant he was deep in sleep.

Briefly, her mind drifted. It was routine for Hallison to show up at Parke and Cheney's house unannounced. That routine ended after seeing Malcolm with his new girlfriend. Old insecurities about her decision resurfaced. Hallison jumped when the phone rang. She checked the caller ID and recognized Cheney's number. "I was just thinking about you."

"Good, because I was just wondering about you," Cheney said with an edge to her voice. "Are you too busy to call, visit, or email? At this point, I'll accept a letter through the mail," she fussed. "When you weren't at church, I assumed you were church-hopping with Paula."

"What are you talking about?" Hallison frowned, confused at her friend's accusation.

"Don't what me. You've given me bits and pieces about a man who might make you forget that Malcolm Jamieson ever existed, and I don't know enough about the brotha."

Hallison accepted her chastening, but Cheney was wrong. No woman could forget a Jamieson man, especially Malcolm. "Well. . . ."

"We need a long girl talk. You know you can come over here—"

"I don't think that's a good idea, Cheney. I feel like I'm invading on Malcolm's domain. How about we meet at a mall or something?"

"Nonsense. You and Malcolm have parted ways. I'm not expecting you to be at every family function, but don't cut us off completely."

Hallison sighed and apologized. "What's been going on in your world?"

"Pure drama," Cheney said. "Momma's gone ballistic, blaming me for moving next door to Grandma BB, as if it were a conspiracy. She's mostly concerned about their reputation if Daddy goes to jail or loses his license. I thought she was changing and wanted a deeper walk with God. This whole situation has messed all of us up."

"Speaking of Grandma BB, have you two spoken again?"

"I've tried not to talk to that crazy woman, but she's like a pimple that won't clear up. Back to you. What's his name?

Bulldog Cheney Jamieson, Hallison called her. Cheney wasn't letting go of her bone. "Derrick 'Trey' Washington," Hallison recited in pride.

"Hmm. Good for you. Then it appears Malcolm isn't the only one who's moved on. Here's a stupid question. Is he really saved and really fine?" she teased.

"Trey is a gorgeous specimen of God's creation. Muscular, long dreads, and sanctified sexy. He's a highway patrol officer who can skate his shoes off."

"Does he have a brother?"

Hallison laughed and Cheney joined her. "Sorry. Paula's got him. What about Prince Parke?"

"Actually," Cheney said, trying to contain her amusement. "I was thinking more for Grandma BB. She is always talking about dating younger men. Talk about a diversion. Okay, back to Mr. Washington."

"Let me get comfortable so this baby won't kick my bladder," she said with labored breath, moaning as she shifted her body. "So, Miss Dinkins, is he finer than Malcolm?"

"You're married to Malcolm's brother. What do you think?"

"Good point. Then he's not that fine," Cheney stated.

Hallison toyed with a stray penny on her table. "Let me put it this way. God knows how to reward for good behavior."

"There's a reason God put emphasis on obedience more than sacrifice. While you thought you were delivering up a sacrifice, you were actually obeying. I'm glad you're finally happy again, although I'm still disappointed that it wasn't with Malcolm. It must've been what God wanted. I need to do a checklist. What don't you like about him?"

"To be truthful, nothing. He enforces the law of the land. He's confident, honest, and thoughtful."

"Hmm," was all Cheney would say. "So what are you thinking?"

"Trey makes it impossible not to care about him. Right now, he's taking a nap after working all night so he can go shopping with me. Isn't that sweet?"

"Mmm-mm, like a box of chocolate."

"Yeah, chocolate-covered strawberries. Plus, he's offered to carry my baggage. I'm not talking about shopping bags, but emotional, heartache baggage."

"Keep talking. I'm taking mental notes."

"I'm beginning to care, Cheney, and I'm scared. Trey calls me before he starts his shift, asks me for a scripture, and we pray together. Now, I can't fall asleep until I've heard from him. I don't want to fall too soon, but I'm definitely slipping."

"I think Parke and I need to check him out," Cheney stated without any hesitation.

"Do you think that's a good idea?"

"Yes. Parke will feel the same way. Name the date, place, and time, and we'll meet you two there."

CHAPTER 21

Cheney chewed her lips after she had hung up with Hallison. She prayed that she hadn't overstepped her boundaries when she committed Parke to check out Malcolm's competition. Jamieson blood was thicker than a twelve-hour pot of coffee. She walked into their sunroom to find Parke sprawled across the sofa and the ceiling fan teasing the newspaper he'd dumped on the floor.

"Hey, sleepyhead." Cheney shook his foot. "I'm the one pregnant. Why are you taking a nap?"

"Your daughter wore me out, that's why. I picked her up from daycare, and she talked me into stopping at Wabash Park to play. I had to drag her away after an hour." Stretching, he rolled his shoulders and sat up. When she sat next to him, he rested his arm around Cheney's shoulder. "So what have you been doing while I played the unpaid babysitter?"

Cheney shoved him in the chest. "That's our daughter you're talking about so you won't be collecting any paychecks."

"Oh, yeah. She *is* ours." He grinned.

She waited for his goofy expression to pass. "I talked to Hali."

On full alert, Parke frowned. "Is she okay?"

"She needs us right now. I was supportive on the phone, but I need you to back me up." Cheney bit her lip, waiting. "If you don't feel comfortable, then she'll understand."

Frowning, he rubbed her stomach. "Of course, she has our support. What's going on, baby?"

"I'm glad you said that because Hali has finally met someone." Cheney paused and waited for Parke to digest the news. His face was blank. "I told her we'll meet him and check him out."

"You did what!"

Shrugging, she batted her lashes. Parke had a thing for her long lashes and shapely brows. "I couldn't help it. It was a toss-up between me being nosy or concerned. We love her as a sister."

"Umm-hmm, did you forget I love my brother like a brother?" Parke bowed his head and let his hand run laps through his hair. He sat quietly as he considered the implications of Hallison's request. "Okay, but God help me if I turn out to like the guy."

A few days later, after Parke had fasted, prayed, and talked to God a little bit more, he told himself he was ready to meet this Trey dude. Before he could get an answer from God, the devil was already calling him a traitor, backstabber, and other names that wouldn't meet God's approval. "There's no reason for me to feel guilty about meeting Hallison's *new* friend." After all, Parke had invited Malcolm and Lisa to an event or dinner twice. It never happened because of their previous engagements. Sometimes, Malcolm never got back to him.

Tonight was the night. He dressed for dinner with mixed emotions. Would he really be backstabbing his brother? Parke didn't voice his concerns. He smiled as Cheney walked into the bedroom with her balloon-shaped belly. Her skin glowed. Her hips were fuller, and she was downright irresistible as she carried their second child.

Meanwhile, despite Cheney's complications from an abortion several years earlier that doctors said left her sterile, she became pregnant less than a year after she and Parke were married. The pregnancy ended with a miscarriage, but they held on to their faith. Parke and Cheney were disappointed, but both were hopeful that Parke Jamieson VII would come through Cheney's womb to continue the Jamieson legacy. Parke and Cheney prayed earnestly for a miracle and tried to live righteously so their request would be granted.

Cheney struggled to wrap her arm around him. She laid her head on his back. "We can back out. Hali will understand." Parke felt her body still. He sighed as Cheney held her breath.

"No, she may understand, but our word is our word. Now." Parke, turned around and patted her behind, shooing her away. "Hurry up or we'll be late."

Kami was watching a Disney movie with a babysitter when they left home. While driving to Westport Plaza, Parke contemplated how he would react to another man with his former sister-in-law-to-be. Would he be jealous, resentful, or rude? "God, help me to be fair," he mumbled.

Cheney squeezed his hand. "Lord, help *us* to be fair."

Parke pulled into a spot, only spaces away from an SUV. Hallison stepped out, patiently assisted by a tall, thick guy with dreads. On the surface, the dude already didn't appear to be Hallison's type.

"He's kinda cute," his wife whispered as he helped her from their vehicle.

Grunting, Parke shut the passenger door and activated the alarm. "I'm not seeing all that. C'mon. Let's get this over with." His sole purpose was to ask questions and scrutinize Trey's answers. *Lord, help me.*

"Hali," Cheney shouted too eagerly for Parke.

With their hands linked, Hallison tugged Trey toward Parke. She released Trey's hand only to hug Cheney who was giggling. *Traitor,* Parke thought. Somebody had to keep the tough exterior. Clearly, his wife was a goner. As Parke sized Trey up, Trey extended his hand.

"It's nice to meet you. I've heard many great things about you and Cheney." Trey grinned and slapped his hand into Parke's for a handshake.

Parke glanced at Hallison. Her eyes pleaded for him to be nice. Parke nodded. He wondered if Trey knew Hallison's ex-fiancé was his brother. Gritting his teeth, Parke expected a long, uncomfortable night. He accepted the handshake with a grip. "Please, call me Parke."

Seemingly satisfied, the women looped their arms and proceeded to the door of the restaurant, leaving the men behind. The night proved to be interesting from the moment they were shown to their booth seating.

"Please, let me treat everyone. I owe Hallison a meal anyway," Trey offered, exchanging some sort of secret with Hallison. Trey winked, causing Hallison to blush.

Parke regulated his breathing as if he were a lamaze student. He wished they would let him in on the joke. Parke was about to let Trey know he could feed his own wife, but Cheney kicked him under the table.

"Ouch." He turned to his wife and frowned.

Cheney blinked. "Oh, honey, I'm sorry. I needed more leg room."

Trey motioned to stand. "Would you ladies like to change seats? There's more room at the end."

"Thanks, but that won't be necessary. My wife just needed to stretch." Parke squinted at Cheney, silently conveying he knew it wasn't an accident. Then he faced Trey. "You sure you want to treat? As you can see, my wife eats enough to feed a horse." He emphasized the last word as a checkmate. This time, Parke winked and blew Cheney a kiss. When her nostrils flared, Parke groaned. Cheney had just declared battle.

"Parke's right. I do have a hearty appetite, but we'll treat next time at EAU Bistro in the Chase Park Plaza Hotel." She batted her lids at her husband.

He nearly choked on his water. The prices at the Bistro were for special occasions, not family dining or buttering up his brother's competition. He shifted his foot and laid it on top of her shoe, barely putting pressure, but enough to let her know he would enjoy paying her back.

"Sounds like a plan." Trey picked up the menus the hostess laid on their tables after they took their seats. "Now, let's get our ladies fed."

Everyone decided on a selection and placed their orders. Cheney and Hallison talked nonstop from baby's clothes to Hallison's new flattering hairstyle, even Mrs. Beacon's name slipped in there. Parke didn't want to know if he had anything in common with Trey, so he listened to the ladies with intensive interest.

When their food arrived, Parke was about to say grace when Cheney double-crossed him and asked Trey to bless their meal. Waiting, Parke expected something along a long-drawn out grandeur prayer, instead, it was a simple bless the food and the fellowship in Jesus name. In unison, they said, "Amen."

Halfway through their meal, Parke began a slow thaw to Trey. For a man who possessed the authority to write a ticket and put someone behind bars, he didn't boast of his power. There was no fault for Parke to find.

"In my line of work, the Lord allows me to recognize the spiritual warfare: sexual predators, missing persons, drunk drivers. The list is endless, and I've seen it all. When I put on my Missouri Highway Patrol uniform, I feel like I'm a soldier for Christ."

As Trey captivated his audience, Parke counted the number of times Hallison reached for Trey's hand, and he welcomed her touch. So far, they were up to five hand holdings.

"Trey, tell them about the men using the bathroom on the side on the road," Hallison urged, laughing before Trey explained.

"That's right," he said, chuckling himself. "Unfortunately, one guy was so intoxicated he pulled to the side of the highway and began urinating against the rocks. The only problem was a skunk had beaten him to the spot. When he saw the critter and yelled, the skunk sprayed him."

Parke didn't want to laugh, but when the others couldn't contain their amusement, he barked out the loudest. Trey turned out to be all right. He had gained Parke's respect for his dedication to his job and the Lord. He had Parke's blessings.

CHAPTER 22

With the motor running, Mrs. Beacon sat in her Cadillac in front of the Jamieson house. Cheney peeked through her wood shutters, watching her every move. She could see Mrs. Beacon in her classic housedress and possibly, her Stacy Adams shoes. When Mrs. Beacon placed her cell phone to her ear and Cheney's house phone rang, Cheney picked up, but didn't say hello.

"We can settle this feud now. Step outside," Mrs. Beacon threatened, without waiting for a greeting.

"What?"

"Okay, okay . . . I'm sorry I shot your father . . ." Mrs. Beacon paused, clearing her throat. "Thanks for accepting my apology. Now that that's out of the way, I've got new clothes for Kami. We can do this the easy way or the hard way. Don't think I won't camp out in front of your house to see my baby, or you can hand over the bundle of energy for a couple of hours for an unsupervised visit."

"Grandma BB, did you forget I don't have to answer the door?" The woman was persistent. Mrs. Beacon called Cheney with her demands in the morning and dropped off packages of goodies outside her door at night. This was her second trip around the corner to Cheney's house in one day. The woman had her faults, but she loved Kami unconditionally. "All right, all right," she said as the baby kicked. "I'll have Parke bring Miss Thang to your house later on. She's been asking for her BB anyway."

"Thank you," Mrs. Beacon whispered humbly. "How's the other baby?"

Cheney smiled at her concern. "Running out of room while practicing for the Olympics."

"It won't be long."

"No. Thank you, Jesus."

Parke was doing something he knew he shouldn't be doing in his own house. He was relaxing on the sofa with his shoes on. In a high back chair, Malcolm sat with his shoeless feet propped on an ottoman. For the past hour, they had watched the highlights on *ESPN* and argued about the plays.

"Malcolm, it's good to hang with you, man. It's been a while."

He grunted. "Yeah, yeah. It's my fault. Lisa and I have had this chemistry since we first met. I don't want just a fling, but man, she is hot and hard to resist! Leave it up to Lisa and my handprints would be all over her body."

"As you might recall, in the beginning that was the total opposite of me and Cheney. We had no chemistry, and the only visible handprints would've been the ones she left up side my head if I had even thought about touching her, but you know me." Parke grinned and shrugged. "I like a challenge. I fell in love with her before I knew about her past. I walked away only to come running back. I couldn't let her go."

"How could I forget?"

Parke aimed a throw pillow at Malcolm's face, which he

blocked. Parke smirked. "I was pretty pathetic. At first, we argued more than we laughed, but that changed when she let me kiss her." Parke licked his lips and winked. "Seriously, Malcolm, we've never let a woman come between us. Don't start now."

Malcolm stared at his brother. "Wrong, Hali did."

"That's where you are wrong. It's Lisa. Hali became a part of our family the day we met her. We all could see the love seed was planted, and frankly, I thought you would beat me to the altar."

"You'll feel the same way about Lisa once you get to know her."

"That's great, but upset Momma one more time with another one of your no-shows on family night, and you're a marked man. I'll personally take one of Grandma BB's guns and come looking for you." Parke tilted his head from side to side, trying to loosen his muscles and crack a bone. If you think I'm bluffing, try me."

"Where did all these threats of bodily harm come from, which don't faze me?"

"I was just being nice since you're a guest, you know. I was holding my tongue until after the highlights were over."

Malcolm nodded. "Just to keep peace and keep you from picking yourself up off the floor, I'll be at the next family night."

"Good. I'm glad we've reached an understanding, because I'd hate to go out and buy you a copy of *How to be a Good Brother for Dummies*."

"You're laying it on kinda thick. I said, I'll be here. Don't make me sorry I dropped by to get a free meal."

"Oh, let me give you a heads up. Since we're hosting family game night this month, Cheney and I invited Hali."

Malcolm's shoulders stiffened. Several expressions

raced across his face before the wheel stopped on blank. Once he was ready to respond, he nodded. "That's cool." Malcolm reached for a sports magazine. He absentmindedly flipped through a magazine he held upside down.

"I'm glad to hear that because she's coming with Trey," Parke raced through his words, grabbed the remote, aimed it at the TV screen and changed the channel.

"Who's Trey?" Malcolm released the publication, and it flopped on the floor.

Parke cleared his throat and forced a cough through a fist he used to shield his mouth. Kami couldn't pick a better time to make an appearance. She crossed the room toward her father, dragging her stuffed animal. Parke sighed at the reprieve.

When Kami noticed Malcolm, she raced to him. "Hi, Uncle Malcolm."

He lifted her on his lap, eyeing Parke, but kissing her cheek. "Hey. Did you just wake up?"

Nodding, she got down. "Daddy, I had a bad dream."

"Really, pumpkin? Tell Daddy all about it," Parke said in a soothing tone, ignoring Malcolm's snarl.

Malcolm would not be denied an answer. "Kami, go find Mommy. You can tell her all about it, and she'll even kiss it and make it better, or whatever mothers do. I'll bet you'll even get a cookie."

Kami's eyes widened as she dashed off, yelling, "Mommy."

"Walk, Kami," Parke ordered, standing. "You know, Malcolm, dinner might be ready." He checked his watch. "We can discuss this after dinner."

Folding his arms, Malcolm relaxed in his chair, then crossed his feet at the ankles. "I don't care how good Cheney's lasagna is. You might as well sit down, because neither of us will be eating for a while. Talk, Parke, or we can take this conversation outside. I guarantee Cheney's not going to like the way her husband looks after we finish our talk." His fingers scratched imaginary quote marks in the air.

"You're making a big deal out of nothing. Trey is Hali's boyfriend."

"Her boyfriend? Since when did she get a boyfriend, and how do you know him?"

"I believe Hali and Trey have been dating maybe a month now. Umm-hmm, I really wasn't keeping notes, but he's a nice guy. Cheney and I met him last night at dinner. Of course, we invited him at the last minute, but he accepted the invitation nevertheless."

"What? You've been sleeping with the enemy?" He sprang up from his chair. The force scooted the ottoman aside. "Unbelievable. Where do you get off about all this talk about the brotherhood?" Malcolm balled his fists, contemplating what he should do with them.

Parke slowly rose and duplicated Malcolm's stance. "No, I've been sleeping with my wife. If you'll recall, every time I attempted to plan a date with the four of us, you two weren't available." He jabbed a finger in the air.

Malcolm paced the room, mumbling, "Again, this is unbelievable. First, you cohort with the woman I thought I'd spend the rest of my life with. Parke, I'm less than one minute from cussing you out with words you can't begin to spell. This is un-be-lie-ve-able. I would do anything for Hali, and what does she do? Toss me aside like an empty box of Kleenex."

"Hali only wanted one thing from you and that was a desire for a deeper and permanent relationship with Christ," Parke argued. "How much longer do you think you two could go without falling in bed? I know you, Malcolm. We've had this discussion before. You were hot in the pants for Hali, but she wasn't ready. God was behind that decision, and she didn't even know it."

Walking within inches of Parke's face, Malcolm's nostrils flared with anger. Parke put on his game face, ready to block his brother's first move.

Malcolm gritted his teeth. "Step outside."

CHAPTER 23

Hallison attended only two Jamieson family nights after she broke it off with Malcolm. Tonight would make three. She wasn't usually an impulsive shopper, but nobody would believe it. Hallison was going overboard at Macy's clearance racks during her lunch break. Paula trailed her, quietly observing Hallison's selection of a black dress and black pumps trimmed in rhinestone. When she added a classy black hat to her pile, Paula snatched it out of her hand.

"Are you attending a funeral or a game night?" Paula whispered while Ursula was distracted, inspecting hidden compartments inside handbags. "What are you doing? I thought you were looking for colorful tops and sandals."

Ursula crept up behind them. "Hey, if we're going to stop by and get our lunch, we'd better hurry. I happen to like my salad cold and my chicken quesadillas hot. First, check out how much these leather purses are marked down." She walked away, expecting them to follow.

To save face, Paula grabbed a few items off the hangers and placed them on Hallison's pile, whispering, "I know your hips can't squeeze into a size three. Mine either, but you can return them later so Miss Nosy Nature won't suspect your gloom and doom behavior."

After they paid for their purchases, they hustled to TGI Fridays for orders they had called in before leaving for lunch. Once they made it back to the bank's courtyard, Hallison dropped her bags by her chair as they prepared to eat. Paranoid, Ursula had begun to join them in prayer to bless her food since word had spread about a salmonella outbreak. Ursula alternated between chewing on a mouthful of pasta salad and sipping on lemonade. Paula frowned at Ursula's marathon eating while Hallison picked at her food.

"Listen," Ursula said, pointing, "If you don't want that salad, I'll eat it. I missed dinner last night. I can't stand it when Anthony makes meatloaf. He's too heavy on the seasoning or something."

Hallison shook her head. "At least he'll cook. You had better stop complaining about that man."

"Then the man farted all night." Ursula turned up her nose while Paula and Hallison snickered. Pasta dangled from Ursula's fork as she twirled it in the air, pointing. "Can you imagine having a husband like Anthony? Can you believe he bought concert tickets to see Norah Jones?"

"No," Hallison mocked.

"You've got you a fine hunk of a man. Anthony's crazy about you," Paula scorned. "Why did you bother marrying him? Listening to you, it's been three years of misery."

"Sex. That's why I married him," Ursula stated.

Hallison choked on her soda. They came to her aid, patting her back. Hallison waved them off once she regulated her breathing. "There's a scripture in Hebrew 13 about marriage and sex."

"There you go with that Bible quoting again. I would dump you two as friends if I didn't enjoy your company so much. Plus, Hallison, you really got me going with this genealogy stuff. I'm still digging into the Palmer families in North Carolina."

"Wait a minute." Paula held up her hands. "I don't want to talk about sex or slaves for the remainder of our lunch. I'd rather talk about Emmanuel." She grinned.

Ursula wiped her mouth, looked at her watch, then folded her arms. "Okay, you've got five minutes. Give me an Emmanuel and Trey update."

Paula blushed. "My pleasure. Emmanuel took me horseback riding last weekend—"

"You on a horse?" Ursula cackled. "Please, tell me someone took pictures. Not only are you and Emmanuel too old, but girl, you're too big to get on a horse."

"Humph! You better go and rent some *Bonanza* videos. I'm not ashamed or shy about my full figure. I'm as comfortable in my size eighteen body as any skinny person."

"You tell her, baby." Emmanuel's voice sliced through the argument-in-the-making. He bent down and placed a kiss on Paula's cheek, then Hallison's, and stepped back when Ursula puckered up. "I was downtown and decided to stop by. I was on my way up to your office when I saw you out here. What are you in the mood for tonight—play, movie, or relaxing? Whatever you want, sweetie."

Standing, Paula winked at her friends as she threw her trash away. Emmanuel waited, then trailed her back inside the building.

"That little scene was interesting. Where's your beau?" Ursula lifted a brow with a smirk.

"I'll see Trey later. We're going to a family game night." Hallison held her breath, waiting for Ursula's questions to begin.

"The Washingtons have game nights like the Jamiesons?" She drained the last of her lemonade.

"Well, no. We've been invited to the Jamiesons' family game night."

Ursula's eyes widened. "Hallison, have you lost your mind? Is Malcolm going to be there? Do you enjoy going into the bear's den or whatever it's called? I want to see God deliver you out of this one. This ought to be good."

"Ursula, Malcolm is dating another woman, I'm happy with Trey. I'm definitely over Malcolm Jamieson." *At least I hope I am. God, give me a sign that reconfirms that I made the right decision*, Hallison prayed.

"Girl, it sounds like it could escalate into a fight night instead of a family night. Does Trey know about your relationship with Malcolm?"

"Yeah, I told him last night. He told me he feels every incident and relationship advances us to the next stage in our lives. I agreed, but I never mentioned Malcolm's name until yesterday."

"Last night, huh? I hope he carries a gun."

Later that evening, when Hallison opened her front door, Trey wrapped her in a hug. He stroked her cheek. "You look pretty," he said, complimenting her red, two-piece ensemble and her trademark strappy sandals. Hallison decided to wear something bright instead of the dark clothes she had picked up during lunch.

"I have to admit, Hali, I feel ambushed. If he's a man like Parke, I could understand a possible attraction." He stared into her eyes. "I'm not concerned about you being over his brother, Mark."

"Malcolm."

He ignored her correction "The question is, if he's over you." Trey's face was a blank. "I hope there won't be any trouble. I'm authorized to carry a gun. I don't like to use it."

"Trey, the best thing that came out of my relationship with Malcolm was meeting Cheney through his brother, Parke. In such a short period of time, we became best friends. We're closer than some sisters are, and we usually do a lot of things together. Otherwise, I wouldn't be going or dragging you."

"Here's the correction, baby. You're not dragging me. I'm going willingly because of you." He stole a kiss from her lips.

She blushed, returning his affection. "One thing I do know is that without meeting Paula, I may have never met you through Emmanuel."

"Hali, my question is," he paused, cupping her face between his hands, "should I be concerned?"

"No," she whispered.

He stepped inside her apartment and shut the door. "Good, but I think we should pray anyway. It wouldn't look good for a trooper to be arrested for assault."

Hallison laughed.

"I'm serious." Taking her hands, he waited for her to bow her head, then he followed. "Lord, in the name of Jesus, your Word is filled with encouragement. You aren't the author of confusion, but of peace. We rebuke the spirit of anger, confusion, strife, and envy. Bless us to show our light that can't be hidden. There is nothing that is going to happen tonight that you don't already know about. Thank you, Jesus, for listening. Amen." They lifted their hands in praise as they magnified the Lord.

The drive from Hallison's apartment to Cheney and Parke's house was less than fifteen minutes. Trey kept Hallison engaged in conversations to keep her mind off the upcoming night. He was confident everything would be peaceful. God would make sure of it.

Trey's feelings toward Hallison had been strong when

he first laid eyes on her. He didn't need to date Hallison for three weeks, six months, or a year to know he had fallen in love with her. She was a woman any God-fearing man would snatch. It had been five weeks to the day, and his feelings were already carved in his heart.

The most appealing thing about Hallison was her determination to walk with God, no matter the cost. Of course, her beauty couldn't be overlooked. When she became quiet, he squeezed her hand.

"Hali, remember you've begun a new chapter in your life, and we're the main characters. Still nervous?" Trey asked, but knew her answer. He encouraged her to smile and she conceded.

"A little."

"I want to tell you something. Maybe it's the right time. Maybe it isn't, but I love you, and tonight when you're facing any demons, remember that I'm with you all the way."

Hallison blinked right before she stopped breathing. Only one other man had uttered those words to her, and she had accepted his marriage proposal. Sniffing, Hallison moved her mouth to respond, but Trey's finger stilled her lips. It was a good thing, but she had no idea what to say. After his declaration, Trey left her to her own thoughts, allowing gospel artist, Ben Tankard's "Song of Solomon" to serenade her.

Once they parked, he helped her out of his vehicle. When she met his eyes, he winked. "Trey, I'm not ready to say—"

"I didn't ask you to. You have time," he cooed. "I'll give you a couple weeks." He grinned.

She punched his arm. He feigned injury before he grabbed her hand and linked their fingers. Hallison took baby steps to the front door of a house that could've been pictured in a storybook, with its perfectly manicured lawn surrounded by colorful plants.

After a brief knock, Cheney opened the restored antique wood door. "Hey, you two. C'mon in."

"Auntee," a toddler called as she ran to Hallison with bright eyes and a big smile.

Scooping up the little girl, Hallison rubbed a loud smack in her cheek. The child giggled and squirmed to get down, so Hallison released her. "Trey, meet my god-niece. Kami, say hi."

She waved, and Trey smiled.

"Are you Auntee's boyfriend?" Kami demanded.

Trey knelt. "Yes, I am. Is that okay?" He offered Kami a smile.

Kami shrugged and squinted. "I don't know. I call it like I see it." Losing interest, she turned as Parke's booming voice rounded the corner. Trey stood and looked at Hallison for an explanation. Hallison shrugged too. Whatever came out of Kami's mouth was becoming as unpredictable as the price of groceries at checkout despite Cheney's attempt to keep a handle on Kami.

Parke sauntered into the living room. He slapped a handshake with Trey and kissed Hallison. "Make yourselves at home. You're the first ones—" The bell chimed throughout the house.

She relaxed, realizing that it wasn't Malcolm unless he had changed his Morse code for announcing his presence. When Cheney opened the door, she confirmed Hallison's hope. Hallison thanked God she had more time to calm her nerves.

Parke's father crossed the threshold. Kami screamed and barreled into him as if she were a mile away instead of a couple of feet. "Grandpa, Grandmommy."

Hallison kept a hand around Trey's arm for support. She didn't know how the elder Parke and Charlotte would greet her. Parke V dispelled her fears when he engulfed her in a bear hug, followed by a warm kiss. "How ya doing, girl? I miss seeing you."

She nodded and smiled. "I'm fine, Mr. Jamieson."

"Hali, you're just as gorgeous as ever," Charlotte complimented as her eyes sparkled. She blew Hallison air kisses since she was carrying a foil-covered pan. Hallison guessed it was Charlotte's seven-layer salad signature dish. Charlotte then turned her attention to Trey. "And who is this young man?" she asked, setting down her food.

He stepped forward and extended his hand. "Mr. and Mrs. Jamieson, I'm Trey Washington."

"Trooper Derrick 'Trey' Washington." Hallison beamed with pride, hoping she wasn't pushing their hospitality. After all, they had loved her as a daughter. Still did, and she still loved them.

Mr. Jamieson clicked his heels and gave Trey a salute in jest. "We stand corrected, Officer Washington." He smiled and winked at Hallison.

"Please, call me Trey."

So far, so good. Two down, one big tremor to go, Hallison thought. Seconds later, the doorbell buzzed twice, paused, and another buzz. *Malcolm*. Hallison's heart jumped as he opened the door with Lisa at his side. She blinked rapidly, afraid to make eye contact. Hallison gave Lisa a brief look-over. She was gorgeous in a two-piece red capri and red stilettos that showed off her calves. Malcolm always was a leg man. Hallison groaned silently. *Great, we're both women in red.* She suddenly wanted to kick herself for not wearing black.

The air around them stilled as movements ceased until Kami shattered the silence, "Hi, Uncle Malcolm." She turned to Lisa and frowned. "Auntee has a new boyfriend. Uncle Malcolm, you should get a pretty lady like her."

"Kami!" Everyone shouted in embarrassment, including Hallison. Trey smirked.

"BB told me to call it like I see it," she explained as Charlotte pulled her granddaughter to the side and made her apologize. Kami did with her fingers crossed behind her back. Parke grimaced. Cheney rolled her eyes, and Trey didn't say a word.

"Lisa, we're sorry. We're glad you could make it, finally," Charlotte said.

"Let the games begin." Malcolm took a deep breath and clasped his hands, eyeing Trey.

Hallison groaned. *God, I'm so glad we prayed.*

CHAPTER 24

Malcolm should've punched Parke in the mouth when he had a chance, but Cheney conveniently interrupted and announced dinner. Cheney squinted, knowing she had walked into a fiery furnace. Her presence delayed the dental appointment Malcolm was confident Parke would need after their talk.

The previous night, Malcolm had refused Cheney's dinner invitation, but she dragged him into the kitchen anyway and shoved a covered plate in his hands and a healthy slice of earthquake cake—his favorite. Still, Malcolm fumed about the enemy infiltrating the Jamieson territory, and he continued to entertain fantasies about getting the job done to his older brother.

He kissed his mother and shook hands with his dad. He debated if Parke deserved a handshake. Lisa watched the two with curiosity. Cheney returned from the table, her stomach guiding the way. She nudged Parke to embrace his brother. Parke did with the strength of a bear, whispering to Malcolm, "Don't act up."

"Unless you want your ear bitten off like Evander Holyfied, I advise you to back off. Remember, I'm a guest." He turned and faced Hallison, Miss Heartbreaker.

So this is Hali's church man, Malcolm surmised. Nodding, he grumbled, "Hali," as he strolled past her, tugging Lisa, whose heels were not meant to be rushed, toward the table. Malcolm ignored Hallison's guest along the way.

"Well." Parke cleared his throat. "Trey, this is my younger brother, Malcolm." The men nodded. "Hallison, this is Lisa."

"We've met," they said in unison.

"Oh," echoed throughout the room. Parke mouthed to Cheney, "I hope you're praying."

"I started when the doorbell rang," she mouthed back.

Everyone began to gather around the dining room table. Cheney stretched out her hands. "Let's bless the food so we can eat first."

Lisa, standing between Malcolm and Parke, stepped back when they reached for her hand. "I prefer a moment of silence," she mumbled.

Malcolm nodded as if he understood, but he didn't. Blessing his food was as routine as brushing his teeth in the morning. Yet, he respected her decision; he didn't want to convert Lisa as Hallison had tried to do with him. No one seemed to make a big deal out of Lisa's decline anyway, including Hallison.

"Trey, since this is your first visit in our home, please offer a blessing?" Cheney requested.

Trey's thumb brushed against Hallison's hand when she bowed her head and closed her eyes. Malcolm chided himself for caring.

"Father, in the name of Jesus, bless this home. Bless the hands that prepared the meal. Sanctify it and bless our bodies to receive it. We speak peace in this place. Let everyone say, Amen."

Begrudgingly, Malcolm did as Trey instructed. Lisa returned to his side with a smile. No words were exchanged as they piled food on their plates. The men went for seconds as the women talked between bites. Kami knew better than to ask for more dessert, when pasta and chicken drumsticks remained on her plate. Malcolm smirked as Kami stole a cookie when she thought no one was looking. Crumbs exploded on the table like a waterfall, exposing Kami's deed. After everyone was stuffed and groaned at the mention of more food, Parke cleared the table of their potluck dinner. His father engaged Trey in conversation. *Traitor*, Malcolm thought, stewing.

Kami raced behind her father in the kitchen and returned with a large garbage bag. Starting with her grandmother, Kami walked around the table and collected trash. She received accolades for being a big girl and Mommy's helper.

Parke returned with a board game. He kissed the top of Kami's ponytail for pitching in before he unloaded the contents from the box. "While buying Kami some toys, we came across this game. This one seemed interesting. Hmm. Black, Bible, & Family Trivia."

Sighing, Lisa crossed and uncrossed her legs. Malcolm concluded this was not going to be her cup of tea. She leaned closer to Malcolm's ear. "We would've had more fun at an arcade or casino."

"Baby, you'll enjoy this. You'll see," Malcolm assured Lisa.

"I'm from Missouri. Show me," she said, paraphrasing the statement tattooed on every state bumper sticker.

Malcolm backed off from an argument. They had had enough of those lately. Plus, he didn't want to make a scene in front of Hallison, suggesting all wasn't well in Malcolm's paradise. When he winked, Lisa smirked as he stretched his arm across her chair, nudging her closer. When he glanced across the table, Trey had Hallison's attention as she almost relaxed in his arms—almost. "Okay, let's get the show on the road. Lisa has an early day to-morrow," he lied, and Lisa grinned.

It took Parke less than five minutes to assemble the three-dimensional pop-up board game. Kami had her own miniature pop-up picture book, which Parke had brought to occupy her.

Three stacks of cards were positioned in different places, forming a triangle. Parke unfolded the instructions. "I've only skimmed through it. The object of the game is the first person to answer five correct questions from each stack wins, and . . ." He held up his finger. "Cheney found this small, engraved trophy. We can pass it around to the winning family member each month. We thought it would add a little heat to the competition."

Mr. Jamieson chuckled. "Like any of us need the incentive." After spinning a wheel to select the first player, Mr. Jamieson started. "Okay, hit me with a card from the black category. This will be a breeze." He flipped it over and recited the challenge. "Name the first colony to abolish slavery." He stroked his chin as if he were perplexed.

"Stop playing around, PJ. We all know the answer," Charlotte fussed at her husband.

"Pennsylvania was the first state in 1780, but Vermont was the first colony or U.S. territory in 1770," the elder Parke answered.

Nodding, Cheney kept tally. "Way to go, Daddy Jamieson."

Lisa was next. She reluctantly spun the wheel and pulled from the black stack. "Name the first black Miss USA," she stated as her face glowed with confidence. "Vanessa Williams. I don't know the exact year, but I think the mid 1980s."

Flipping through the pages for the answer, Cheney was the bearer of bad news. "Nope, sorry, Lisa."

Her frown looked as if she would challenge the answer.

Black history was tricky. Textbooks weren't always accurate, and popular answers weren't always the right ones. Lisa's shoulders slumped as Cheney went around the table, asking for the correct answer. "Anybody can pick up an extra point. Name the first black Miss USA."

The room was quiet. Hallison knew the answer, Malcolm would bet on it. Not only was his former fiancé proficient at trivia games, she was well versed about beauty products, fashion, and celebrities, yet, she held her peace. As former teammates, they played to win, chalking up more victories than losses.

"Buzz." Cheney mimicked, checking the game's stopwatch. "The correct answer is Carole Gist in 1990. Gist was crowned in Wichita, Kansas. She was twenty years old and six feet tall. A year later, she was first runner-up in the Miss Universe pageant."

Why didn't she grab the point? Malcolm wondered again. Hallison wasn't six feet, but she was five-feet-eight and still gorgeous. Hallison could've easily competed in a pageant and won.

"Okay, Mal, spin the wheel," Cheney prompted.

"Get ready to get whipped," Malcolm boasted. Just his luck he would be the first one to pull a Bible question. Eyeing Hallison and Trey through the hood of his lashes, neither wore mockery expressions.

"What was the name of the first woman judge in Biblical Israel?" Malcolm amazingly remembered the answer from fifth grade. At the time, he thought Mrs. Green was lying about a woman ruling men. That tidbit had stuck with him. "Deborah."

"Correct," Cheney congratulated.

"Yay, Uncle Malcolm." Kami clapped.

Across the table, Hallison took a spin and playfully shoved Trey, before picking a card. "Who said, 'Is there anything too hard for the Lord?'"

* * *

Of all the Bible questions in the stack, Hallison pulled the scripture she had prayed many times over the past months. "God, in Genesis 19." It was also the scripture Paula shared with Hallison when she learned about the volatile situation Hallison had Trey walking into it. Paula prayed with Hallison then advised she expected a full report.

"Yeah," Trey shouted, giving Hallison a high-five.

"Yay, Auntee," Kami shouted, clapping again before going back to her pop-up game.

Hallison was having a great time, and to think the night would be awkward. God had dispatched peace, and the Holy Ghost was actually allowing Hallison to enjoy herself. Yes, both she and Malcolm had moved on. Hallison turned to Trey. "Okay, let's see what you can do."

When Trey flexed his biceps, Hallison giggled. She didn't know if she was giddy with his antics or his admission earlier that he loved her. This was what a relationship should be, two people who loved the Lord. Although she hadn't returned his declaration, it was comforting to know how much he cared. She could build on that. The night of Mrs. Beacon's arrest, Hallison gave up hope that Malcolm would ever do an about-face and surrender to God

"Hmm," Trey mumbled after his arrow steered him to the untouched family trivia stack.

"Finally, this category, I'm anxious to hear this question," Charlotte said.

Trey's voice boomed as if he were a game show host. "How much do you know about your parents and grandparents?"

Hallison already knew about his father and his two marriages, one ending in the death of his first wife. Hallison had met Trey's mother, Sharon, and his father, Derrick Jr.

"I'll start with my maternal great-great-grandparents, Callie Lowe and Winston Wade. Callie was born in the Cherokee tribe, which is one of the five civilized Native Indian tribes. All I know is Winston died while slavery still existed. Callie was listed on the Indian 1906 Dawes roll as a freed Cherokee-owned slave. . . ."

Trey captivated everyone as he spoke eloquently about his heritage. Hallison didn't want to rub anything in Malcolm's face, but she was glad God had sent her a good, God-fearing man.

Charlotte interrupted, "Trey, what's the big hoopla that's going on in Congress about the Cherokee Nation wanting to cut off African Americans?"

"The Nation amended its constitution, which would revoke Cherokee citizenship to almost three thousand black descendants if their Indian ancestors weren't listed on the Dawes roll. If they're successful to dishonor our ancestors, the federal government could withhold three hundred million dollars in funding and suspend the Nation's gambling license. It's amazing how the tribe enslaved my ancestors and then basically said that if you can't prove it, then you're not entitled to all the benefits afforded the Cherokee Nation—"

Lisa frowned and interrupted, "I never understood why tribes were considered civilized."

Malcolm didn't seem too pleased with Lisa's sudden interest, although he wondered about the answer.

"The white race considered the Cherokee, Choctaw, Chickasaw, Creek, and Seminole civilized because they mimicked the Whites' mannerisms and lifestyles, including owning slaves. The Cherokees are believed to have owned the most slaves." Trey encouraged the group to visit Cahokia Mounds. "Did you know that across the Mississippi River in Collinsville, Illinois, the *only* prehistoric Indian city north of Mexico still exists?"

Malcolm cleared his throat, and Hallison pinched Trey's arm.

"I'm sorry, I'm talking too much," Trey apologized.

Hallison scrunched her nose. "Yep." And she enjoyed it. Every day she learned Trey was so much more than a man who wore a uniform, carried a gun, and worked for an agency that patrolled and protected the state's highway. *Yes*, she thought, *Trey's definitely one of God's treasures*.

"We came to play a game, not listen to a lecture," Malcolm stated as if he were the game spokesman.

"Sorry, man," Trey told Malcolm, then faced Cheney. "Do I still get my point?" He gave Cheney a lazy grin that he used on Hallison to bribe her into getting some frozen custard.

Out of the blue, Kami shouted, "Yeah."

Cheney glanced around the table for the consensus. Hallison held her breath, hoping Malcolm wouldn't cause a scene. She could feel his vibes. Clearly, he wasn't happy seeing her, Trey, or both of them together.

She did feel guilty about coming on Malcolm's turf. Why did she agree? Any other normal ex-fiancée wouldn't have yielded, but somehow Cheney's invitation gave Hallison an excuse to see Malcolm. He had a beautiful new girlfriend. She had Trey. Hallison shrugged away the discomfort. She and Trey were invited guests, and even Malcolm's parents had treated her cordially.

The game continued until the turn fell on Lisa. "Bible trivia," she mumbled, annoyed. Lisa sighed as she reached for a card and scanned it silently before reading it aloud. "Where did the wise men come from? Hmm. Somewhere in the East," she answered with certainty.

"Correct. Matthew 2:1." Cheney grinned.

Malcolm and Lisa celebrated with a kiss. Hallison felt a slight prick in her heart, but she smiled anyway at the affection she once shared with Malcolm. She prayed silently as Trey reached under the table and squeezed her hand. *Lord, let your perfect will be done.* Cheney called the winner at ten points instead of fifteen, allowing Parke to edge past Malcolm by one point. "This game is almost as long as Monopoly," Cheney complained, shifting a sleepy Kami on her lap around her emerging belly.

"I got her, babe." Parke stood and lifted his daughter into his arms.

Trey checked his watch. "Yeah, it's getting late. We'd better head out. I have a twelve-hour shift tomorrow." He pulled back Hallison's chair so she could stand.

Hallison offered to help clean up, but Cheney waved her off.

"I'll do it," Lisa volunteered.

Hallison froze. She swiftly rebuked the sweeping bout of jealousy. The devil urged her to play a game of tug-of-war with Cheney's friendship as the prize. *Lord, help me through this. I've moved on—I guess,* she thought. "Are you sure, Lisa?"

"Yes, I am, Hallison," she said with an underlying challenge.

What did Hallison expect? Lisa was staking her territory. "Okay. I'm sure Cheney would appreciate it."

"Yes, she will," Lisa replied as she folded up the game. Malcolm turned around, but not without a flicker of a smirk.

Nodding, Hallison proceeded to hug everyone, bypassing Malcolm and Lisa. Trey followed with handshakes. Once outside, Hallison looped her arm through Trey's and rested her head against him. "Trey, your love made a difference."

CHAPTER 25

Malcolm survived the night without getting into a brawl. He bid his parents goodnight while Lisa helped Cheney. His ex-fiancé and her Christian man bailed out first. As Malcolm peeped through the slits in the living room shutters, Malcolm calculated the bottom line of his previous relationship. Slipping his hands in his pants pockets, he huffed.

He would always respect Hallison. She was honest, beautiful, and committed to her beliefs—whether religious, social, or family. Lilly had been keeping a checklist and so had he, but without a pad and pencil. Lisa was fresh, exciting, and a little demanding. That was a sexy quality.

Parke stirred behind Malcolm. "Wanna talk?"

"Sure," Malcolm answered, but didn't budge.

"Whenever you're ready." Parke headed for the sunporch. That's when Malcolm followed. Behind closed French doors, Parke walked to the wicker furniture and flopped down. Leaning back, he watched Malcolm pace. "What's on your mind, bro?"

"Like you don't know." Malcolm felt like someone was

slapping, kicking, and punching his emotions all at the same time. "I can't believe you invited that woman stealer in your house," he hissed to keep from shouting.

"Didn't you accuse God of stealing your former fiancée?"

"The board game is over, Parke. I don't feel like starting another. You broke all the rules under the brotherhood code of ethics." Malcolm rambled, rubbing his hair in frustration. "I could've been somewhere making love to my woman."

"Don't let God stop you."

"He already has," Malcolm snapped.

Flowers were delivered to Hallison's office. Without pulling the card out of the accompanying envelope, she knew the sender. Hallison picked up the phone and punched in his cell number. "Thank you," she said with a smile. "They're beautiful, Trey. I never knew there were so many colors in a rainbow."

Trey was amused. "The colors reflect all the beautiful things God created in you."

"I thank God for sending you into my life."

Before Trey could respond, a radio dispatch interrupted their conversation with urgent chatter. "Baby, I've got to go. I've got an emergency call. I'll pick you up later for dinner."

"Okay, Trey. May God keep you safe," Hallison said, disconnecting.

Four hours later, Hallison's assistant knocked and opened the door, carrying a larger bouquet. She sucked in her breath. "Trey." Picking up the phone, Hallison pushed in his number, without opening the small envelope. As soon as he said hello, she exaggerated kisses over the phone. "Two deliveries in one day? You're spoiling me."

"That's my intent."

"Trey, they're gorgeous."

"And so are you."

"You wouldn't have said that if you'd seen me last night in the hair salon," she teased.

"Hali, you're beautiful naturally."

"You believe in adding whipped cream to all your desserts, don't you?"

"Only if the waiter is serving me up some Hallison Dinkins," Trey cooed into the phone.

She smiled. "Save your sweet talking for later over dinner. I'll be ready at seven."

She threw him a kiss. He returned the gesture before they both disconnected.

An hour before she planned to go home, Hallison received another floral delivery. Hallison shook her head. "Trey, you're unbelievable," she whispered as she opened the flap on the envelope. It wasn't from Trey.

Hali, I'm sorry if I made you feel uncomfortable at Parke's house a week ago. I tried to make you happy, but I failed. I tried to love you, but I failed. I hope Trey doesn't fail to make you happy. Malcolm.

Hallison sucked on her breath. Her heart dropped, then bounced back in surprise. Speechless, Hallison decided it was the perfect time to head home early. She was trying to eradicate memories of Malcolm and his flowers wouldn't help, so she locked up. On her way out, she took Malcolm's flowers, minus his note, and placed them on Gloria's desk.

That night, under strategically dimmed lights and attentive service, Trey and Hallison enjoyed specialty appetizers, salmon, sautéed vegetables, and garlic potatoes. Throughout the night, a mischievous sparkle stayed in Trey's eyes, causing Hallison to blush. She was falling, but was it love?

Their server approached their table carrying a platter, showing off a selection of fresh desserts: luscious cheese-cakes, a triple scoop of rich old-fashioned, homemade vanilla ice cream topped with fresh berries, and a combination sweet potato and pecan pie. Hallison eyed the cheesecake, but Trey waved the man away.

"What are you doing? That's white chocolate and caramel cheesecake," she protested. Hallison's eyes continued to trail the server until he disappeared around a wall.

Trey chuckled, which aggravated her more. "I have a better idea." He reached for her hands. She pulled back, pouting. Trey reached for them again, trapping her fingers in a forceful, yet gentle grip. "These are soft."

"Thank you, but I was planning to eat cheesecake with them," she mumbled.

Trey lifted her left hand to his lips and placed a soft kiss on it. "But one thing is missing," he paused. "My ring. Remember the night I told you I loved you?"

Hallison nodded, swallowing. She was afraid to ask what was going on.

"Since then, I've waited to hear those words from you, but I haven't." He shrugged nonchalantly. "It's amazing how a person's eyes speak things her mouth won't, but I see it, Hali." He took a deep breath. "If I ask you to marry me, would you say yes?"

Would I? Should I? He makes me happy. He's saved. Go for it, her mind commanded so she nodded again.

Moving his chair back, Trey's knee cracked as he bent. Looking up, he smiled. "I'm not quite ready for Geritol yet," he joked, and she chuckled. He wiped the humor from his face and stared. "Hallison Dinkins, I love you so much. I'm paid to protect and serve the community. It would be my honor to protect and serve the woman I love. Spend the rest of your life with me, Hali. Marry me, and I promise you'll never regret it."

For the third time, she nodded.

Trey shook his head. "Ah, ah, ah, you can utter, whisper, or shout, but I want to hear only one word that begins with a 'y' and ends with an 's'."

Hallison closed her eyes, released a tear then opened them. "Yes, Trey. I'll marry you."

"Yes!" Trey leaped up, pumping his fist in the air. Patrons turned their heads as forks clattered against the plates. Servers frowned in concern. Once Trey's outburst was understood, some cheered. Others stood, but most clapped. After pulling Hallison from her chair, he realized he had forgotten to give her the ring. "Oops." He grinned and dug inside his pants pocket for the ring box. He slipped it on Hallison's finger and kissed her long enough for more tears to fall.

Saturday morning, Hallison woke with a smile. She hadn't dreamt it. She was engaged again. Yawning, she slid on her knees. "Good morning, Lord. Thank you for making your will known to me. I love Trey. Not as strong as I felt for Malcolm, but you know that, and what's best for me." The phone rang as she said, "amen" and got up.

"Good morning, baby," Trey's charged energy greeted her.

She laughed. "Well, somebody had a good night's rest."

"Why not? I'm engaged to a beautiful and saved woman. What's more to ask for except for her to set a date? Emmanuel said congratulations, but in the same breath said we could've waited until after he asked Paula."

Hallison shook her head, loosing curlers. "That means Paula knows. I guess I'd better go and call my mom, Cheney, Tavia, my cousins Faye and Tammy. Momma's crazy about you. Well, except for your dreadlocks and the gun, otherwise, you're a shoo in."

"Don't play, woman."

"Trey, there is nothing I would change about you. I love you the way you are."

"Hmm. It's good to hear you can say I love you, especially before you say, I do."

Hallison twisted her lips. She did say it, didn't she?

"Cat got your tongue? Hali, don't be afraid to love again. God knows my intentions are pure. I love you."

She closed her eyes as her heart beat wildly. "I know you do. It's so hard to say it again, that's all." She needed a little bit more time to grow into the degree she loved Malcolm. She didn't know if she ever would. After all, nothing compares to a first love. "Listen, you. Since I'm now pressured to set a date, I think my mother would like to know you asked, and I said yes."

"Okay. I'll see you later, and we'll do whatever you like today."

Once they disconnected, Hallison took a deep breath and pushed in her mother's number. "Hi, Mom. I'm engaged! Again."

Addison released, "Thank you, Jesus. Lord, we praise you. Hallelujah. What's he going to do with his hair? He's not going to strap a gun under his tuxedo on the wedding day, is he?"

"Momma, just start planning. I've got to call Cheney and Paula." Addison agreed and hurried off the phone. Hallison's cordless rang immediately. "Hello? Tavia, I'm engaged," she screamed into the phone.

"Again?" Octavia attempted humor, then grew quiet. "Hali, the doctors found another lump. I'll go for a biopsy on Tuesday." A soft sniff turned into a wailing cry. "I can't keep doing this. Prayer doesn't work, so I'm not even going to try this go-round."

"Prayer does work," Hallison mustered a whisper as her joy deflated. While God was giving her a second chance at happiness, Hallison's top priority was praying that Octavia got a second chance at surviving.

"If it did, I would be healed. I'd be a wife, a PTA mom, and everything else that comes with a healthy, normal life. About now, I would be on my way to the shopping mall, movies, or reading a book, instead I'm fighting to beat the big 'c' again."

Lord, I really don't have any problems, do I?

CHAPTER 26

A few weeks later

"Hey, I need to talk to you. It's important," Malcolm informed his brother, already heading over to Parke's house, uninvited.

Ten minutes later, when Parke opened his door, Malcolm crossed the threshold without speaking. The animosity still lingered. Malcolm couldn't recall a time in his life where he couldn't shake a grudge. He had sent flowers to Hallison as a peace offering. Of course, Lisa would've had a fit if she found out he ordered them from *another* florist for his *ex*.

The morning after family game night, Malcolm had a long talk with his dad, which made him late picking up Lisa. He had always respected his father's wisdom except that day.

"Hey, son. How are you this morning?" Parke V didn't wait for his son's reply. "Before you answer, remember you're talking to your dad. I reared you, and I know you, so don't waste my time."

Malcolm twisted his mouth to spit out the words. "If she's happy, then I'm happy."

"I told you not to waste my time. You're lying."

"Dad, you know I loved Hali. She knew I loved her. God knew I loved her, but I'm a Jamieson. I wished she hadn't flaunted that sissy of a man in my brother's house. I mean, does he have a complex about going bald and that's why he's wearing all that hair?"

His father waited before responding. "Hali is a sweet lady. Wish her the best and move on. It appears you and Lisa have some strong chemistry between you. Be patient, and see where that goes."

For almost a half hour, Malcolm vented, and his father consoled. This was one of those times where he wished his father would take sides. Malcolm had a new resolve. If his father could be neutral, so could he. That's when he ordered Hallison flowers.

Parke caught him off guard when he trapped Malcolm in a bear hug. Within minutes, Malcolm had wrestled himself free. "All right, already. I love you, too. I'm still mad at you, but . . . I . . . I came to apologize."

Parke slapped his brother on the back. "We don't have to agree on everything, but blood is blood. Our DNA will never change," he said over his shoulder as he led the way to the back of the house.

Once Malcolm took a seat, he checked his watch. "Listen, I don't have much time. Lisa is working on a big project, and I promised to bring her dinner." He took a deep breath and dropped his head then clasped his hands, thinking. When he looked up, Parke was watching him.

"Here it goes. I admit I was a little upset about—"

"Define a little, because you and I don't have the same definitions."

"Okay, Parke. The last family night was good therapy

for me. At first, I felt like a lost soul without Hali, but Lisa is smart, sexy, and a classy entrepreneur. After doing a mental checklist, the only fault I have with Lisa is sometimes she works too hard, yet she'll rearrange her plans for me if I ask her, which I've only done once on family night. We click, and I see a future with her. "

"I never thought you and Hallison wouldn't make it to the altar." Parke threw his arms up in the air. "I would've never thought *this* was God's plan either, you dating Lisa and Trey proposing."

"What? What did you say? Speak slower, Parke, real slow."

He shrugged. "I said, Trey asked Hali to marry him last week. We just found out the other day since her friend, Tavia, is going through—"

"What did she say?" Malcolm's voice took on an eerie calm as he squinted.

"She said yes. Now, don't go ballistic. Cheney already thinks you and I shouldn't be left alone. I told her our babysitting days ended before we were teenagers."

Frowning, Malcolm drew in his face until his nostrils flared. He stood abruptly and stormed out the room.

"Where are you going?"

"To Hali's."

"For what? I thought you said Lisa complemented you?"

"I lied," Malcolm tossed over his shoulder. He stormed to Parke's front door without looking back. He couldn't drive fast enough to Hallison's. Although he had a sporty Monte Carlo, he had never received a ticket for speeding. He had never had a good reason.

At the curb of the Pelican Cove Apartments, he shifted into park. Climbing out, he nearly choked when he forgot to unbuckle his seat belt. Finally, freed from the contraption, he pinched his finger in the crack as he shut the car door. Cursing, he sucked on the bruise until he reached the landing, then he hopped two steps at a time.

Once Malcolm reached her apartment, he used all his strength, including his throbbing hand, to bang on her door. He didn't have time for his signature buzzes. She opened it, displaying three emotions on her face: surprise, love, and anger.

"Malcolm? What is wrong with you? Why are you here?"

"Take it off, Hali," he ordered, snarling. His balled fist proved he was ready to carry out his demand.

She continued drying her hands on a towel, but didn't allow him entry. "Take what off, Malcolm? What are you talking about?"

"Take that ring off." He gritted his teeth as he leaned closer.

Trey appeared behind Hallison. "What seems to be the problem, baby?" He eyed Malcolm and got his answer. "If I heard correctly, which I think I did, I put that ring on Hallison's finger, and I'm the only one who can take it off. That's not going to happen."

When Hallison tilted her head to the right, Malcolm threw the first punch to Trey's left jaw. With Hallison trapped between them, Trey retaliated with a fist jammed into Malcolm's chin, barely missing Hallison's shoulder. Malcolm hadn't been in a fight since he was a freshman in college. The University of Missouri at Columbia, a.k.a. MIZZOU Tigers, lost the football game, but the home team won the fight. Malcolm didn't plan to lose this one either, but he was losing his mind.

"Stop it, Malcolm," Hallison shouted, pushing against his chest. When he didn't budge, she faced Trey, dodging his uppercut. Shoving him back out the doorway, she shouted, "No, Trey. You two are animals." Hallison's voice trembled as her tears and requests were ignored. Finally, she became Trey's body-shield, causing Trey to stop and growl.

Huffing, Malcolm kept his fists ready and his eyes focused. "Hali, you aren't marrying this guy."

That's when Trey shoved Hallison behind him. "You thug. Only God can stop me."

"No, you didn't just call me a—" Malcolm's cell rang, saving Trey's eye. He shifted, but kept his foot in the door-jamb. Snatching the phone off his belt, he snarled at Parke's 911 text message. Malcolm hit redial. "Unless you're on your way for backup—"

Hallison used the intermission to push Trey into her apartment and kick Malcolm's foot out the doorway.

"What's that blaring noise? The ambulance . . . Cheney's what? I'm on my way." Malcolm left his opponent and began jumping down the steps.

"What about Cheney?" Hallison screamed after him.

"The baby's coming."

CHAPTER 27

Hallison and Trey beat Malcolm to Missouri Baptist Hospital. After overhearing bits of Malcolm's conversation, Hallison raced to her kitchen. Haphazardly, she yanked ice cubes from the freezer and threw them in a Ziploc sandwich bag. Most landed on the floor. Scooping them up, she tried it again. After three tries, Hallison successfully slapped the meager first-aid patch to Trey's jaw. He jumped as she ran back into the living room and snatched a set of keys off her table and slipped on her mules.

Hallison hurried to the door, then remembered Trey. She turned around as Trey walked out the kitchen, watching her. "C'mon," she ordered, tugging at his arm.

"I think I should drive," Trey mumbled as he allowed her to lead him.

Hallison frowned and scrutinized his battle wounds. "Are you sure? I'm in a hurry."

He retrieved his keys from her hands. "I'm up to living, and baby, considering you can't put your shoes on the right feet, you may not see the red lights."

After she had locked up and they were sitting in his

SUV, he drove while she held the ice bag to his jaw. They needed to talk about what just happened with Malcolm, but later. Presently, the baby was more important, and she prayed all the way to the hospital that Cheney and the little Jamieson would be all right.

At the hospital, Hallison had the door open and one leg out before Trey could park. He restrained her. "Wait."

Flustered, Hallison gritted her teeth before speaking. "Trey, we've got to get in there. Let's go." Agitated, she almost yanked her arm from his grip.

"Let's pray." He bowed his head without waiting for her. "Oh, right."

"Jesus, please let the mother and child have a safe delivery. We need you, God, with us right now. Save Malcolm, and keep me from—"

"In Jesus' name. Amen." Hallison ended the supplication, jumped out the vehicle, and sprinted toward the hospital entrance. Trey locked up his SUV and scrambled to catch up.

Minutes later, Malcolm entered the emergency room with duplicate bruises. *I should've made him an ice pack too*, Hallison thought. She rolled her eyes. Malcolm Jamieson was no longer her concern. Let Lisa kiss him and make him feel better.

Gripping a speeding ticket, Malcolm stormed past Hallison and Trey for the nurse's station. A woman looked up and handed him a clipboard. "Sir, if you'll fill this out, a nurse will see you soon."

"I don't need to see a nurse or doctor," he snapped. He took a deep breath and calmed down as a nearby security guard closed his magazine and stood. "Sorry," he mumbled. "I'm here to see my sister-in-law, Cherry . . . I mean Cheney Reynolds . . . no, no . . . Cheney Jamieson. That's right."

Hallison and Trey tentatively found a seat.

"Sir, did you know you're bleeding?" she questioned suspiciously, observing his face.

"Of course I know that I'm bleeding. I just got into a fight! Look at the damage I did to that guy over there." Malcolm tilted his head over his shoulder.

Hallison tightened her hold on Trey's shoulder and shook her head. She didn't need a repeat demonstration of testosterone.

"I have no problem pressing charges for assault on a law enforcement officer," Trey advised Hallison, but kept his eyes on Malcolm.

"Please, don't," she pleaded.

"Only because I love you," he said, winking then wincing.

The woman peeped over the counter at Trey holding the ice bag against his swollen jaw. She twisted her lips in thought. "Hmm. Maybe you should see a doctor too."

Trey was about to challenge the woman's across-the-room assessment, but Hallison squeezed his hand. He stood anyway, dragging Hallison to her feet. Malcolm looked at him with a mocking glare. Hallison could tell the gesture hurt Malcolm's face, but the stubborn man did it again anyway.

Hallison had never before seen Malcolm exhibit such aggressive behavior. Maybe she could get Parke to suggest anger management classes for him until God saved him. Hallison silently prayed as two security officers approached Malcolm at the same time Parke walked between two automatic doors with his shoulders slumped. "It doesn't look good," he stated before breaking down as his chest heaved for air. "I need my wife and child."

Malcolm went to him. The brothers held onto each other and wept. Hallison waved off the security guards and walked to them. Parke was overreacting, even for a first-time father. Malcolm and Parke opened their arms and Hallison entered their embrace.

"Stop upsetting yourself, Parke." Hallison squeezed his neck. "Hopefully, Cheney will soon give you that son."

Parke dropped his arms, revealing his swollen face as he made eye contact. "Something's wrong, Hali. We thought she was going into labor. I mean she was only two weeks away. Then she started bleeding . . . the ambulance came. . . ."

First Octavia, now Cheney. Hallison didn't hear anymore as she became hysterical at the alarming news. Malcolm and Parke barely composed themselves, only to lose it again.

"I'm sorry, Hali. I thought you knew," Parke whispered, taking a deep breath. "I'd better call my neighbor who took Kami when the ambulance came." He sighed. "It could be a long night," he said, turning around. He left Malcolm and Hallison still clutching each other. Hallison rubbed his back and whispered soothing words.

"If you don't get your hands off my man, you're going to leave here with stitches up and down your body," Lisa warned, sounding like a seventeen-year-old hood girl, but resembling a professional.

Hallison and Malcolm slowly released each other. When Malcolm shook his head in disbelief, Lisa saw his facial bruises. She charged Hallison with the intent to hurt her. Blocking the blows, Hallison prayed for strength not to retaliate. She wanted to represent Christ, but she was close to losing it.

The recognizable voice of Mrs. Beacon tore through the ruckus. "Listen, hussy. Touch Hal one more time and I'll cut you. I mean that. I'm out on bail. Don't give me a reason to forfeit."

The second hit never came as Malcolm dragged Hallison away at the same moment Trey was reaching to save her. The officers had Lisa in a body grip while she unsuccessfully struggled to free herself.

Hallison looked toward the emergency room's sliding

doors. First, she saw the Stacy Adams shoes then the house dress. As Mrs. Beacon started to approach, the security guard blocked her path.

"Don't you know it's rude to walk in front of people?" Mrs. Beacon lifted her walking cane and pointed. "She assaulted that sweet, young lady. I want to press charges. I witnessed the crime. Good thing I came when I could."

"You're one to call the kettle black, you criminal," Cheney's mother spat as she and Mr. Reynolds rushed through the doors.

"I need backup, emergency room," the guard called on his radio. His request didn't quiet the group. Parke had disappeared in the pandemonium.

More officers arrived and threatened to arrest everyone if they didn't retreat to their respective corners. The group was slow to retreat. Mrs. Beacon didn't back down from her challenge to Lisa to step outside. Mrs. Reynolds warned Mrs. Beacon to keep away from her daughter; Trey advised Malcolm that he could comfort his own fiancée.

"I mean it. If I can't hear a pin drop, I'll put all of you out. Do I make myself clear?" the first officer barked out his order.

Everyone froze, except Mrs. Beacon who was rambling through her purse. Finding what she wanted, she taunted the authority by dropping a safety pin on the floor. She looked up at the officer. "Oops, pin drop."

Forty-two minutes later, when Parke returned to the waiting room, he was greeted with an eerie silence. Everyone was sitting as if seat belted to chairs. Their peaceful, friendly expressions were merely a pretense as eyes and worried brows followed his movement.

"He's gone. My boy is gone," he mumbled. He would've collapsed if Malcolm hadn't been near.

More chaos erupted. Mrs. Beacon jumped up and released an ear-piercing wail. "Oh, my God. I killed my great-godson." Shaking her head, she staggered for another seat near Lisa. Tapping her cane, she motioned for assistance from a security guard. When he obliged, she slumped into the chair and cried louder and harder than Parke.

Parke's parents almost ran into the glass doors of the emergency room as they waited impatiently for the automatic doors to open. Without asking any questions, they headed straight to their eldest son. Malcolm deserted his post next as his tears went unchecked. Mrs. Jamieson wept openly without shame while her husband paced near Parke, wiping his eyes.

Malcolm's attempt to stop the tears only caused him to break down further. Hallison couldn't hold it together. She left Trey's side to join the circle of the Jamieson family. Malcolm hugged her until she patted his back. Squinting, Lisa immediately stood and took one step as Mrs. Beacon shifted her cane, forcing Lisa to stop or trip. "Oops. Sorry, missy. I get stiff sometimes."

Lisa jutted her chin and switched her hips as she went to Malcolm. Untangling him from Hallison, she comforted him with soft kisses to his bruises.

"Hali, if you can pray right now, God knows I'll listen," Malcolm stated.

Glancing over her shoulder, Hallison nodded for Trey to join her. Without hesitation, Trey was there. Despite his ruckus, Trey hadn't usurped his authority, allowing the hospital security to handle it first, but Hallison knew Trey wouldn't stay passive too much longer.

"It's interesting how your little desperate behind keeps popping up, silly woman." Lisa shot Hallison fiery darts.

Visitors in the waiting room perked up. *Remember Christ, remember Christ. Don't take the devil's bait. Resist the devil and he or she will flee*, the Holy Ghost warned Hallison. "Listen, I'm trying to be the sensible person here."

"None of this is necessary. Death is temporary. It regen-

erates in another living form. Women miscarry all the
time. Get over it and move on," Lisa shouted her frustration.

If Mrs. Beacon had another safety pin, everyone could've
heard the pin drop. *Lisa has done it now*, Hallison thought.
The woman was about to witness the Jamieson wrath,
knowing how much they valued family. Hallison turned to
Trey and mouthed, "Pray."

Parke sobered and stalked over to Lisa. "Before my
wife reached twenty weeks, she miscarried our first baby.
Less than one hour ago, our son was delivered stillborn.
You don't even know what you're talking about, lady. It
would be best if you leave."

Lisa lifted her face in superiority. "Parke, let me point
out your error. Stillbirths are common. As a matter of fact,
one in every one hundred and fifteen deliveries ends in
stillbirths," she said matter-of-factly.

"I don't need you to recite figures to me." Parke thumped
his thumb in his chest. "I'm a living statistic. My prayer is
that my brother chooses wisely about the woman he brings
into this family. Excuse me, I need to get back to my wife,"
Parke did an about-face. He nodded to Cheney's parents
to follow and all three disappeared behind the double doors.

Malcolm faced Lisa, disappointment shining in his eyes.
His fists were balled and his teeth gritted. His nostrils
flared as he struggled to control his breathing. "Lisa?"

She shrugged. "I'll send Cheney a nice floral arrangement."

"Keep it." Malcolm walked away.

"Ah naw," Mrs. Beacon said, fumbling with her cane to
stand. "It's going to be worth me going to jail today over
this chile."

"Sit down, lady," a security guard demanded. His order
seemed to infuriate Mrs. Beacon.

She squinted. "Is that the way you talk to your mother or grandma?"

"Ah, well, no, ma'am," he stuttered.

"Then don't try it with me, buddy," she said with a game face that hinted she could back up what she said.

The guard regained his self-respect and turned to Lisa. "Madam, I'm going to ask you to leave. You're upsetting family members."

As if they weren't interrupted, Malcolm joined hands with Hallison and reluctantly with Trey as Trey led the prayer. "Lord, in your magnificent name, we profess our faults for the world to see, but the world also wants to witness your glory and power. You already knew about the loss here today, but you know the blessing that will follow. Let it come more abundantly, Lord. We ask in Jesus, believing. Amen."

Malcolm repeated amen along with some visitors in the waiting room.

Afterward, Trey pulled Hallison aside. "Sweetheart, I'm sorry about taking Malcolm's bait earlier. There was no excuse to you or God. Please, don't hold it against me. I know you don't want to leave, but you know I'm working the overnight shift, and I need to get home and get a few hours of sleep. Let me drop you off at home."

"I can't believe the baby's gone," Hallison mumbled as she hugged Trey for comfort. Slowly, they walked away. "I forgot you had to work. I doubt Bank of Missouri will see me tomorrow. I'm taking a vacation day. Plus, I can't see me getting any sleep tonight. I might come back."

"If you do, be careful, baby. Try not to stay out too late, and have one of these officers walk you to your car." He paused to think of additional instructions. "Wait," he said, turning around. He backtracked to Malcolm and offered an apology. It was accepted when Malcolm shook Trey's hand.

CHAPTER 28

Mrs. Beacon managed to tiptoe across the room and bypassed the new guard on duty who was watching a ballgame. She made it inside the maternity ward unnoticed until her oversized Stacy Adams shoes clumped on the floor, blowing her cover. Peeping through a crack in the door, Cheney and Parke stopped whispering and looked up.

"Cheney, I'm so sorry," she said, sniffing with a bowed head. "I didn't mean to cause you so much stress to lose our baby. I blame myself. I should've waited until after you had the baby before taking an aim—"

"Grandma," they warned before Cheney mustered a tender smile.

Mrs. Beacon smiled back, then blinked. She thought she heard a voice, but dismissed it. The voice came again as God spoke to her mind. She couldn't shut it out.

Only I have the power to judge the deeds of men. Vengeance is mine, I will repay every man according to their works, He chastened.

Disconcerted, Mrs. Beacon shuttered. *Talk about the fear of God*, she told herself. "I love you, Cheney; I really do. Sometimes, it's more fun acting like a fool."

Cheney stretched out her arms. Mrs. Beacon clunked to Cheney's bedside, hugged her, and left.

In the parking lot, Malcolm walked off his anger, pain, and confusion until he had circled the perimeter of the hospital. "It's not about you, Jamieson," he chided himself. Taking a deep breath, he strolled back inside, a marked contrast to him storming out.

Once he was told Cheney had been moved to a private room, Malcolm detoured to the gift shop. It was closed. He had nothing to offer them: no flowers, no words of encouragement, no moral support. That little baby meant so much to his family. Finally getting on the elevator, he punched the button for the designated floor.

"You two all right?" Malcolm asked, cautiously entering the room where he found Cheney and Parke holding hands.

"Hey." Cheney attempted to smile. "We're waiting for the nurse to bring us Parke VII to hold our little angel and say goodbye."

They had consented to an autopsy in hopes that the doctors might find the cause of Baby Parke's death. The doctor cautioned they might never know. The more Cheney talked about their baby, Parke motioned for Malcolm to take a seat. Her face brightened until she began another crying spree, which caused Parke to fret. Malcolm couldn't contain his emotions as he broke down worse than he had earlier.

Parke hadn't seen Malcolm cry this much since he shattered his mother's expensive vase after playing football in the house. Parke was at his side consoling him. "Mal, we've got to believe God. He'll give us another son."

Malcolm slicked down wavy hair as he rubbed his head. "Yeah, but will I get another chance at Hali? She's engaged."

"What?" Parke frowned. "Is that what you're bawling about?"

Malcolm nodded. "Yeah. I've got to let her go, man. I've got to." Granted, he was near hysteria when he called Lisa while en route to the hospital. Minutes later, he was pulled over for a speeding ticket. As Malcolm rambled, Cheney began to doze. Parke elbowed Malcolm to complain in hushed tones.

Parke listened without interruption until Malcolm was composed, then Parke left the room to inquire about staying overnight. When he returned, Malcolm was watching Cheney sleep.

Malcolm seemed to sense Parke's presence. He released a mock chuckle. "Lisa shocked me tonight. Shoot, I shocked myself. Lisa made a heartless comment. Then me—a CPA—popped an armed state trooper, and I started it. I must not love my life, but that did feel good." He sighed. "Can it get any worse?"

"Trey's a good guy. I'll ask him not to press charges, but Malcolm, it can get worse. God is calling you, and it's about time you pick up the phone."

"He'd better be a good guy to have Hali, but he still ain't good enough, and I can't believe you're talking about God's love. He just let your baby die, man."

"I don't know God's reason for my firstborn son being a stillborn, but now is not the time to stop praying. I need to be there for my wife. God, I love her. My job is to comfort her and let her know that she's not guilty of causing the baby's death."

Malcolm agreed and stood. He stretched his muscles before stepping to the bed. Malcolm leaned down and kissed Cheney's head, causing her to stir. "I guess I don't see God in this at all. Even with Hali, none of this is making a believer out of me."

"Yet," Parke added.

Malcolm shook his head and strolled to the door. He stopped and turned around. "Hey, I'm not heading home yet. I'll just hang out here for a while. I wouldn't get much sleep anyway. Hit me on my cell if you need me."

Minutes later, Cheney woke in pain. Parke pressed the call button. Two nurses came in together. One carried a syringe; the other cradled their baby wrapped in a blanket. Cheney shook her head. "I'll hold off on the pain medicine."

After placing the bundle in Cheney's arms, the nurses left. Struggling, Cheney carefully scooted over, giving Parke room to join her in the bed. "He's beautiful," she whispered in awe.

"PJ 7 is so little." Parke fingered the toy-size fingers. "We're holding our love," he choked.

They caressed his head, stomach, and feet before repeating the ritual.

"He would've looked like you." Cheney sighed.

"Yep. He would've been handsome too." Parke grinned and released a chuckle.

"Funny." She playfully shoved him just before a sharp pain hit. Cheney gritted her teeth. Clutching their baby to her chest, she began to weep. "Parke, I tried. I tried to give you a son. I know it's because of the abortion years ago. God may have forgiven me, but He hasn't restored my body. I'll always be guilty of murdering my baby."

Wrapping his wife in an embrace, Parke held his family. "Baby, it's okay. Don't let the devil taunt you. You're no longer guilty." Teary eyed, he looked up and silently questioned, *God, why did You do this?*

* * *

How can Parke suffer a devastating loss and still trust God? Malcolm asked himself again. Stuffing his hands in his pants pocket, he fingered his copy of the speeding ticket. Yes, it had gotten worse. Turning the corner, he found a family waiting room empty on the maternity floor. He scooted two chairs together and stretched out. For the first time in hours, his chin began to throb. He moved his makeshift bed and went to the nurse's station.

"Uh-oh," two nurses said when Malcolm stood at the counter. One backed away. "Listen, we've heard about you. Don't think you're going to come up to my floor and bother our patients. Security is one phone call away."

Holding out his hands, he shook his head. "Look, I'm sorry about spearheading the commotion down in the emergency room."

"I'm not going to put up with it."

"Yes, ma'am. If you've got an extra ice pack, I'd appreciate it."

Keeping an eye on Malcolm, she went into a utility closet for an insulated paper water bottle. Getting ice from a freezer, she dumped it inside the bag. The nurse returned to the counter and placed it in Malcolm's hand. "Here you go, and we're sorry about your loss."

He nodded, then winced when he accidently slapped the ice pack on his chin, then retraced his steps to the waiting room. "When did my life get this messed up?" Malcolm mumbled. He went back to his corner of two chairs. Laying his head back against the wall, he closed his eyes and fell asleep.

"Malcolm," Hallison's sweet voice called sometime later.

"Yeah, baby," he answered. His dreams seemed to be the only time he could talk to Hallison.

"How's Cheney?" Hallison's voice was more forceful as a finger jabbed his shoulder.

He struggled to open one eye. The ice had frozen the

wrong side of his face. Once he managed to focus, he recognized the beautiful brown eyes. "Hali, what are you doing back here? And where's your guard dog—I mean, Trey?" he slurred, fighting exhaustion.

"Malcolm Jamieson, wake up and tell me how they're doing."

"Cheney's asleep, and Parke's in there with her."

She sat next to him. "Malcolm, be the strong black man I know you are. I'm here for the same reason you are. I love Cheney and Parke. I just can't believe it . . ."

Fully alert and enjoying the sound of Hallison's voice, Malcolm shifted and reached for her hand, then linked his fingers through Hallison's. "Hali, I'm sorry . . . I was crazy back there."

"Yes, you were."

He scrutinized her other hand with the engagement ring. "I still think you should take that thing off."

"Of course you would." She scooted down in her chair and rested her head against the wall. Malcolm wrapped his arm protectively around her shoulders. Hallison didn't protest as she drifted to sleep snugly against his chest. He wasn't dreaming.

CHAPTER 29

When Trey's shift ended at six the next morning, he stopped to get flowers for Cheney before heading home. He heard good things about Gertie's Garden. He had ordered from them over the phone, but today he wanted to look at their selections. Once inside the showroom, it took him fifteen minutes before deciding on a large basket with a mixture of plants and flowers.

Taking his selection to the counter, the previous day's nightmare awaited him. "Lisa?" He frowned. "Well, good morning." *Lord, what am I about to face today?* "You work here?"

"I own it," she stated, ignoring the proper business pleasantries. "What can I do for you, Officer Washington? Here to buy your fiancée flowers? You know, you really need to keep your lady in check."

"Excuse me?"

"Your woman is out of control. Any other *man* wouldn't have allowed his girlfriend—oh that's right—fiancée—to do all she did at the hospital. Malcolm's girlfriend," she paused, pointing to herself, "meaning me . . . is not that gullible." She gave Trey a warm and inviting smile. "Fair warning. If you can't control Hallison, then I will."

Trey was praying and counting the minutes before he would lose his temper. He didn't ignore threats—subtly or openly. *Beloved, believe not every spirit, but try the spirits whether they are of God because many false prophets are gone out into the world*, he thought, recalling 1 John 4:1.

"Lady, I'm engaged, so Hali isn't a threat to you, but here is a threat. Don't you ever lay hands on her again. There're two laws you should be concerned with—the spiritual and natural."

Lisa arched a brow and twitched her nose. "Really? Your gun doesn't scare me. The gods I serve have great power to destroy you and your little girlfriend."

"Don't try me, Lisa. I can back up my words, and I don't need this gun to prove it." He laid his item on the glass counter and swaggered toward the door with his shoulders lifted and hand close to his holster in case he needed to play cowboy. If he had to buy flowers from a peddler on the street, he would. Gertie's Garden wouldn't make another dime from him.

Trey arrived at Missouri Baptist Hospital with flowers he purchased from Stems Florist Shop. The owner, Jenny, had greeted him and helped in record time. At the receptionist's desk, he inquired about Cheney's room, then he rode the elevator to the third floor as instructed. Double-checking the room number, he knocked softly on Cheney's door. It was too early to visit, but he wouldn't have time to get back to check on her later. He opened the door. Cheney was resting, and Parke was sprawled in a reclining chair beside her. His hand was still latched unto her's as he snored.

Quietly placing the flowers on a nearby table, Trey left. Taking a wrong turn, he bypassed the family visitors' room and froze. He wasn't surprised to see Malcolm camped out in a corner asleep. However, he was shocked to see his fiancée snuggled in Malcolm's arms, asleep. Lisa was wrong: Hallison wasn't a threat to her. It was Malcolm who Trey had to worry about.

Trey's nostrils flared like a bull. If he thought he could get away with snatching Malcolm up by his T-shirt and imprinting his fist print on the other side of Malcolm's head, he would. Unfortunately, that wasn't an option. It wasn't the image he wanted to portray to God, his sergeant, and again to Hallison. The list was endless.

Trey calmed his breathing, but he couldn't stop staring. He was trying to send the telepathy thing where Hallison could feel his presence, wake, and run into his arms, then he would whip out his gun and fire shots at the villain. Too bad he couldn't play out the scene that had been on a recent *CSI* episode.

At that moment, Trey wouldn't give the devil the satisfaction of another fight. The previous day, Trey took Malcolm's bait; he wouldn't take Lisa's today. Once he got some rest, he would talk to Hallison about her compromising position. Retracing his steps, he left the hospital, fighting every thought the devil was trying to put in his head.

The first order of business for Trey when he got home was to pray. He trusted Hallison. Malcolm was a suspect in a man-acting-like-a-fool-in-love case.

In hindsight, Trey should've arrested Malcolm the moment he lunged at him. "No, I chose to push my Holy Ghost aside. My flesh had some fun at the expense of shaming God." He was sure Malcolm was taking pleasure in calling him one of God's hypocrites. "Why didn't you stop me, Lord?"

Going into his bedroom, Trey didn't undress, but removed his gun holster as he fell on his knees. Sighing, he unloaded, praying for forgiveness. "Lord, I slipped last night. I know I've disappointed you. I've failed you by not using your restraining power. I've quoted Romans 12:21 so many times on my job, *Be not overcome with evil, but overcome evil with good.* Yet, when it came time for a trial, I forgot it. Lord, please don't let me lose your favor or become a hindrance in Malcolm's salvation. Amen." Trey heaved his body on the mattress and fell asleep.

I have forgiven you. Do not be angry about what you saw today. It's my will that Hallison and Malcolm are together, God spoke.

"What!" Trey slurred as he stirred.

God continued, *You are the vessel I have chosen to accomplish that task. Finish that work that I have begun through you.*

Trey rolled over, alarmed. When he didn't get enough rest, he had the wildest dreams, sometimes nightmares. After Trey got up, showered, shaved, and performed other grooming necessities, he couldn't shake the dream. Did God really speak to him? If so, was it ludicrous to hand over the woman he loved? Not to any man, but to Malcolm? It was absurd, but the nightmare got stranger. God said not to mention a word of His plan to Hallison.

God didn't say anything about talking to Malcolm, but Trey wasn't feeling that. The request was almost enough to cause Trey to backslide in rebellion. *Let no man take your crown,* God whispered Revelation 3:11. Trey gritted his teeth in frustration. "How did I become a main character to advance God's story?" In the past, when God spoke, Trey listened and tried to obey, but this was an emotional suicide.

He needed confirmation. Opening his Bible, he scanned the pages, looking for a scripture. Instead God spoke again. *I will present you faultless before the presence of my glory with exceeding joy.*

Frustrated and still confused, Trey picked up the phone. His brother was a skillful listener who could decipher meanings behind words without explanation. Once Emmanuel answered, Trey recapped the entire scenario, starting at Malcolm pounding on Hallison's door to his dream.

"You almost got in a fight?" Emmanuel couldn't stop laughing. It was as if he didn't hear a word about what God had instructed Trey.

"No, keyword. I *did* get in a fight with Hallison's ex."

Emmanuel hollered, barked, and spit out a laugh. Finally, he sobered. "You're going to lose your Holy Ghost or career over some fool."

God had already chastised Trey, so he didn't need another reprimand. "E, listen. God said Malcolm was Hallison's blessing for her obedience and steadfastness to His Word. What about my blessing? What about my obedience to God? What about me?"

His brother sighed. "Hmm. That's deep. At least we know God is still in the blessing business," he said solemnly.

"Man, did you hear me? Evidently, I'm not a part of Hallison's blessing."

"Trey, calm down. You must've found favor with God for such a heavy task. I don't know what to say. All I know is God doesn't always reveal the whole picture. Look at Job, Abraham sacrificing Isaac, or Moses' forty years in the wilderness."

"I don't want to be lost in the wilderness for forty years! God mentioned He's preparing my wife. I wish I'd known that *before* I proposed. The future Mrs. Washington must be a nutcase. It seems as if I'm the go-between man between Hali and Malcolm because she needed encouragement. Malcolm needed to be brought to his knees. He wanted no part of a godly life, so He sent Malcolm a woman who was not after His own heart."

"I need to see you work this. How about a double date?"

"E, you aren't helping."

"You don't need my help, my brother. God's got your back. Just remember, Paula is mine."

"We need to talk," Malcolm told Lisa on his way back to the office after seeing a client. Two days had passed since Lisa's showdown at the hospital. Since then, Malcolm had done a lot of soul searching.

"I tried to give you time for your family, but I've been waiting for you to call. You want to have dinner at my house or yours?" Lisa replied.

"Neither. I'm in Chesterfield. How about meeting me halfway at the Gashouse Grill in Creve Coeur? I know the owner and can eat him out of his sweet potato fries. We might as well grab a bite to eat there."

"That's doable. Although I prefer for you to pick me up. Oh, how is Cheney? I've been sending good vibes her way. I hope she enjoyed the flowers from Gertie's Garden."

"She received them," Malcolm said, becoming bored with the conversation. "Thank you, Lisa. We appreciated it. See you in a few."

Hours later, Malcolm relaxed on the patio outside Gashouse Grill, waiting for Lisa. He had already put away two orders of sweet potato fries. When she pulled into the lot, Malcolm stood. By the time Lisa parked, Malcolm was at her car door.

"Hi," she said, breathless. "Sorry I'm late."

Malcolm kissed her on her cheek and swept his arm out for her to lead the way back to the patio. In her classic black attire, she swayed her hips with the wind. Malcolm shook his head. *What a waste*, he thought. Pointing to their table, he held out her chair before he sat. They ordered and ate, and then Malcolm unloaded his memorized speech. "Lisa—"

She reached out and laid her hand on top of his. "I overreacted the other day. I'm secure in your feelings for me." She paused, lifted her face in superiority, and sighed. "It's another bump in the road in our relationship, but we can work out the kinks." She displayed a bright, enticing smile.

Loosening her hold, Malcolm leaned back. He formed a teepee when he folded his hands. Even though her eyes were pulling at him, he blinked to break her spell and looked away. Finally, he cleared his throat and carefully explained his position. "I have three don'ts, Lisa. Don't you ever, ever lay your hands on Hallison again. The woman has too much class for that, and I thought you did too." He glared as she gasped in shock, but he continued. "The Jamiesons are a proud family. Babies in our family are a big deal. Losing little Parke was a generation lost. For you to say Cheney can have another *one* was not only the worst timed comment I've ever heard, it was calloused too. We don't know if another baby will come from her womb."

"Sorry, but I like to deal in reality. Sometimes I get emotional, but rarely. I didn't know." Suddenly moisture covered her eyes, hinting at her sincerity.

"I know you didn't." He squeezed her hands, accepting her apology. Very few people could comprehend his family's obsession with the birth of Parke VII. An African ceremony, savings bonds, yearly treasures stored away, and property listed in his name for later use and more were waiting for him at his birth. No one outside his family would understand the depth of their celebration.

"I'll send her more flowers. The Sympathy Ship is our most popular."

"That won't be necessary, which brings me to my next point. The past few days have been a wake-up call for me.

I saw God's power of life and death. I also witnessed how my brother and sister-in-law are recovering despite the loss. While they were holding it together, I broke down. I don't know if He was listening, but I talked to Jesus. Lisa, my life can't continue as it is—unsettled. I don't know if Jesus has all my answers, but I want to find out. Care to join me on this spiritual expedition?"

"I can't."

"Why?" If Lisa had the same aversion to religion, he could understand. It had taken him a year, and losing two people close to him, for him to wake and smell the flowers from Gertie's Garden.

"Malcolm, I practice Wicca," she stated boldly as if he should've known.

He froze, waiting for any sign that she was joking. She didn't blink, but he exhaled. Parke was right. It did get worse. He was dating a modern day witch. No wonder he felt he was being pulled in two opposite directions. "Well, I'm not a warlock or whatever the male counterpart is. I'm not into that. Our relationship isn't going to work."

"I'm not ready to let you go."

"I am." He reached into his back pocket for his wallet to pay their bill.

"It's because of Hallison, isn't it?"

"Unfortunately, Hallison is engaged, but I'm finally hearing what she, and my brother, and sister-in-law have been telling me for a long time. I've got nothing to lose by trying Jesus."

"If possible, you could lose me."

Malcolm didn't say anything, but he sure did think that may not be a bad thing.

CHAPTER 30

When Hallison opened her front door, Trey was leaning against the doorjamb with a large bouquet of flowers and a smile. "Hi."

Hallison stood on her toes and brushed a kiss against his lips. He swiftly wrapped his arms around her, causing her to squirm. His embrace was also a death grip, as if he were saving her from drowning.

"Sorry, baby. I've missed you."

She grinned. "Can't fault a man for loving a woman. I missed you, too." She stepped back to let him in. She closed her eyes and enjoyed his cologne, which drifted in after him. Their clothes matched, different shades, but the same color scheme of mint green or sage. The most important thing was their souls matched.

He whistled. He shook his head and whistled again. "You look gorgeous," Trey complimented as he strolled to her sofa and relaxed. His eyes seemed to dance as he followed her on the way to the kitchen with the flowers. Hallison thought she saw a flash of longing. She surmised he was ready to set a date.

Trey shouted from the living room, "What's the latest with Cheney and Parke? I haven't seen them since I took her flowers early—real early—the morning after she lost the baby."

Hallison walked out the kitchen, arranging the flowers. She thanked God he didn't find her in Malcolm's arms as she found herself when she awoke. Malcolm had still been knocked out, but she was able to slip from under his arms. That was one scenario Trey wouldn't have understood.

"It's going to take time for them to emotionally recover. Let's continue to pray for them and Tavia, too. She's halfway though her chemotherapy."

He nodded. "I haven't stopped since you told me."

"Me either. You know Parke and Cheney really wanted that baby. I also want to mention Malcolm."

"If you must," Trey said dryly as Hallison gathered her purse and keys from her sofa table.

She chuckled. "Trey, be nice. I believe the prayer in the hospital helped calm his spirit."

Standing, Trey reached for her hand. "Speaking of prayer, I could use a short one right now myself."

Alarmed, Hallison squinted, studying his face. "Is everything all right?"

"Can't a man get a little prayer every now and then?" he teased.

Hallison seemed suspicious. People didn't ask for prayer randomly. Either they or someone close was going through something. There were no intentional secrets between them, so Hallison shrugged away the negative thoughts. Bowing their heads, Hallison led, praying for strength, encouragement, and the Jamiesons. After they said amen, she ran back into her bedroom to grab her banana-and sage-colored shawl that complemented her attire and strappy shoes—a gift from Alexis from one of her shoe safari parties after seeing Hallison's dress.

During the thirty-minute drive downtown, Trey's conversation was filled with spiritual growth and recognizing the voice of God.

"You know I'm back with the Lord today because I recognized His voice. I didn't want to hear it. I wasn't seeking Him, but God was talking to me, whether I wanted to hear it or not," Hallison reminded him.

"His ways are not our ways neither is His will our will," Trey said, paraphrasing Isaiah 55:8.

Hallison chuckled and squeezed his hand. "Just think, I responded to God out of obedience. God sent you to me, and I thank Him." She turned their linked hands over to brush a kiss against his knuckles. Before she looked out the window, she noticed a glaze over his eyes. She smiled that her words could touch him so deeply.

They arrived at the Millennium Hotel and rode the elevator twenty-eight stories to the top where a restaurant revolved 360 degrees, overlooking St. Louis' Riverfront. Paula and Emmanuel, who suggested a double date, were already there. They stood from the table to greet Trey and Hallison.

Paula and Hallison exchanged hugs. Emmanuel slapped Trey's hand in a handshake. "I've got your back, man."

Trey shoved him. It was a playful gesture between brothers, but Trey gave him a look as if saying, *don't start nothing, and it won't be nothing.* Paula shrugged and Hallison frowned. She wondered if the two had an unresolved dispute and that's why Trey had asked for prayer.

Once seated, their server appeared and suggested Asian duck tacos and Peekytoe crab cakes as appetizers. Emmanuel licked his lips. "Sounds good to me."

Everyone laughed at Emmanuel's appetite, even Trey. Hallison relaxed. Prayer did change things. It was going to be a great night. When the platters arrived, Hallison and Paula hesitated to sample it. Once they did, Trey and Emmanuel interpreted their moans and smiles as signs to help themselves.

Throughout the night, Hallison caught Trey staring at her. "Why are you looking at me like you've never seen me before?" she teased. Breaking off a piece of bread, she gave him a nibble then she took a bite.

He exhaled. "Can't I admire God's beauty?"

"Good answer, bro." Emmanuel grinned.

Twisting his mouth, Trey squinted at his brother. Hallison rolled her eyes. *Brothers.* Paula ignored them as she inquired about Cheney, her family, and Mrs. Beacon. Hallison also told her about Octavia.

Paula frowned. "She's the doll lady, right?"

Hallison chuckled. "I guess you can call her that. She seems to escape in a world of fairytales, creating black princesses, queens, and superwomen dolls. I'm worried about Tavia." She had Trey and Emmanuel's attention as she explained, "I'm so afraid that she's going to die—eventually, yes, but sooner. I don't know how to interpret her avoidance of talking about it. Is she scared or in denial? I want to know what's going on with the cancer. How long does she have to live? Is she prepared to die? Those questions are always in the back of my head." Hallison shrugged. "Anyway, she's going through chemotherapy again. I want to go and be with her, but she refuses until after her treatments. She says she doesn't want me to see her sickly. I can't take anymore bad news right now."

"I'm sorry, Hali." Paula shook her head in sympathy. "What about Cheney? Is Cheney still in the hospital?"

"Oh, no. She's been home. I plan to stop and check on her after church."

Trey cleared his throat. "Is Malcolm going to be there?"

"I don't know. Why? Please tell me you're not still holding a grudge."

"You have no idea," Trey mumbled.

CHAPTER 31

Monday morning, Malcolm strolled into his office, whistling. He had succumbed to attending church with Parke while Cheney was still convalescing at home, plus, he couldn't refuse a Sunday service after reading a humorous billboard, "Shock your Momma, Go to Church this Weekend." *God is advertising on billboards.* The message humored Malcolm. Surprisingly, Malcolm didn't feel any pressure to commit and had survived. When he left service, he couldn't remember why he was so dead set against it.

"Good morning, sunshine," Malcolm said, nodding toward Lilly.

"Excuse me? Are you coming down from a weekend hangover or has another personality invaded your body?"

"Nope. I just went to church," Malcolm stated nonchalantly as he picked up his messages.

Lilly lifted her brow and came from behind her desk. Her fingers were set to snap. "Praise the Lord—"

"Don't put your dancing shoes on yet. I said I went to

church. I didn't join. I was comfortable being a visitor—at least for now."

"Humph. A visitor today could be a preacher tomorrow," Lilly mumbled, dismissing him as she returned to her seat. She perched her reading glasses on her nose and resumed pecking away on her computer keyboard. "Oh, by the way, is that witch Lisa, still on the list?"

He stopped and looked at Lilly, frowning. "You can erase her off your pad. How did you know she practiced Wicca?" He shivered. "That's creepy, even for me."

Lilly stopped typing and reached inside her desk drawer for her pen and paper. "When you're my age, you've seen it all. I don't care how bright the smile, the darkness never leaves those kind of folks." She took out a first-grade size eraser and performed the task. "Okay, Hali still reigns in the list."

Malcolm snorted. *Oh yeah, Hali still reigns, period. God, all I need is a second chance.* He had hoped Hallison would be in attendance at service, but per Parke, she was visiting Paula's church. Although he wasn't going to Sunday worship to impress Hallison, it would've been nice if she'd been there.

It hadn't really mattered. Sunday service had been directed at him. Malcolm jotted down Psalms 68, 102, and 116 to rethink later in the day, but he never got around to it. Pastor Scott seemed to answer a silent question in his sermon, "Try going to the doctor without insurance. I guarantee, you'll be charged full price, but if you've got benefits, your costs are reduced to maybe ten or twenty-dollar co-pays," he continued citing other examples. "What's the conclusion of what I'm preaching today? God's benefits make you a cut above the rest."

When the altar call came, and the pastor asked those who wanted the extra benefits to come, Malcolm didn't budge, and Parke didn't nudge him. He witnessed several people get baptized, and then rejoiced. Yet he still wasn't persuaded. It would definitely take more than one visit for him to make a move.

Sometime later, Malcolm sat at his brother's table while Kami entertained them. "Daddy, Mommy says you didn't add enough salt yesterday to our hamburgers."

"Kami, hush," Cheney scolded, blushing. Parke waited for her to make eye contact and she never did.

"I'm just calling it like I see it," Kami stated, scrunching her nose at the baked chicken.

The adults laughed, and Kami grinned. Parke cooked one of the basic five dishes Cheney taught him, one for every day of the week. Actually, Parke's baked chicken, green beans, mashed potatoes, and fresh salad was decent minus the pepper. Kami was right.

Despite Cheney's smiles, the sadness peeked through. If God was a fairy godfather, Malcolm would ask for one wish—a baby for Parke and Cheney. Malcolm fingered his napkin, stalling to broach the subject of God without becoming defensive. "I can't believe I acted a fool about going to church."

"We can," Cheney and Parke answered in unison.

"You're a fool, Uncle Malcolm," Kami repeated, grinning. Everybody chuckled, including Malcolm. She repeated fool at least two more times before her parents stopped her.

Malcolm cleared his throat. "Have Hallison and Trey set a date?"

Cheney frowned, thinking. "You know, we haven't talked about that. I honestly don't know."

Malcolm ended his inquires about Hallison. No sense in torturing himself about something that was his own doing, and he couldn't change. Trey was a lucky man. Lisa was hot, but she sure knew how to cool off a brother with her antics at the hospital and her declaration of magic, voodoo, witchcraft, or whatever else she did.

The following week, Malcolm attended church again with Parke and Kami. The pastor preached Proverbs 29:23: *A man's pride shall bring him low. But honor shall uphold the humble in the spirit.* Since birth, he was taught to wear the Jamieson name with pride. He was proud to be a black man, a CPA, a homeowner, an uncle, and a lover. There was not a humble bone in his body and he wasn't ashamed to admit it. The message didn't convict him, although it gave him pause to consider it.

Hallison groaned as she parked in front of Parke's house at the same time as Malcolm. They had reached some kind of truce the night they stayed at the hospital more than a month ago. She watched as he came around to her car door to open it. Always a gentleman, always fine.

"Hey, Hali," he greeted, leaning in to place a kiss on her cheek. He waited for her permission.

Any other time, his endearing gesture would've seemed harmless, but with the frail ceasefire between him and Trey, Hallison didn't think that would be a good idea. "Hi, Malcolm, you wouldn't be offended if I say no, would you?" She smiled and hoped he understood.

"Offended? No. Am I disappointed? Yes." Malcolm always said what he meant. He stepped back and allowed her to lead the way. Hallison expected Malcolm to perform his customary wacky doorbell ring, but he never touched the bell. Instead, they scrutinized each other under hooded lashes. Malcolm gave off the same vibe when they first met—attraction. She remembered his compliment: "I'm in awe of your beauty." From another man's lips, it would have been a lie, but Hallison sensed his sincerity. Malcolm was a good man.

Malcolm was also handsome, despite the bruise near his eye like a code of honor. The discoloration was fading, but on a light-skinned man, it was obvious that it wasn't a birthmark. He could've easily concealed some of it with large sunglasses, but that wasn't Malcolm Jamieson's style.

She watched as he scrutinized her from head to toe. She had her eyes trained on him. When he finished his appraisal, their eyes met. *She who gets Malcolm as a husband, will have a good man,* Hallison thought, twisting the Proverbs 18:22 verse: *Whosoever findeth a wife, findeth a good thing.*

"I guess neither one of you planned to knock. It's a good thing I saw both your cars from the window," Parke said as he opened his front door. As they crossed the threshold, Parke teased, "Since you're not arguing, does this mean you two kissed and made up?"

"She wouldn't let me," Malcolm said, pouting as he rubbed his hands together.

"You're still suffering from dry skin, bro?"

Malcolm glared at Parke as the two exchanged a silent message. *Brothers and their antics.* Hallison smiled. Something was happening. Hallison couldn't put her finger on it, but the air between her and Malcolm was changing. Peace had somehow replaced their storm.

"Well, Parke, you know your brother. He can't just stop at one kiss." Hallison shrugged and headed for the upstairs. While Parke claimed the sunporch as his private domain, a large sitting room off the master bedroom was often Cheney's hideaway.

"Yeah, Parke, Hali's like a bag of chips, and I can't eat just one."

Hallison hadn't taken two steps, when Malcolm called her name. She stopped and glanced over her shoulder. "Yes?"

"You were right. I was wrong." He walked away.

She wanted to cry at Malcolm's tender apology. There could be so many things she may have been right about, but she didn't ask. Her heart warmed. That was the Malcolm she knew. Blushing, Hallison nodded and continued upstairs.

Situated near French doors, Cheney sat reading a thin, paperback book. She looked up when Hallison knocked before entering. "Hey."

"Praise God no matter what, huh?" Cheney mustered a pathetic grin.

"Yeah, no matter what," Hallison repeated, coming closer and settling in a La-Z-Boy recliner. She lifted the book, *Sleeping Angel: A True Story of a Mother of a Still-born Baby.*

"Imani picked it up at a bookstore in San Diego. Parke VII was my second angel."

"I know." Hallison could see the despair about to descend on Cheney. Clearing her throat, Hallison perked up. "What, San Diego? Is that the best your friend can do? How come she's not in Amsterdam or the Congo or someplace overseas?" she asked about Cheney's longtime flight attendant girlfriend.

"That's a long story." Cheney laughed. "Anyway, it's about time you visited your dear sister-girl who's an invalid. Daily calls don't count. I've been meaning to ask, how are the wedding plans going?"

"I haven't set a date, picked a dress, or shopped for china—per my mother."

Cheney leaned forward and squinted. "What's going on, Hali? You don't sound excited."

"I think I'm still in love with the man downstairs." Hallison couldn't meet Cheney's eyes.

Slowly sitting back, Cheney nodded and arched a brow.

"Really? Hali, don't take this the wrong way, but Parke ain't interested."

"I'm not talking about Parke. Malcolm's here, too. Somehow, we arrived at the same time."

"Oh," Cheney mumbled and sat back. She opened her book and suddenly found renewed interest.

"Oh? Is that all you have to say? Cheney, I'm having some serious multiple personalities going on right now. I need help. I need advice. I need prayer." Hallison closed her eyes.

"Malcolm is a man your heart will never forget. Accept it and get over it. Even after you and Trey celebrate your fiftieth wedding anniversary and have three-point-seven or something kids, you'll always love Malcolm."

Hallison frowned. "What kind of friend are you? You're not supposed to confirm what I just said. You're supposed to wave the notion away and say, 'oh, that's puppy love,' and the rest of that nonsense."

"You just said it for yourself. I'm not saying Trey isn't the one."

"What are you saying, oh wise one?"

"Absolutely nothing." Cheney went back to her book, flipping pages too fast for her to read.

"God, what is going on with me? Why are my feelings for Malcolm resurrecting with a vengeance?"

Hallison's plan was to check on Cheney. The topic of Malcolm hadn't been on the agenda. Hallison sat quietly until Cheney began to talk about her angel baby—Parke VII. When Cheney ran out of words and tears, the two hugged and prayed. "I'm going to head home. Love you, sis." Again, Hallison chided herself about the simplicity of her love relationship issues compared to the life-altering events in her friends' lives.

"Thanks for coming." Cheney grabbed Hallison's hand

before she walked out the room. "Pray, Hali. God wants His people to be happy."

"I know," Hallison whispered. Once downstairs, Hallison was almost at the front door, but Malcolm's husky voice stopped her again.

"If God told you that we belonged together, what would you do?"

Malcolm was into mocking God now? Hallison wondered. She wouldn't even dignify the question with an answer. She reached for the door handle at the same time Malcolm closed the distance between them.

"Hali? What if God told you we belonged together? What would you do?"

She was becoming irritated with his stall tactics. "Malcolm," she said, keeping her tone even, "this isn't about *what if* God told me. It's about *what* God told me."

"Woman, you always could be stubborn. I asked you *if* God told you that we belonged together, what would you do?"

Sighing, she whispered, "Then I would be with you, Malcolm."

His expression became unreadable as she prepared herself for a smirk or tease, but neither surfaced. Instead, he took her other hand. "How have you been Hali, really? I'm sorry I acted a fool over you."

"Your caveman style was corny, but flattering." She couldn't help but blush.

Malcolm let go of her hands. "C'mon. I'm leaving, too. Parke will figure I'm gone when I don't return from the little boy's room. I'd rather walk you out, make sure you're safe." He opened the door and let her go ahead.

She stepped off the porch. "Malcolm, it's daylight."

He frowned and looked up. "Hmm. Imagine that. What are the crime stats in this neighborhood, anyway?" He slowed his gait to match her steps.

"I heard that!" Parke yelled. "Goodbye, you two, and thanks for visiting." Laughing, Parke slammed his front door.

They smiled, and Malcolm waved without looking back. He stuffed in hands in his pockets. "Truth or dare, Hali?"

"I don't want to play any games, Malcolm. Family game night is over."

"Oh, I can play this one all by myself. The truth is I couldn't bear seeing you sitting alone without me in the Old Courthouse. The truth is I can look at you all day and never fall asleep. The truth is I had a problem with this Trey dude from the moment you smiled at him, and the last truth is, Hali, I can't shut off loving you. The next dare is I challenge myself to seek God for all His benefits."

Hallison unsuccessfully wiped at her tears. Once she could focus, she punched Malcolm in his shoulder. Her fist bounced off his bicep. He snickered.

"The only way you can hurt me, Hali, is to say yes at the altar to another man."

"Why did you wait for me to move on and become engaged to act a fool, or tell me this?" She balled her hands and stomped her heel in frustration.

Shrugging, Malcolm leaned in and kissed her on her cheek without permission. "I like drama. I dare you to walk down that aisle with any other man besides me, Malcolm Jamieson. I will stop it. That's the truth. Dare me."

Monday, while lunching with Paula and Ursula, Hallison lost her appetite before she could take the first bite. She sighed. "I'm in love with Malcolm."

"What else is new? I'm getting a divorce," Ursula griped, without looking away from her food.

Dropping her fork, Paula didn't blink. She shifted and sucked in her breath before jabbing a manicured nail in the air. "Hold up. First, Ursula, you're always getting a divorce. Second, Hallison, Hali, or Miss Dinkins, I think I had temporary hearing loss. What did you say?"

"I'm in love with Malcolm," Hallison repeated, perplexed.

"That's what I thought you said. Do you suffer from multiple personalities? Were we not together a few weeks ago on a double date? You looked absolutely in love to me with Trey. Hali, I—"

"Girls, I'm really getting a divorce this time. Let me tell you what your nice, sweet friend, Anthony, did. That man filed an EZ divorce on line. I don't know when, but yesterday when I got home from work, I was served papers on my doorsteps," Ursula shouted, snatching back the attention.

Paula looked from Hallison to Ursula. She held up her finger to Hallison. "I'll get back to you later." Paula got out of her seat and wrapped her arms around Ursula as she slumped against Paula and cried.

Once Ursula composed herself, Paula snapped her head back to Hallison. "Don't think I'm finished with my inquisition."

"Yeah," Ursula muffled through a makeshift tissue, using a napkin.

"Humph! She's all right, Paula. Now, tell us what happened, Ursula," Hallison said.

Ursula strung her words together without taking a breath. "One minute we're talking about ordering Chinese food—you know that's my favorite with crab Rangoon and extra eggs—"

"I didn't ask you the ingredients in your fried rice. I'm talking about the divorce," Hallison insisted.

Straightening her body, Ursula jutted her chin. "In the middle of me talking about food, he said he wanted a divorce. His stupid reason was because I nag him too much, even while I'm sleeping. I threw him those scriptures you had been trying to teach me, *Whosoever shall put away his wife, except it be for fornication, and shall marry another, committeth adultery: and whoso marrieth her which is put away doth commit adultery.*"

"Matthew 19:9," Hallison recalled in awe.

"Yeah, I guess. See, I was listening." She twisted a sandy brown lock on her wig. "Anyway, I told him point blank, 'If you're sleeping with a woman or man, I'm suing her or him for breaking up my marriage.' Then it just slipped. I cursed him out without learning the truth. That made him mad."

Hallison ran her hands through her hair and shook her curls. "No, no, no, Ursula. You can't quote scriptures and curse him out in the same breath."

Ursula nodded and grabbed a sip from her cup. "I know, I know. You're right. I should've waited a few minutes. Do you know that man had the nerve to quote a scripture about it's *better to dwell in a corner of the housetop, on the flat oriental roof, exposed to all kinds of weather than in a house shared with a nagging, quarrelsome, and fault-finding woman.*

"I asked him where did he pick up that nonsense, and he said Proverbs 21, the Amplified version. Girl—"

"With all this scripture talking, you two should've resolved your issues," Paula suggested.

"I can quote them just by listening to you two. I didn't say I believe them. As of last night, we're sleeping in separate bedrooms. That way he can't hear me nag, which is probably good because he passes gas." Ursula picked up her fork and resumed eating her leftover fried rice as Paula and Cheney smothered their laughs.

Later, a few minutes before five o'clock, Samuel walked into Hallison's office without an appointment. He knocked, unlike Paula or Ursula. Hallison kept a blank expression while she admired a fine specimen God had created. Too bad it was going to waste with another man.

Hallison stood and pointed. "Have a seat, Samuel." She retook hers. "How's everything going in the IT department? Is there a problem?"

Relaxing in his chair, he teased his mustache with his finger. He stared at her and formulated his thoughts. "Hallison, I'm just going to lay my cards on the table."

She nodded and folded her hands. She didn't think Samuel was going to quit. He needed the job for health benefits, but his demeanor suggested it was something serious. She sighed and prepared herself for whatever might come next.

"I'm attracted to you," he said with nostrils flaring and chest heaving.

She blinked wildly while her heart missed a beat. *God, what is going on with me and these men?* "Samuel, I'm not a homosexual," were the first words out of her mouth. She wanted to laugh at the parody. *Lord, please give me a hint what is happening in my life.*

"That's why I'm drawn to you. It's something about you that makes me want to come out of the closet and be what God created me to be."

"Umm-hmm. What does your, your . . . ah . . . the other man, your partner, say about your change of heart?" This would be a good moment to testify or pray, but Hallison needed to get over the shock. *Why do I feel like I'm playing enny, meeny, miny, moe with Trey, Malcolm, and now Samuel?*

Treat him as a lost sheep coming home. You are the light on the hill that can't be hidden. Show him the way, the Lord spoke to her spirit.

"He's devastated, but my attraction to you is getting stronger every day."

Hallison took a deep breath. Her spirit calmed, and her

words were sure of the authority given to her. "Samuel, you're attracted to Jesus. That's the light you see in me. God's giving you strength to leave your sins behind. God's calling you to repentance. Salvation is free. Do you want it?"

Samuel nodded. "Yes. Yes, I do."

"Good." Hallison smiled as her heart pumped wildly at the unexpected turn of events. She reached across her desk for his hands. "Let's pray right now. Afterward, if you want to get baptized, I'll call the church and ask them to warm the water." Without waiting for Samuel's response, Hallison closed her eyes. "Father God, in the name of Jesus, we come boldly to your throne of grace and mercy. We come baring our sins before you. Lord, Samuel's ready for a change. You've called him, and he's answering . . ."

Before Hallison could say, amen, Samuel said, "Let's go."

CHAPTER 32

For one soul, Faith Miracle Church opened its doors. When Samuel said, "Let's go," Hallison didn't hesitate to grab her car keys. With swiftness, she signed off her computer and offered to drive. During the car ride, Samuel revealed his tormented thoughts and lifestyle.

"I've had this uncontrollable appetite for men since I was a teenager. It's not as if I planned to be different. I thought I had the willpower to give up my urges, but the pull was too strong not to fall back into temptation, so I gave up and just lived with it."

"Sam, it sounds like God gave you over to a reprobate mind. He allowed you to be swallowed up in your own desires and lusts, and that's not limited to homosexuality. The Bible says we were all born in sin, but God doesn't expect us to continue in sin. Repentance is the only way to shed our sins."

Thirty-five minutes later, standing in the sanctuary, Hallison clutched her Bible as tears streamed down her cheeks. She was about to witness Samuel's new birth. The pool's water swished as all of Samuel Smith's six feet three inches descended down the steps. He had exchanged his suit and tie for a pair of white socks, pants, and a T-shirt. Following the directions of the minister, Samuel crossed his arms against his chest.

The minister raised his right hand and gripped the back of Samuel's T-shirt with his left. Within seconds, he baptized Samuel in the name of Jesus with His promise of the Holy Ghost. One hour later, at one minute past seven, God filled Samuel with the Holy Ghost. The tongues rambled from his stomach, climbed up his throat, and exploded out his mouth like a volcanic eruption. Once Samuel stopped praising God and praying, he asked question after question until both the minister and Hallison were exhausted. Eventually, Hallison and the new convert left church after midnight.

Hallison thought she would be sluggish the next morning, but she was alert and full of praise energy when she walked into her office late. She was prepared to apply extra makeup to cover up any puffiness and dark circles around her eyes, but after patting it with cold water, there was no tell-tale signs of her abbreviated night's sleep. She smiled, knowing Samuel was removed from the devil's hit list. Hallison had even stayed on her knees a little longer, asking God to bless her and protect her from unseen dangers.

Before she could get comfortable in her chair behind her desk, Samuel called her office with questions about scriptures. She had patiently answered them, then reminded him she needed his department's report. "Church is church and business is business. I need your report, my new sanctified employee, on time, please." Hallison chuckled. She would've never guessed Samuel would've willingly sought redemption without her reading, preaching, and testifying about holiness. She hung up the phone, only to have it ring again.

"I don't have much time because my department's reviews are due to the director of personnel this afternoon. You know, she's a task master and just happens to be on the other end of the phone," Paula complained sarcastically. "But seriously, Hali, your love life trumps business, at least at the moment. How can you compare Trey to Malcolm? We've got to talk. We've got to pray, and we may have to fast."

Hallison ignored Paula's dramatics while glancing at the reports already stacked on her desk. Her second priority was to review the revised employee handbook with updated dress code and random drug testing. If she ate lunch that day, it would be a luxury.

She relented. "Okay, but I've got better news." She grinned, thinking. "I've got a praise report! Guess who got saved?"

"Who?"

Hallison's sigh was heavy as she mumbled, "I'll tell you all about it when you bribe me with a chicken salad and mango juice from the deli. I can only spare ten, maybe fifteen minutes tops," Hallison bargained. "If you can come now with it, then I'll squeeze you in for twenty minutes."

"See you in a few." Paula hurried off the phone.

As Hallison disconnected, her assistant carried in a vase of dark flowers, as if they were burnt, into her office. The arrangement was odd. She was accustomed to strong, bold, vibrant flowers. "These are for you, Miss Dinkins," she said, forcing a smile as she laid them on her desk then pushed them toward Hallison and left.

"Ooh. Who sent you those, Trey or Malcolm?" Paula wrinkled her nose as soon as she walked in.

"Neither." Hallison twisted her mouth, silently reading the card. "They're from Lisa Nixon. That woman hates me, so why would she want to send me flowers? These don't look like a friendship bouquet," Hallison stated as she read the card. 'Take my advice. Stay away from Malcolm. You don't want me as your enemy. Unfortunately for you, you already are.' Paula, can you believe this woman?" Hallison rolled her eyes at the unwarranted threat. She understood why God had her pray a little longer earlier that morning. *Resist the devil and he will flee.* Hallison planned to pray, resist, and keep her distance. "Malcolm has himself a barracuda."

"I would pitch that thing in the trash and stay at least five feet, or whatever the guidelines are in a restraining order, away from Malcolm." Paula handed Hallison her order, then unwrapped her sandwich, but she didn't take a bite. "Let's pray. Lord, please sanctify the food before us, the hands that prepared it, and fill the stomachs that are hungry. Your Word says in Psalm 27, that in the time of trouble you shall hide us. Jesus, we know no weapon formed against Hali should prosper. Cover her with the blood of Jesus and protect her from the enemy. Amen."

They ate quietly for a few minutes before Paula began singing the praises of Trey, from his spiritual devotion to his fine stallion looks. "I can't believe you're yielding to temptation when Trey's been so good to and for you. Go ahead and act on your worldly emotions, and you're going to break Trey's heart, which in turn will break my baby's heart, which—"

"I've already talked to God about this sudden attraction or distraction, or whatever you want to call it." Hallison glanced at her watch.

"And?"

"Amen," she said, forking up a heap of salad and purposely stuffing it in her mouth, making her unable to respond. Hallison swallowed and answered confidently. "I heard Him tell me to trust Him."

Paula gathered her trash and stood to leave. "Just make sure your ears are free of wax."

"Hold on. You'll never guess who repented, got sins washed away and filled with God's Spirit last night."

Paula stopped in her tracks. Tilting her head, she stared. "If you tell me Malcolm, I won't believe it. That man would need a whole slew of witnesses and then some."

"Umm-hmm, then I won't tell you it was Malcolm. It was Samuel Smith." Hallison grinned and waited for it to register with Paula.

When it did, Paula screamed, "Oh, my God. Oh, my God. Fine, deep-voiced, and needed to be some woman's husband is delivered? Well, praise God. Some say God can't deliver. Hallelujah." She threw her hands up in the air before slapping them flat on Hallison's desk. "I need details, girl. When? What happened? Did someone die? Does he have AIDS?"

"Paula, go back to your office and finish your report. Samuel freely came."

God had given Trey the gift to discern spirits. The Lord had manifested the gift the day after the hospital incident in the floral store. God revealed Lisa was a sorcerer. To overcome the adversary, Trey had to couple his prayer with fasting to bring that spirit under subjection.

I will allow her lusts to consume her because of her reprobate mind, God said.

Trey arrived home from work still trying to come to terms with God's edict to give Hallison back to Malcolm. "How can I love her and leave her, Lord?" Surely she would notice his lack of interest or affections. Again, he didn't see how God's plan was going to work.

Your purpose is to bring them back together. My thoughts are not your thoughts. Neither are your ways mine, God said.

He checked his watch. Hallison had at least twenty minutes before she left her office. Trey planned to enjoy his current fiancée until God gave him direction. He picked up the phone and called her.

"Hallison Dinkins, director of human resources."

Trey fell in love with her professional tone all over again. "Hi. Do you feel up to a picnic at Forest Park? We could watch the sun set or stroll to the Muny to see if there is an outdoor performance."

"Although I'm not too hungry, I like the sound of your company. Is seven too late? I had a late lunch with Paula so I want to finish up here before I head home."

"I'll starve just for you," he joked.

A few hours later, with his long, muscular legs stretched out on a light weight throw blanket at the bottom of Art Hill in Forest Park, Trey admired the sun's rays as they bounced off Hallison's engagement ring each time she moved her hand to eat. He shook his head. "So how was your day at work?"

"Blessed, busy, and odd." She frowned as she took another bite into her fried catfish.

Leaning back on his elbows, he twisted his mouth in amusement. "You're going to explain all that, right?"

Hallison grinned. "Of course. One of my employees, a professed gay guy, repented, saying he was seeking something he couldn't get in his current relationship. At first he thought he was attracted to me. . . . "

Trey lifted his brow. He wasn't amused.

"Anyway, I told him it was the Holy Ghost that drew him, not me. He got baptized in Jesus, and it wasn't long until Samuel Smith was made a new creature."

"Okay. That's the story behind your text message last night, that you were at church and you didn't know how long you would be there." He nodded his understanding.

"Yeah." She frowned. "Then remember Malcolm's girlfriend, Lisa?"

Oh God, what has Lisa done? "Yeah." Trey tensed as he waited for Hallison to elaborate.

Wiping her mouth, Hallison shook her head in disbelief. "First, I don't know how she found out where I work, but she sent me flowers."

Because I purchased flowers for you and had them delivered, not knowing she owned the place, Trey thought, not confessing his blunder.

"They probably would've been pretty if they were other colors, but I had never seen flowers so dark. It was almost eerie, reminding me of death," she explained, shivering and wrinkling her nose.

"Where are they?" he asked. Hallison didn't need to know the woman dabbled in black magic. Trey grunted. God had the situation under His control, but Trey would have to continue to fast and pray. If Lisa didn't repent, then Trey would enjoy God taking her down.

"Trash."

He laughed. "Good for you."

"She had this cryptic message about staying away from Malcolm, along with a threat that I don't want her as my enemy. In her next sentence, she stated she had already tagged me as one. It's weird, because I'm already with you," she added in a whisper as if she was trying to convince herself.

"Hali, you know she has a spirit on her."

"You don't have to be saved to see that." Hallison shuddered. "Can we talk about something else?"

Nodding, he reached for her hands. She squeezed his and sighed. When she looked up, Trey could tell she had something to say.

"Trey, I don't know when or why, but somehow, my feelings for Malcolm have resurfaced." She held up her hand. "Before you say or think anything, I want you to know I have been faithful to you. I haven't snuck around or anything. It's hard to explain, but if I marry you, it wouldn't be a lie. You're so easy to love . . ." She poured out her soul to Trey.

He listened, knowing this was God's will. Still, it didn't keep his heart from breaking. She finished, sniffing and waited for his reaction.

Her admission didn't mean Malcolm was still in love with her, too. *Yeah, right.* His jaw begged to differ. He guided her face closer, wanting that last lingering kiss. "Hali," he whispered, "thank you for being truthful. I love you, and now I wished I'd gotten in a few extra punches." Hallison laughed and slapped his shoulder. "I accept that you and Malcolm have a history. That's all I'll accept."

"You're not cross-examining me about his lack of salvation?" she probed.

He shrugged and squinted. "Should I?"

"As a matter of fact, I've already been cross-examined. Paula certainly didn't hold back when I mentioned the same thing to her."

"Hali, despite what you just told me, I'm going to continue loving you until you tell me it's over." His heart pounded and dropped as he reluctantly said the words that needed to be said.

"It's over," Hallison said tearfully, twisting the ring off her finger.

CHAPTER 33

Ursula stormed into Hallison's office before Hallison could sit down. She threw a folded piece of paper on her desk. Hallison lifted her brow. "What is wrong with you, and what is that?" She pointed.

Huffing, Ursula took a seat that wasn't offered. "These are the results of my DNA test."

"What?" Hallison asked, frowning as she sat in her chair. Reaching across her desk, Hallison unfolded the paper and read it. She stared at Ursula. "Okay. Why do I care?"

"Can't you see? I'm seventeen percent Sahara African, seventy-five percent European, and eight percent Asian."

"Umm-hmm," Hallison mumbled and sat down to boot up her computer. "Congratulations."

Ursula stood and leaned against Hallison's desk. "You don't get it, do you? Now I can check the multi-cultural box when asked my race on all my applications," she said proudly. "I'm mixed. I can't believe it. All these years I thought I was Anglo-Saxon. Who knew? I might even have some Jamaican in me, man." Throwing her arms up, she twirled around and headed for the door, mimicking a bad imitation of the once popular Superman dance craze. "And just think, I owe it all to you, cuz," she tossed over her shoulder. "Anthony and I are definitely getting a divorce. He served me papers. Maybe it's time to cross the color line," Ursula added before dancing out of Hallison's office.

Shaking her head, Hallison smiled. "Maybe it's time for random drug testing." She made a note to invite Ursula to the upcoming Missouri Black Expo so Ursula could explore her black roots.

It had been four days since she made her confession to Trey. She felt unstable: two engagements, two broken engagements. Trey was a sure thing. Malcolm was still Malcolm, and he was tangled up with a crazy woman. She missed Trey—the hand holding, the morning wake-up calls that included prayer, the lazy weekends wherein they planned nothing, but only wanted to be together. It had been longer since she last saw Malcolm. She wondered about him and prayed for him, especially with a woman like Lisa. "Lord, save him soon."

Paula had put her friendship with Hallison on hiatus because of her decision with Trey. Paula seemed more upset than Trey and Emmanuel. "She'll get over it," Hallison mumbled to herself. Friendships should never be tied to a man. Her cousin, Tammy, had drilled that rule into her head while growing up.

With summer winding down, Hallison used her lunch hour to stroll outside since she wasn't really hungry. She passed the waterfall and fountain at Keiner Plaza. Her Blackberry alerted her to a text message: *Hey, I'm finished with chemo. Doctors believe they got it. Praise God for that . . . Tavia.* Lifting her hand, Hallison whispered, "Hallelujah." Claiming a nearby empty bench, Hallison exchanged a few more text messages before Octavia advised she had to get back to a doll mold in her world of make-believe. Hallison shook her head.

Octavia had won her battle. Hallison was still battling two emotions. Standing, it seemed like something from inside the Old Courthouse was beckoning to Hallison. Shrugging, she crossed the street, walked up the steps, and opened the door. She bypassed the gift shop and entered the rotunda, recalling her last visit—heartbreaking. Her heels clicked as she walked a few steps to a wooden bench.

"It's about time you got here," the familiar voice scolded as hard steps casually approached from behind.

Hallison inhaled and closed her eyes. She glanced over her shoulder. "What are you doing here again? You've been waiting for me?" She scooted over so that the six foot three inch, golden brown skinned, bearded man would have more than enough room. Malcolm leaned down and kissed her cheek before sitting.

She didn't protest. Scanning the empty room, Malcolm rested his arms on his thighs. He didn't look at her. "In a way, I have. I had an urge today to walk down here. I wanted to feel your presence, although I know you're engage—" He turned and stared at her hand. His expression asked the question without him opening his mouth.

She looked away and shrugged. "I took it off."

"Why?"

"My reasons are my own." Hallison would rather live with their memories than make new ones with someone else. She begged the Lord to save Malcolm—God didn't; she asked the Lord to mend her aching heart, which He did; then Hallison made peace with the good and bad memories, but wrestled to hold on to them. "Where's your sidekick? Not that you care about my opinion."

"I do care." His voice was low and tender. His stare was intense.

She broke eye contact to regain her focus. "I never thought you would go for that type of woman."

"Hmm. I'm glad you brought that up. I never thought you would go for a dread-wearing guy," he said amusingly, not accusatory.

"Oh, so we're doing tit for tat, are we? Well, at least Trey isn't nuts. Your little woman is either chemically imbalanced or plain crazy for sending flowers that looked too dead for a gravesite. She's creepy. I'd be scared if it weren't for the fact that light has power over darkness."

Malcolm stood abruptly with his hands balled into fists. He startled her. "Hali, I've never hit a woman, but I'm coming close. I warned her about ever laying her hands on you again. She was too much drama, so I broke it off with her." Nostrils flaring and his teeth gritting, Malcolm checked his watch, and his eyes showed him mentally calculating something. "Listen, I need to take care of a few things before I head back to work."

She yanked him closer. "If that something is Lisa, leave her alone. No weapon formed against me will prosper. Her stunts make me fast and pray longer, harder, and more often. I'm not afraid of that trial. Besides—" She paused and pulled on his hands again. "I thought you were waiting for me."

He wrapped his large hands around Hallison's smaller ones. "All my life."

She couldn't face him. Malcolm was the only man she knew who could say so much with so few words. Clearing her throat, Hallison broke their point of contact. "I have to head back."

Nodding, he stood first, then pulled her up. Hallison knew he wanted to kiss her. God help her because she wanted to be kissed, but saved and unsaved still separated them. *If only in my dreams.* She smiled, and he stepped back, giving her space. When she walked out, he followed and escorted her down the street.

At the bank's entrance, Malcolm stuffed his hands in his pockets. He concentrated on her lips. Malcolm didn't blink as he read her expression. "If I said I'll be good and keep my hands to myself—"

"Your lips?" she challenged, wrinkling her nose.

Malcolm gritted his teeth and looked away in frustration. He rubbed his forehead before stroking his beard. He appeared tortured when he opened his mouth. "Okay, okay. I'll keep my lips to myself, too. Hali, I just want to spend some time with you. Maybe tomorrow?" he asked with an angelic expression Hallison hadn't seen since they first met.

She wasn't falling for it. "I'm sorry," she said to his dejected expression. "I'll be busy at the library."

Folding his arms, Malcolm rocked on his heels. His brow lifted in arrogance. His full mustache outlined his lips, which curled into a smirk. "Who are you researching?"

"I'm back on the Palmers, trying to dig up the last slave owner of Minerva Palmer."

"Hmm. You're still stuck on your maternal great-grandmother." Malcolm's eyes sparkled with mischief. "We'll find her."

"Did you hear the news?" Parke called Malcolm on his cell phone as Malcolm was driving home in a euphoric mood. Nothing his brother could say would spoil it. "Turn on KMOX radio. A three-alarm fire burned two buildings and it's spreading fast. Mal, Gertie's Garden has already been destroyed."

Shocked, Malcolm's heart sank for Lisa. The business was her family's legacy. Their romantic relationship was over, but he wasn't callous. Parke had definitely ruined his good mood. He sighed. "I'd better head over there to see if I can comfort her."

"Oh, you're a Jamieson man. You can provide comfort, but keep it at a three-mile distance. That woman has no place in our family."

Agreeing, Malcolm let Parke have the last word as they disconnected. He had witnessed Lisa's aggressive behavior in the emergency room after her insensitive remarks about the baby. When she turned ghetto and attacked Hallison, Malcolm had had enough. After he really thought about it, he and Lisa weren't a good fit. Malcolm groaned in agitation. He'd rather go home, shower, grab a beer, and call Hallison. He wouldn't make up an excuse for calling her. Even if she recited the entire Book of Psalms, he would listen.

Malcolm didn't remember how long it took to drive to Mid-town St. Louis, but he could smell the acid and see the remnants of dark smoke in the air before he made it to the scene. Parking as close as he could, Malcolm got out. He locked his door and immediately joined the onlookers to find Lisa. It didn't take him long. She was slumped on a curb. Her hands covered her face, and her shoulders shook with grief. Malcolm stretched his long legs over the curb and sat next to her. "Lisa." He touched her elbow.

She turned and presented a tear-stained face. Her meticulous look was disheveled. When she gripped him, Malcolm swallowed her up in his arms. "My life is over, Malcolm. That's all I had," she mumbled and stared across the street at the charred remains. "Generations gone."

He rocked her petite body. So many times they neared the threshold of becoming lovers, but a force seemed to hold him back. Now he knew why. The woman who practiced Wicca wanted to possess him. Thank God Parke had been praying for him; probably Hallison, and many he probably didn't know about.

Pulling her away, he scanned her face, refusing to look into her eyes, for fear of being pulled into her darkness. "I'm sorry, Lisa. What happened? Does anyone know how it started?"

She shook her head. "I don't know. I was in the back room working. I don't know what happened. I almost didn't make it out alive."

Malcolm squeezed her shoulder. "I'm sorry again, but you can start over, Lisa. People can always start over."

She sniffed. "Does that include us?" She searched his face, but Malcolm refused prolonged eye contact. He shuddered, feeling as if she wanted to suck the life out of his soul.

"No." Malcolm stood. He didn't like how she had flipped the conversation from her livelihood to another chance at a relationship. Lisa had insurance. She would be just fine. He walked away without feeling guilty about his actions.

CHAPTER 34

Saturday morning, Malcolm waited for Hallison to arrive at the St. Louis County Library. As he chatted with the familiar faces of library's genealogy staff, Hallison bounced up the stairs with her notebook, folder, and the magnifying glass he had bought her. His heart swelled. She was the only woman he wanted. Why had he let God come between them? Why had he been so bullheaded about at least trying Christ?

He almost leaped from his seat. In a few strides he met her and relieved her load as if she were carrying a fifty-pound box. Hallison nodded her thanks; spoke to the staff, then chose a working area.

"You smell good," he complimented, sniffing.

"Mr. Jamieson, if you're going to flirt, then you can take a seat in the corner," she teased. "C'mon. Let's get started because I plan to get my money's worth out of you."

"Did you forget how much money I have in my account? C'mon, baby, break my bank," Malcolm challenged.

"I'm trying to establish some sort of rules for friendship

here. I like the peace we used to share. The bickering is unproductive."

"Hali, neither one of us can reduce our past love affair to a friendship."

"Watch me." She slapped him in his chest and sat down near one of the microfilm machines. He leaned over her shoulder, perusing her notes and documents.

Finally, scooting a chair closer, he sat down. Hallison was right about one thing: there was no longer turmoil between them. He enjoyed her company. Separating the census copies from the 1850 Arkansas Slave Schedule, Malcolm grabbed the magnifying glass and read a few pages line by line. "According to what you've uncovered, Minerva Palmer would have been two years old and most likely still with her mother, if she were lucky to be one of the many children who weren't separated from their mother until ages six or seven."

"I think her last slave owner might've been Eliza Palmer who hailed from North Carolina between 1850 and 1860 to take possession of slaves," Hallison said, explaining her thought process.

"Not so fast, babe. Let's see. It looks like Eliza was thirty-one years old. She could've inherited the slaves when she was a child, or Eliza might have taken ownership after her husband died. The scenarios are endless." The hunt was on. Malcolm moved to the bank of computers. He typed in an advance search on ancestry.com while Hallison combed through slave books and copied Palmer slave schedules from 1840 to1860. Frustrated, Hallison turned to North Carolina, hoping to find Eliza as a teenager before she married a Palmer.

After four hours, Malcolm suggested they break for lunch and come back. Packing up Hallison's notes and folders, they left the library. Walking to the corner, they waited at the stop light facing the ritzy Plaza Frontenac. "Feel up to some window shopping?" he asked, grabbing her hand as they jogged across Lindbergh Boulevard. If she wanted a hundred and twenty pairs of shoes from one of the upscale shops, he would buy them. He was already smiling at the possibility. When they were together, they would often go shopping and buy clothes that pleased each other: shoes, dresses, suits, and other accessories.

As soon as Hallison's foot hit the sidewalk, she released his hand. "Nope. I want to eat and get back."

Hallison chose the Brio Tuscan Grill although reservations were required up to a week in advance for the weekend. However, with the lunch crowd thinning, they were seated within fifteen minutes. Malcolm suggested the outdoor terrace. The waitress took their drink orders and returned for their main selections. Since Hallison wanted something light, they agreed to share a spinach-and-artichoke dip appetizer and homemade Bruschetta. When the waitress left, Malcolm stared, making Hallison uncomfortable by his scrutiny. Obviously, it was pure enjoyment for him.

"So, how's work?" She cleared her throat, forcing an interest Malcolm knew she didn't have.

Tapping his finger on the table, he leaned back. "Hali, you know everything about me. My job, how much I make, my family's background, where I live—everything. Small talk between us is artificial. Don't worry about me. I can entertain myself by enjoying your beauty." After their dishes were laid on the table, Malcolm reached for her hands to pray. "God, thank you. Amen." Malcolm didn't need a lot of words to give thanks for his food, health, and a moment with Hallison.

What am I doing? Hallison scolded her heart. Why had she given up a good, God-fearing man? Paula was right;

Hallison had lost her Holy Ghost mind. As soon as they finished eating, she would end her genealogy hunt for the day. She would check on Cheney, then go home.

Lunch was uneventful. After his brief, curious prayer, Malcolm didn't touch her again with his hands, but his tell-all eyes whispered he still was very much in love with her. Silently praying was the only way she endured the temptation. Without a doubt, if she called Trey and asked him for more patience as she worked through her new unsettled feelings, his ring would be back on her finger, but Trey was no fool. They wouldn't walk down the aisle until she said three words: *I'm over Malcolm.*

On the library's parking lot, Malcolm hugged her as they parted ways. He drove in one direction and Hallison in another. Somehow they wound up at Parke and Cheney's house five minutes apart. *Lord, this is more than a coincidence.*

Malcolm had just rung the doorbell when Hallison stepped onto the porch. He lifted his brow and stretched a grin across his face. "It seems like we keep meeting, but I'm not complaining." He winked.

Parke opened the door and grinned. "Well, it's nice to see my favorite people. C'mon in—"

"Auntee. Uncle Malcolm." Kami's high-pitched scream raced toward them as Malcolm scooped her up and smacked a kiss on her cheek. Fighting back his affection, Kami reached for Hallison.

"Auntee, I got a new stuffed animal and new shoes and new toys . . ."

Hallison listened attentively, but her ear turned bionic, overhearing Parke mention to Malcolm that Lisa was suspected of arson. *What is that all about? What has she set on fire?* Hallison prayed no one was hurt. Nothing about Malcolm's former ex would surprise her. Kami squirmed her way to the floor, dragging Hallison toward the back of the house.

Kami's playroom favored the fictional Santa's workshop. In the midst of chaos, Cheney sat on the floor, completing a triple-level castle. In the background on the shelf, there were five collectable porcelain dolls, including the one Hallison purchased at the doll exhibition. Octavia came to mind, so Hallison said a quick prayer for her and made a mental note to call Octavia again since she hadn't returned any of Hallison's last few calls.

"Hey, stranger." Cheney stood to give Hallison a hug.

"How are you doing?" Hallison whispered into her ear then held on to Cheney longer than normal.

Cheney disengaged from Hallison and squinted, trying to read Hallison's mood. When Hallison gave nothing away, Cheney continued to stare as she returned to the floor with Kami.

She pointed to Hallison's attire. "Short dress or not, you might as well get on the floor and help build this monstrosity of a dollhouse."

Scouring through miniature pieces of pink doll furniture, Hallison started decorating the toy-size living room. "I can't shake Malcolm," she confided, "not physically, emotionally, or perhaps spiritually."

"I agree," Malcolm's booming voice confirmed from behind Hallison.

Hallison's heart pounded rapidly as she slowly glanced over her shoulder and tilted her head. Malcolm's imposing body was within feet of her. His biceps rippled as he folded his arms. From her quick assessment, she found no challenge in his eyes, but Hallison couldn't read his expression either.

Facing Cheney, Hallison sighed. "See what I mean?" Somehow Hallison had misplaced the handout of the rules on what God was trying to tell her.

CHAPTER 35

Malcolm had made up his mind. Since salvation was free, he was going to take a sample of the Holy Ghost hoopla. He purposely and fashionably arrived late at Faith Miracle Church on Sunday. He was surprised to see Hallison sitting with Cheney and Parke. According to Parke, Hallison had started to attend services at Trey's church. A few times, she had fellowshipped with Paula. He would've loved to have known what went down between Hallison and Trey. He grinned, hoping he had something to do with it.

The trio, plus Kami, had no idea that he was present. If Malcolm was going to do this conversion thing right, he didn't want any distractions. He settled in a space on the back pew. Unfortunately, he was the middleman for a group of teenage girls to his left and boys nearing manhood on his right.

If God spoke to him today as He had done in the past, Malcolm was walking down that aisle. The praise team was good, the choir was better, but Malcolm eagerly awaited the sermon. His newly purchased Parallel Bible, which included four versions, was ready to open.

Pastor Scott didn't allow the congregation a respite
after worship. He quickly delved right into the sermon.
"Slavery is over, but servitude still exists, not color or
class. I'm talking about flesh worshipping, obeying, and
cherishing different spirits. Turn with me to Luke 16:13:
*No servant can serve two masters: for either he will hate
the one, and love the other; or else he will hold to the one,
and despise the other. Ye cannot serve God and mammon.*
This is not Burger King. No, you cannot have it your way.
Who are you going to serve today? I can't choose for you.
God won't choose the way for you. This is a free will-
world. You can't have a wife and girlfriend, or husband and
boyfriend, or be both male and female. You must decide."

Malcolm had already made his choice. When the appeal
for discipleship began, Malcolm was repenting. He wasn't
naïve enough not to know of his sins, but he was sure
God's list was much longer.

"The Lord Jesus is waiting on the throne. God is faster than
a speeding bullet. You want to be forgiven of your deeds?
Okay. Check. You want the grit of your sins washed off your
spirit? He's got that too. Check. You want a reservation on the
next flight out of this world? Check. You don't need an appointment for all those things. Come, repenting. Make your
way to one of our ministers and have him pray for you. We
have a change of clothes for you to be buried in the water in
the name of Jesus. Then the icing on the cake is the Holy
Ghost. Talk one on one with God with the evidence of speaking in other tongues. . . ." Pastor Scott continued his appeal.

Malcolm stood and climbed over the male teenagers.
He straightened his silk tie and unbuttoned his Armani
navy suit jacket. He began the trek to the front; the distance seemed a mile away. As the pastor beckoned for
him and others to continue coming, a voice reminded him
he had time to turn back. *Don't be hasty. You've been fine
without God up until this point. Just turn around. Now!*

The excuses slowed him down, but his feet propelled him faster as the singing and praising pulled him closer. Malcolm walked past his brother's pew. Kami called his name, but he was on track and couldn't stop. Once Malcolm stood before a minister, he raised his arms as instructed.

"What do you want today, brother?" a tall woman dressed in black with a white clergy collar asked.

Closing his eyes, Malcolm spoke without shame, "I want God to save me." He didn't add anything else on his long list of requests. Salvation was his top priority.

Nodding, the minister motioned for a man to come and lead Malcolm to a back room for the baptismal. After changing into a white T-shirt, white pants, white socks and a long hospital-length-gown, Malcolm walked to the platform and stepped down into the water.

A short man was in the pool, waiting for him. Malcolm doubted the man had the strength to dip him. "Cross your arms," the minister instructed. Malcolm complied. The man asked Malcolm his name before continuing. "Brother Malcolm, you have confessed your sins. In Philippians 2, God exalted the name of Jesus to the highest place above every name and at the name of Jesus every knee should bow, in heaven and on earth and under the earth so it is in Jesus I baptize you for the remission of your sins. God will give you the evidence of the Holy Ghost through speaking in other tongues, according to the Book of Acts. Amen."

Malcolm's submersion was so swift, it caught him off guard. Once he broke though the threshold of the water, shouts of praise burst from his mouth. Malcolm was in awe. He never thought he would shout that loud for anything, other than a football game. The minister directed him out of the pool. It took Malcolm a few minutes, because some spiritual power got a hold of Malcolm, and Malcolm didn't want to let the feeling go.

Finally, back in the changing room, Malcolm dried off

and redressed, then he was ushered into a small chapel. When Parke, Hallison, and Cheney, with Kami in tow, entered the chapel, Malcolm was stretched across the carpet, trying to compose himself and utter a word in English. Instead of helping Malcolm up, the group knelt beside him, praying and praising God. Malcolm's cheeks were numb from nonstop speaking in unknown tongues. When the Lord got through with him, Malcolm was panting and out of breath. He didn't realize his face was wet until Hallison dabbed at his tears.

Hallison couldn't control her weeping, neither could she stand. On the floor, they hugged each other until there were no more tears. Quietness greeted them as everyone had vacated the room. "Malcolm, I'm so glad you know Jesus for yourself."

She straightened his suit as he stood and pulled her up. She wrapped her arms around him. Within minutes the others re-entered the chapel and joined them in a group hug. When they separated, Malcolm pulled Hallison back into his arms and whispered in her hair, "I was wrong about Jesus and you were right, Hali." She squeezed him tighter. "But don't expect me to become a minister."

Through misty eyes, she shook her head, smiling. "I won't."

Slapping Malcolm on his back, Parke announced a feast at his house. One minister, who prayed with Malcolm, took his information for the church records. Malcolm shook all their hands and thanked them.

Less than an hour later, Hallison helped Cheney set the table while Malcolm recapped his experience at church to Parke. Gathered around the dining room table, Malcolm volunteered to say grace. Linking hands, they bowed their heads and waited.

"Lord Jesus, this is my first prayer coming to you as a changed man, God, thank you for your mercy and patience with me. Bless our food in Jesus' name. Amen."

* * *

Monday evening, Parke was still riding high from the weekend's events. One family member saved, three more to go for salvation—his dad, mother, and youngest brother, Cameron. Walking through his front door after work, Parke grabbed the phone on the second ring as he laid down his keys.

Minutes later, he slammed it down, disconnecting the call. His mission wouldn't be accomplished until Cheney's mother was double-dipped in water in Jesus' name. He wouldn't allow Mrs. Reynolds to spoil a good day and stress Cheney by blaming her for warrants being served on Roland earlier that day. Roland was responsible for his own actions. It wasn't Cheney's fault his sins were uncovered.

Shaking off the anger, he walked to the kitchen and kissed his wife. Parke held his breath when his cell phone played the Mickey Mouse ringtone Kami had chosen. Cheney smiled every time she heard it.

Clearing his throat, Parke answered, hoping Mrs. Reynolds wasn't now harassing him on his cell. He listened to the caller. "Are you sure?"

Cheney grabbed his sleeve. "What, Parke? What's wrong?"

Parke snapped the cell phone shut. His eyes watered as he stuttered, "That was the private investigator. He's almost ninety percent sure he's located my son, the first Parke K. Jamieson VII."

Tears flashed in Cheney's eyes. "Oh, Parke, praise God. Where is he? We can leave now and get him." Cheney hurried around the kitchen to grab her purse, but Parke stopped her.

"There's one issue, baby. He's being adopted."

"What?"

"That means nothing to me. He's a Jamieson, and I'm going to get my son—our son. Count on it."

CHAPTER 36

Malcolm sat in his office, smiling and sipping on a cup of decaf. Everything was okay in his world. His love for Hallison was stronger than ever. His commitment to God was sweet and calming, not as confined as he had first believed it would. Malcolm had just hung up from telling her good morning . . . again. He grinned as he opened the *St. Louis Post-Dispatch*.

Lisa had been charged with arson in the fire that engulfed five buildings and caused millions of dollars in damages. The state fire marshal's investigation had uncovered hundreds of lit candles and highly flammable items in one area of her store. At least three firefighters were injured, one critically. Lisa's bond was set at five-hundred thousand dollars.

Malcolm shook his head in disbelief. Why would she destroy something that had been handed down in her family? Briefly, Malcolm wondered if Lisa was performing some type of ceremony. He didn't want to know. Malcolm shrugged. He was glad he'd come to Jesus when he did. Prior to his salvation, Malcolm had believed that witch-

craft in sitcoms and the sorcery in children's books were
harmless and sensationalized. At first, he hadn't noticed
anything out the ordinary or flashing warning lights with
Lisa, but every time he thought about his relationship
with Lisa, maybe the signs were there, but his spiritual
eyes weren't open to see them.

He had shared Lisa's admission with Parke; however,
they agreed that knowledge was the key to arm themselves against that form of wickedness. Malcolm stopped
daydreaming when he heard voices outside his door.

Folding the paper he wasn't reading, he saw Trey in his
uniform, clearing Lilly's office area and heading straight
toward him. Malcolm groaned. He hadn't been saved a
month and his first confrontation with his nemesis was
moments away.

"Can I help you?" Lilly blocked Trey's path. "Is this a
raid? Do you have a search warrant? I don't know anything about my son's criminal activity. I can be granted im-
punity—"

"Immunity," Trey corrected. "Actually, I'm here to see
him," he said, tilting his head toward Malcolm.

Lilly sighed, but didn't move. "He's in a meeting. You
can have a seat."

Malcolm was going to have to talk to Lilly about lying,
especially in association with him.

"He doesn't look like he's in a meeting to me." Trey
squinted around Lilly, making eye contact with Malcolm.

Fastening a hand on her hip, Lilly tapped her shoe on
the carpet. "Well, I'm about to meet with him, so you can
have a seat."

Malcolm stood to intervene, waving his assistant off.
"It's okay, Lilly. I can take care of this. Trey, I'm telling you
right now, my fist is in retirement. I don't want any trouble."

Stepping around Lilly, Trey proceeded to Malcolm's office and took a seat without an invitation or permission. He crossed his ankle over his knee, making himself comfortable. "I'm here for a peaceful resolution."

"Umm-hmm." Malcolm didn't believe him. Hallison was permanently off the market to Trey or any other man. Malcolm perched on the corner of his desk, folded his arms, and nodded for Trey to explain.

"Listen, man. This is going to sound unbelievable. I still can't believe God played me, but He never intended for Hallison to marry me." He grunted and shook his head. "It would've helped to have known that before I fell in love with Hali *and* asked her to marry me." Trey paused and took a deep breath. "My sole purpose in my relationship with Hali, I guess, was to be some sort of middle man to protect her physically and encourage her spiritually until you got your act together and repented."

Malcolm stood abruptly. He wasn't about to allow Trey to point fingers at him.

"Watch yourself, man." Trey cautioned. "You're at a disadvantage because I carry a gun. Anyway, you have Hali, leaving me empty-handed. To be honest, if I want to see Jesus, I had no choice but to obey God, even though the whole thing didn't make sense to me." He grunted. "It still doesn't. I began to pray for you because God wanted you to see the difference in an ungodly woman and a woman after God's own heart. Personally," he said, shrugging, "I thought you were too slow to see it. I did."

Malcolm laughed. "Are you kidding? Lisa was crazy. If I had known up front what I know now, I could've saved God the trouble."

"Believe it. Our ways are definitely not His."

Malcolm grinned as their fists met in agreement. "No hard feelings, man." Malcolm retook his seat behind his desk. He should've, but he didn't feel one ounce of guilt for Trey forfeiting Hallison. "What do you get out the deal? The least I can do is set you up."

"That's okay." Trey shook his head then shrugged. "Who knows God's mind or His plan for me? Somehow, I believe she ain't meek and humble. God hinted she's already been selected, but she's still in the oven. If I didn't have so much confidence in God, I would run the other way from His matchmaking scheme. Hopefully, I can put in a request for what I would like." Trey chuckled as his mind seemed to wander.

Saved or unsaved, Malcolm wasn't giving Trey any pity. "Better you, man, than me."

"Don't think I won't specify a tall, shapely woman, honey-tone skin, shoulder-length hair, almond-shaped eyes—"

"Watch it, Trey. That sounds too much like Hali, and she doesn't have any sisters."

Trey dropped his foot to the floor and leaned closer to Malcolm. "Hali is one beautiful woman. Don't mess up again, Jamieson. God doesn't always give second chances."

"I know."

CHAPTER 37

Two months and not a day later . . .

Malcolm stood at the same altar for a second time. The first time, he dedicated his life to Christ. Now, he would profess his love to Hallison until death they would part. Malcolm was praying for a long life as he glanced at his watch. Hallison should've walked down the aisle three minutes ago.

Parke, Malcolm's best man, taunted him with a snicker. His younger brother and lone groomsman, Cameron, cleared his throat in amusement. Minutes earlier, Cameron had escorted Hallison's best friend, Octavia, down the aisle. She looked healthy and happy. Hallison still continued to pray for her body and spirit.

Malcolm took a deep breath to regulate his nerves. Cheney winked as she walked down the aisle as Hallison's matron of honor. Despite the loss of another baby and the family drama, Cheney appeared happy. Malcolm prayed she would hold up during the trial that was set to begin soon.

Malcolm's drifting mind came back to the moment. Hallison Dinkins was now five minutes late. *She had better not leave me standing at the altar,* he thought, reflecting on his second proposal. It was different. It was bold, and it could've backfired.

The Sunday after Malcolm had received the Holy Ghost, the pastor invited all converts, if they chose to do so, to testify to the congregation about their Holy Ghost experience. Malcolm was the third person to accept the microphone handed to him while he and ten others were lined up behind the pulpit.

"To the saints of God, I can truly say God is merciful and very real. He's not in some far-away land or place. I'm still in awe about His presence, His closeness, and His power to show me He's in control." He gathered his thoughts.

"I praise God today that He chose me by giving me His spirit with the evidence I had once read about in the Bible, and honestly, didn't believe." He had taken a deep breath as his eyes skipped over faces and pews until he found her. *"Hallison, you were right about salvation, and I was wrong about God. I have come humbly before God, repented, and received His invitation to the kingdom. The one thing I need before Jesus comes back is you. Hali, will you marry me?"*

The congregation had gasped at his unexpected declaration. From the pulpit, Malcolm got on one knee and pulled out a black velvet ring box. When he flipped it open, God gave Malcolm a little help—the Lord blinked, allowing the diamond to sparkle like a star for the audience, including Hallison, to see.

She stood, with her hands clasped. The air ceased as the congregation waited along with him for her response. "Yes, Malcolm, I would be honored to be your wife."

The cheers were louder than the fans at a football game. That was the only encouragement he needed.

"I've got a wedding to plan," Malcolm mumbled into the microphone before shoving it into the hands of the next convert.

Later, she teased him. "What if I had said no or let me think about it?"

His nostrils flared with passion as he winked. "Baby, have you ever heard of a late dismissal? I wasn't going anywhere."

The wedding guests stood as the sanctuary doors opened, alerting Malcolm of Hallison's entrance. *Angels must have dressed her,* Malcolm thought. She was already gorgeous, but wings were the only things missing. Her face glowed along with her ballroom dress. He hoped Hallison's hairdresser, Alexis, hadn't weighed down Hallison's fancy hairdo with hair pins, because the curls were coming down.

Hallison's uncle escorted her down the white runner, crushing the random piles of rose petals Kami had dropped in her haste to get to her father. If their hired photographer didn't capture that vision, Malcolm would re-stage the moment.

Malcolm huffed. Hallison was torturing him by walking much too slow. He didn't recall Hallison's stand-in during the rehearsal walking so slow. If she didn't pick up the pace, he would go and get his bride himself. She didn't need an escort, anyway. They could've walked in together as far as he was concerned.

Once she read his expression, Hallison appeared to miss a step. When she was within three pews of the altar, Malcolm made good on his threat, leaving his post to meet her.

Wrapping his arm securely around his bride's waist, Malcolm glanced over her shoulder and caught Trey's eye with an unreadable expression. Malcolm nodded and Trey returned the gesture.

* * *

Hallison sucked in her breath. *Thank you, Lord, for my blessing.* Although Paula remained skeptical about Malcolm's genuine conversion, Hallison knew in her heart that no man could make a stubborn Jamieson man do anything, but God knew how to bring a man down to his knees. She made eye contact with her mother, who blew her a kiss. Hallison smiled brighter.

Lord, teach me how to be a good, saved wife to Malcolm, she prayed as Malcolm came to her and possessively took her away from her uncle, who relinquished his duty, once he recognized Malcolm's determination. She loved that about Malcolm—his public and private shows of affection. "You couldn't wait? I was almost there," she teased, whispering.

He rubbed his mouth against the veil near her ear. "I could've married you the first day I saw you." Falling in step with the music, Malcolm laid her lace-covered arm on top of his. With a flare of dramatics and precision, he escorted her the remaining distance to the altar.

Once they stopped and faced each other, Hallison leaned in and whispered, "Thank you for saying yes to Jesus."

"I'm going to say thank you to Pastor Scott once he says I can kiss my bride." They shared soft chuckles until Mrs. Beacon made her presence known.

"I had trouble finding a parking space. Scoot over, Charlotte," Mrs. Beacon ordered Malcolm's mother. "I'm the fairy grandma. I bought this new digital camera just for this. I want to get Malcolm fumbling over his vows for YouTube. Have you seen those 'Oh Glory' wedding videos? Mine will trump theirs."

Charlotte hushed Mrs. Beacon as the minister began, "Dearly beloved, we are gathered here today . . . you may now recite your personal vows."

Malcolm gathered Hallison's hands and brought them to his lips. "I love you."

Hallison gazed into his eyes. "I love you."

He whispered again, "I love you," with more power to his declaration.

"I love you," she repeated with the same determination.

The minister cleared his throat. "Recite your vows, Mr. Jamieson." The guests chuckled.

Frowning, he turned to Pastor Scott. "I'm trying, but I love her."

"Yes, you've established that, and we're your witnesses," he advised.

"This is good stuff. I told you that man would forget his vows," Mrs. Beacon stated, adjusting the camera to zoom in.

Reluctantly, Malcolm broke eye contact with Hallison. First, he turned to Mrs. Beacon and winked for her camera. He faced his bride again. "Hallison, Hali . . . God knows what's best for me, and He gave me you and the Holy Ghost. I promise to fulfill your desires, dreams, and needs. I promise to pray for direction and understanding in our marriage. I promise to be true to you and place your happiness above mine. Again, I profess my love to you."

When the pastor instructed Hallison to go ahead, she didn't blink. "Malcolm, I'm so blessed that God chose me to be your helpmate. I love you so much. I will trust you, honor you, and obey you. . . ." Hallison wasn't among the women who were afraid to obey their husbands because they didn't trust them to do right. Malcolm wouldn't dictate to her. She knew he would consult with her, and together they would make decisions.

"By the power God has given me, I now pronounce you husband and wi—"

Malcolm threw back Hallison's veil. His touch was so tender Hallison didn't care about ruining her makeup—

well, maybe a little for pictures' sake. She waited for Malcolm's lips. He was torturing her as he stared as if deciding how to tackle the task. The kiss came and lasted until Parke attempted to pull them apart. Malcolm let go of her lips, but not Hallison. He kept her in his embrace.

Parke smirked as Malcolm fed his wife cake. Some of the children's antics at the reception briefly distracted him. When he looked back, the newlyweds were escaping. He was glad his brother and Hallison were finally married. They had more drama than he and Cheney. He prayed, when the time came, Cameron would elope.

"Beatrice, I tell you this has been a year for everyone. I think you need a man to keep you out of trouble," Charlotte joked as she introduced Mrs. Beacon to other family members.

Mrs. Beacon waved the air. "I've already got one."

Several heads turned in sync. "Huh?"

"Yep, I've got to have some fun before my trial starts, which is weeks away, but I ain't worried. I got this. If you ever need to spice up your love life, then you've got to enter second life—the high-tech video world. Girl, let me tell you, I'm dating a thirty-something Italian tycoon, and. . . ."

Epilogue

Malcolm and Hallison Jamieson's marriage was blissful. They enjoyed indoor and outdoor picnics and movies on Saturdays. They never missed church on Sundays. Breakfast in bed on Mondays was mandatory. Love lunches on Tuesdays were expected.

Lessons at Bible classes on Wednesdays were thought-provoking. Pampering on Thursdays was for downtime. They didn't lose their competitive edge at family game night on the fourth Friday of every month.

Nothing trumped pillow talk every night of the week with a goal of starting their own little dynasty—Malcolm Jamieson, Jr.

BOOK CLUB QUESTIONS:

1. How big of an issue was Hallison breaking off her engagement with Malcolm because of her religion?

2. Did Lisa exhibit any signs that she worshipped the spirits of darkness?

3. Have you ever been in a situation where God told you to give up something you really wanted? For example, Hallison and Trey walked away from people they loved. If so, did you feel that God was unfair?

4. Is it possible for a person to be spiritually-attracted to an individual without knowing it, like Samuel was to Hallison?

5. When was the last time God spoke to you and you listened?

6. Discuss the circle of unending forgiveness: Grandma BB, Cheney, and Cheney's mother.

7. Why did Grandma BB feel she had to take matters into her own hands?

8. Cheney suffered two losses in her pregnancies. How do you think that affected her spiritual walk?

9. Did Ursula and Anthony have grounds for a divorce, even if they weren't churchgoers?

About the author . . .

Pat Simmons is a recipient of the Katherine D. Jones Award, presented at the 2008 Romance Slam Jam in Chicago, IL, for humility and grace. She is a Jesus baptized believer and received the gift of Holy Ghost by the evidence of speaking in other tongues. She is a news writer and assignment editor for a St. Louis television station. Prior to that position, she worked as a talk show host, board operator, and news reporter for various radio stations for ten years. She recently celebrated her twenty-fifth wedding anniversary, and she is the mother of two.

Pat Simmons holds a B.S. in Mass Communications from Emerson College in Boston, MA. Her hobbies/interests include digging up dirt on dead people while researching her genealogy. She is considered a connoisseur of board games, and is always on the hunt for off-brand games that nobody wants to play so she bribes them with her tetrazzini. She praises God for the inspiration to write, and the "village people" for helping her get the job done. Her works include *Guilty of Love, Talk To Me, Book II: Not Guilty of Love,* and upcoming Book III: *Still Guilty* (April 2010), and Book IV: *Free from Guilt* (2011). Please visit her website at www.patsimmons.net where you can take a look at pictures or sign up for her monthly e-newsletter. She enjoys hearing from readers. Send her an e-mail at pat@patsimmons.net, or snail mail at 3831 Vaile Ave., Box 58, Florissant, MO 63034.

Be Blessed!

About the **Palmers** in *Not Guilty of Love* . . .

My fourth-great grandmother, Minerva Palmer, was founded on 1870 Monroe County, Arkansas. She was 22 and the mother of George (1866), Wyat(t) (1867), and Sam (1870). By December 1, 1870, she was married to Spence(r) Lambert (possibly once owned by the Lamberts slaveholders).

June 25, 1880, Spence and Minerva "Nervie" had the following children, Henry, Nellie (my great-great grandmother) who was a twin to Solomon, Mary, Caroline, Washington, and another son and daughter.

1n 1900, Nellie Palmer married Joseph Brown. Together they had Minerva (yes, another one who was my great-grandmother), Hattie, and a set of twins: Louis and Ellis.

In 1910, My great-grandmother, Minerva, married Odell Wade. Together they had Timothy, Ivory, Ann, Theaster, Jessie (my grandmother) and Jessie's twin, Louis.

Still Guilty
Book III of the *Guilty Series*
An excerpt

CHAPTER 1

How did my life become so complicated? Parke Kokumuo Jamieson VI wondered. He was the firstborn son
of the tenth descendant of Paki Kokumuo Jaja; the chief
prince of the Diomande tribe of Cote d'Ivoire, Africa.
Parke was destined to produce the next generation.

It was an honorable task that Parke had relished to ful-
filling until he met Cheney Reynolds. He had tossed caution,
common sense, and responsibility to hurricane-strength
winds. Cheney was his destiny, and Parke was determined
to have her even after being advised she was sterile. Addicted to her strength, determination and beauty, Parke
proposed anyway—more than once.

Six feet without heels, Cheney's height complemented
his six feet five inch frame. Her long lashes and shapely
brows were showstoppers, but it was Cheney's delicate
feet that were his weakness, after her hips. Her feet were
always manicured and soft, and seemed to nurture a
slight bounce to her catwalk.

Cheney's skin held a touch of lemon coloring and her
lips were a temptation for kisses. Within a year of their

marriage, God performed a miracle against medical odds. Cheney became pregnant twice. Both times, they lost: first through a miscarriage, the second—a precious son— delivered stillborn.

Late one night, while studying his Bible, Parke petitioned God for a sign as to whether a son would ever come through his seed. When he stumbled across Genesis 16: the story of Abram, his wife Sarai, and Sarai's handmaiden Hagar, Parke read the passage three times. "What are you telling me, God?"

Cheney could've portrayed Sarai. Although, he had just turned thirty-seven, Parke prayed his family reproduction bank wasn't dried as Abram in order for God to perform a miracle. Maybe there was hope. Closing his Bible, he climbed into the bed and wrapped his arms around his wife. Before he turned off the light, he wondered who was Hagar.

The next day, his private investigator called. "I hope you're sitting down."

Sipping his cup of coffee, Parke didn't answer right away. As a senior financial analyst, he was mentally contemplating his client appointments for the day. "Nope. What's up?"

"Good news. I've located your son," Ellis said.

Two years earlier, Parke had initiated a search, after a social worker who was screening him and Cheney for the foster care program, questioned Parke's name similarity to Park Jamie who was somewhere in the system. The woman risked discipline or termination for breaching client confidentiality. "I feel God wants me to say something to you," she had explained.

Almost immediately, Parke contacted his long time friend and Lincoln University Kappa Alpha Psi frat brother. Ellis Brown was the CEO of Brown Investigations. The last time they had spoken, Ellis had basically told Parke the rumor was unfounded.

Parke froze—his hand, mouth, and breathing—as his heart collided against his chest. Once he thawed, he spewed coffee across the counter like a wayward water sprinkler. Dumping his cup in the sink, Parke used all his strength to gulp pockets of air. Somewhat composed, he sniffed as his vision blurred.

He stretched up his hands in praise, almost forgetting about the cordless phone. "Yes! Thank you, Jesus. Praise God—"

"Wait, Parke. Parke!" Ellis interrupted. "Ah, there's a slight twist."

Parke grinned, not caring. He couldn't help it. *This was great news. Thank God for Hagar*, he silently praised.

Ellis sighed heavily. "He's about to be adopted."

"What?" Parke shouted. As the words sunk in, visions of his life seemed to appear in slow motion before fury raced to the surface. He glanced around the room, searching for any moveable object to throw that Cheney wouldn't miss. "When? Where? Who?"

Parke hadn't liked Ellis's answers.

Fast-forward almost three months later, and Parke wasn't any closer to getting his son. "I'm tired of waiting. If I need to prick my finger, rub a swab in my mouth, pee in a cup, or pull out a hair sample, bring the DNA test on," Parke barked, anchoring his cell phone on his shoulder, thumb-steering his new Escalade Hybrid and swerving around a pothole.

The vehicle's brakes suffered the abuse of Parke's frustration. He squinted at the clock on the dashboard and increased his speed to pick up his daughter. Racing through traffic on Chambers Road, Parke calculated the minutes to his destination—Mrs. Beacon's house on Benton Street in Ferguson, Missouri. Mrs. Beatrice Tilley Beacon was his wife's former neighbor, surrogate grandmother known as Grandma BB, reliable babysitter, and the only suspect in shooting Cheney's father.

A traffic light snagged him. He huffed, venting. "Ellis, I'm capable of doing two things at one time, but arguing while driving isn't a preferable combination. A cop is right behind me, and I'm not up to hearing the wrath of little diva if she's late for her marital arts lesson. That girl has a mean left kick."

"I'm not scared of your four-year-old. As a matter of fact, Kami loves me. Anyway, did you forget you're not paying me? The last time I checked, I quit after you fired me the second time."

That was true. Parke hadn't really meant to lose control and almost his Holy Ghost. When it came to anything remotely Jamieson-related, his emotions often overrode his sensibility. "Ah, yeah. I hope you didn't take me seriously, did you? I'll double my last offer."

"You can quadruple it, buddy, but four times zero is still nothing, so stop harassing me," Ellis retorted. "You asked me to check out a rumor that you had a son in the foster care system. Do you know how long that took?"

Parke shrugged. It was a good thing Ellis couldn't see his nonchalant behavior.

"I located a Park Jamie. His mother was a petite Latina who died in a car crash and—"

"I don't need a summary of your report. I remember Rachel Blackberry. God help me if I could forget that woman's legs—whew." Parke shook himself and refocused. "I want Parke Kokumuo Jamieson VII." He scowled. "As his birth father, I have a right not only to see my son, but to take immediate custody."

"Parke, Gilbert Junior was adopted nine months ago.

Even if a judge grants a paternity test, you'll have to prove you didn't give up your rights as a parent," Ellis tried to console. "You can't bake a cake and have a clean pan too."

"You know that didn't make any sense, right?"

"It didn't, did it?" There was a pause. "My point is you're an adoptive parent. You know the process. What if Kami's parents had challenged your adoption?"

Parke didn't answer. It wasn't the same. Kami's natural family was so dysfunctional they probably didn't notice her missing when she was put into the system. With a blink of an eye, the teenage mother and father had signed the papers, dissolving their parental rights.

"Call your attorney, man."

"I did. Can you believe he removed himself from the case, then hung up on me?" Parke snarled.

Ellis exploded with untamed laughter. "That makes how many attorneys—two? I'm telling you, you should call my cousin, Twinkie. Don't let the name fool you. She's more than a butterball. The girl squashes their competition. If there's a loophole in the law, she'll widen the gap. Until then, wait on the Lord as you always tell me. Quote a scripture, and you'll be all right."

Parke grunted and disconnected without saying goodbye. *I'm tired of waiting.*

Urban Christian His Glory Book Club!

Established January 2007, **UC His Glory Book Club** is another way to introduce **Urban Christian** and its authors. We are an online book club supporting Urban Christian authors by purchasing, reading and providing written reviews of the authors' books that are read. *UC His Glory* welcomes both men and women of the literary world who have a passion for reading Christian based fiction.

UC His Glory is the brainchild of Joylynn Jossel, Author and Executive Editor of Urban Christian and Kendra Norman-Bellamy, Copy Editor for Urban Christian. The book club will provide support, positive feedback, encouragement and a forum whereby members can openly discuss and review the literary works of Urban Christian authors. In the future, we anticipate broadening our spectrum of services to include: online author chats, author spotlights, interviews with your favorite Urban Christian author(s), special online groups for *UC His Glory Book Club* members, ability to post reviews on the website and amazon.com, membership ID cards, *UC His Glory* Yahoo Group and much more.

Even though there will be no membership fees attached to becoming a member of *UC His Glory Book Club*, we do expect our members to be active, committed and to follow the guidelines of the Book Club.

UC His Glory members pledge to:

- Follow the guidelines of *UC His Glory Book Club*.
- Provide input, opinions, and reviews that build up, rather than tear down.
- Commit to purchasing, reading and discussing featured book(s) of the month.

- Respect the Christian beliefs of *UC His Glory Book Club*.
- Believe that Jesus is the Christ, Son of the Living God

We look forward to the online fellowship.

Many Blessings to You!

Shelia E. Lipsey
President
UC His Glory Book Club

**Visit the official Urban Christian Book Club website at *www.uchisglorybookclub.net*